REST IN PEACE

EVA RAE THOMAS MYSTERY - BOOK 15

WILLOW ROSE

What's coming next from Willow Rose?

Get on the list to find out about coming titles, bargains, giveaways, and more.
Join the WILLOW ROSE VIP NEWSLETTER.

Just scan this QR code with your phone and click on the link:

Prologue

CAPE CANAVERAL, FL

Thursday Evening

As the rain poured down heavily, Sarah gripped the steering wheel of her car, her knuckles turning white. Her mind was clouded with a mixture of anger, hurt, and frustration. The familiar streets blurred as she drove through town, her vision distorted by the raindrops cascading down the windshield.

She knew it was a terrible idea to confront Steven while in such a state. But the alcohol coursing through her veins drowned out any rational thought she had left. She had convinced herself that this confrontation was long overdue—her chance to finally express all the pent-up emotions that had been simmering inside her for far too long.

Lost in her turbulent thoughts, Sarah failed to notice the trash can standing defiantly in the middle of the road until it was too late. With an abrupt thud, the car collided with it, sending a cacophony of clattering sounds echoing through the empty street. A torrent of expletives escaped Sarah's lips as she slammed her foot on the brake, her heart pounding in her chest. She stared at the dented trash can, its contents spilling onto the wet asphalt.

"Great," Sarah grumbled, her anger further fueled by this unexpected obstacle. She glanced around nervously, praying no one had witnessed her reckless driving. If she were caught, this wouldn't be her first DUI, and she couldn't afford one more. The rain continued to pelt against the roof of her car, adding an extra layer of frustration to her already chaotic state.

Taking a deep breath, she willed herself to calm down and regain control of her emotions. This was not the time for distractions or accidents. She needed to focus on the real reason she was here—to face her husband head-on and tell him just what she thought of him and his actions. He wasn't fooling her anymore.

With trembling hands, Sarah shifted back into drive and accelerated down the street. Her headlights cut through the darkness, illuminating the path toward his house. Each passing minute brought her closer to the confrontation she had been building up in her mind for months. The rain intensified, pounding against her car with a relentless fury that mirrored the storm inside her.

Finally, Sarah arrived at the house. She parked her car haphazardly, not caring about the crooked angle or that she had hit the curb in her haste. She reached for the door handle, her hand trembling with nerves and anger.

As she exited the car, raindrops plastered her hair to her forehead and soaked through her clothes. But she hardly noticed; she was too consumed by the fire raging within her. She marched up the driveway, leaving muddy footprints in her wake. As she approached the porch, Sarah stumbled slightly, her unsteady gait a testament to her intoxication. Yet, fueled by anger and determination, she pressed forward, marching toward the front door with newfound purpose. The porch light flickered, casting an eerie glow on her flushed face. Sarah took a deep breath to steady herself before pounding on the door. Each thud echoed through the house like a declaration of war.

Seconds stretched into minutes, but there was no response. Frustration etched deep lines into Sarah's face as she pounded harder, her voice rising in a crescendo of anger.

"Open this door, you coward! We need to talk!"

With every passing moment of silence, Sarah's fury grew. The rain continued to drum against her back as if mocking her desperation. She stepped back and kicked the door with a force she didn't know she possessed. The sound reverberated through the quiet neighborhood, shattering the calm night like a thunderclap.

Prologue

Adam peered through the window, his heart sinking as he saw Sarah's familiar figure sprinting up to the front door next door. A sigh escaped his lips, and he turned to his wife, Nicki, who stood beside him.

"Oh, no," Adam muttered, his voice laced with weariness. "She's at it again."

Nicki's eyes widened, mirroring Adam's concern. "Oh, dear," she replied softly. "Should we call the cops again?"

Adam hesitated for a moment, contemplating the best course of action. Deep down, he knew reaching out to Sarah might be more productive than involving the authorities. He placed a reassuring hand on Nicki's arm and offered her a small smile.

"It might not be necessary," Adam said gently. "Let me go over there and talk to her."

Nicki nodded, her brow furrowed with worry. "Please, be careful," she urged, her voice filled with genuine concern.

Adam kissed her forehead, feeling a surge of warmth and

love for his wife. "I will, I promise," he assured her, his eyes meeting hers. "I won't let anything happen to myself."

With a determined nod, Adam grabbed his raincoat from the hook by the door and slipped it on. He knew the importance of addressing this situation with empathy and understanding. Sarah had always been a troubled soul, lost amidst the chaos of her mind. He almost felt sorry for her, but he knew it was always the drinking that got her in trouble. If only she would stay away from the bottle....

As he stepped out onto their porch, Adam's heart raced with apprehension and compassion. He ran across the neatly trimmed lawn, jumping over puddles of water left by the passing thunderstorm.

Reaching their doorstep, Adam noticed that the door was still open and that it seemed like Sarah had kicked it in.

"Oh, no, what have you gotten yourself into this time, Sarah?" he mumbled, primarily worried about the family's daughter, Victoria, who was most likely asleep in there somewhere, unaware of what was happening.

Adam stepped onto the porch, his heart heavy. The storm had ceased, leaving a trail of wet leaves and scattered debris in its wake. The front door was swinging eerily in the wind, revealing a glimpse of darkness within.

A chilling breeze brushed against his face as Adam took a tentative step forward. Suddenly, from within the house, he heard a scream that pierced through his bones.

Without hesitation, Adam's instincts kicked into overdrive. He dashed across the threshold and rushed through the dimly lit hallway. The house seemed to hold its breath, suffocating under an oppressive silence broken only by the sound of his racing heartbeat.

As he neared the bedroom door, fear tangled with dread

inside him like an intricate knot. A flickering light spilled out from within, casting macabre shadows on the walls. Adam forced himself to push forward, his entire body trembling with horror and determination.

He flung open the door, the wooden frame creaking in protest, and his eyes were instantly drawn to the scene unfolding before him.

The bed was a mess of disheveled sheets and pillows, but that wasn't what caught his attention. There, sprawled across the bed, was Steven, Sarah's husband. His body was limp and unresponsive, blood seeping out from a gaping wound on his forehead.

Adam's heart practically stopped, grief and shock washing over him in waves. His eyes darted around the room, taking in the sight of the blood-stained walls behind Steven's lifeless form.

But his attention was soon drawn back to Sarah. She stood by the bed, trembling and looking like she had seen a ghost. There was a gun in her hand; she was holding it between two fingers, staring at it while sobbing relentlessly. She looked absolutely terrified.

"Sarah? What have you done?"

Adam's heart shattered into a million pieces, realizing the gravity of the situation. He rushed toward Sarah, trying to reach out to her to make sure she didn't hurt herself or him.

"Sarah, come on, we need to call an ambulance," he pleaded, his voice trembling with emotion.

But Sarah was beyond any help he could offer. Her eyes were empty, her face a pale mask of horror. She looked like she had lost her soul, her grip on reality slipping through her fingers.

For a moment, time seemed to stand still. Adam could hear

the sound of his own breathing, his heart pounding, and the distant thunder from storm clouds gathering again outside. It felt like everything was crashing down around him.

Then, suddenly, Sarah's grip on the gun faltered, and it fell to the floor. Adam lunged forward, wrapping his arms around her and pulling her away from the weapon. She was shaking in his hands.

"It's alright, Sarah, it's okay."

He could feel her body trembling, convulsing with sorrow and guilt as she sobbed onto his shoulder. Adam knew that he couldn't leave her like this. He had to get help for both of them... for Victoria.

Gripping the phone tightly, Adam dialed 911, his voice barely more than a whisper.

"Yes, I'd like to report a... an incident. I'm at 139 East Suwannee Lane. Yes, there's been a... a shooting. I think you need to hurry."

Part I

FRIDAY MORNING IN COCOA BEACH, FL

Chapter 1

The morning light spilled across the kitchen counter, casting a warm glow on the neatly arranged sandwiches, fruit cups, and carrot sticks. I sighed, feeling the absence of a third lunch that no longer needed making. Olivia's departure for college had left a hollow space in both the kitchen and my heart.

"Mom, where's my history book?" Christine's voice brought me back from the edge of melancholy as she bounded into the kitchen, her ponytail swinging with youthful energy.

"Did you check the living room?" I suggested, sealing the last sandwich with practiced finality.

"Found it!" she proclaimed seconds later, returning to grab an apple from the bowl on the table. Alex followed closely behind; his eyes were still sleepy, but a soft smile played on his lips. He mumbled a grateful "Thanks, Mom," before digging into his cereal.

I glanced at the clock, tension knotting in my stomach. Any minute now, Matt would be coming down. The anticipation felt like waiting for thunder after the flash of lightning. And then, there it was—the rhythmic thud of crutches on the upstairs floorboards.

Matt appeared at the top of the stairs, his jaw set in a hard line, eyes narrowed with a familiar frustration. Every step seemed to echo his bitterness, a stark reminder of the price he paid on duty—with me by his side, unable to prevent the irreversible.

"Good morning," I said, my voice treading a fine line between casual and cautious.

"Is it really?" Matt's response was terse and acidic. He descended the last step with a graceless thump of wood against the tile.

"Sit down; I'll get you some coffee," I offered, reaching for the pot.

"I'm not hungry," he snapped, maneuvering awkwardly to the table, the crutches clattering against the chair legs.

"Matt, you need to eat something," I pressed, feeling the weight of his dark mood pressing in around us.

"Stop mothering me," he retorted, a scowl etched deep into his features. His anger was a palpable force, charging the air between us.

"Maybe if you didn't act like a child—" The words slipped out before I could stop them, igniting the kindling of our constant conflict.

"Act like a child? I'm not the one who needs to fill the silence with pointless chatter because they can't handle their daughter leaving for college!"

His words stung, finding their mark with brutal precision. I gripped the edge of the counter, feeling the sting of tears threatening behind my eyes. I wanted to scream, to unleash the storm of emotions that whirled within me—grief for Olivia's absence, guilt over Matt's injury that caused him to lose a part of his leg, the suffocating helplessness.

"Maybe if you'd try to see past your own pain, you'd realize we're all hurting," I managed through clenched teeth, my heart pounding with fury and sorrow.

"Save it. I'm not the one falling apart," he shot back, the venom in his voice cutting through the remnants of family harmony like a knife.

"Mom, Matt, please stop," Christine's plea broke through our escalating war of words, pulling us back from the brink.

"Sorry, sweetheart," I murmured, deflated, the fight draining out of me as quickly as it had surged. It wasn't their battle to bear.

"Me too," Matt muttered, though his apology was directed more at the floor than Christine or me.

The kids gathered their things, escaping the battleground that our home had become. I watched them go, each step away from us a tiny ache, and wondered how many mornings we could endure before we were nothing but fragments, held together by habit and shared history rather than love and understanding.

That's when my phone vibrated on the counter. I grabbed it, relieved to be pulled away from our conversation. The past couple of months hadn't been easy on us. We were fighting a lot, and I felt so guilty every time because I knew he was struggling. Matt's son, Elijah, had been at his grandmother's for a few weeks, and we didn't know when he would be back. Matt hadn't had the energy to be a father to him since he was shot on duty and lost his leg. But it was painful to watch how Elijah still tried to connect with his dad, but Matt wouldn't let him in. He didn't like for his son to see him like this. Our three-year-old, Angel, had been spending a lot of time at my mom's house lately and was there for a few days now, giving me the extra time and space to take care of Matt or at least help him the best I could. He was going to rehabilitation five days of the week but still not making a lot of progress. His physical therapist, Dan, said it was hard to keep him motivated.

I picked up my phone, the weight of the situation heavy on my shoulders. The room seemed to hold its breath.

"Hello?" I answered, my voice betraying my worry.

It was Emily on the other end of the line, a friend I had met at the support group I had recently joined to help me navigate this new situation. She understood the unique pain that came with being a spouse or relative of someone who had been injured in war or on the job. Her voice trembled with concern and disbelief as she began speaking.

"Hey, it's me," she started, her words faltering slightly. "Something's happened... to Sarah Chapman."

My heart skipped a beat at the mention of Sarah's name. In the support group sessions, Sarah and I had connected on a level that felt profound. We shared our fears, our frustrations, and our journey toward healing. She appeared fragile and vulnerable, but beneath that facade was a strength I knew she could use to make it if only she stayed sober, which she had been good at lately.

"What happened to her?" I asked.

"She... she was arrested last night. For murder."

Chapter 2

THEN:

THE AFTERNOON LIGHT spilled like molten gold through the half-open blinds, casting long, lazy shadows across Victoria's bedroom. Sarah stood in the doorway, her silhouette elongated on the pastel carpet, watching her daughter's chest rise and fall as she napped. The room was a sanctuary of soft pinks and stuffed animals, each chosen with love to create a haven for their little girl.

"Sweet dreams, my angel," Sarah whispered, tiptoeing closer to plant a tender kiss on Victoria's forehead. But as she drew near, her maternal instincts prickled with unease. Victoria's cheeks had a pallor that didn't belong amidst the rosy décor, a stillness too pronounced for the gentle flutter of slumber.

"Steven!" Her voice cut through the calm, sharp with fear. Footsteps thudded against the hardwood floor, growing louder as her husband approached from downstairs, where they had been watching TV.

"What's wrong?" Steven's words were breathless, tinged with the edge of his profession. His eyes, trained to notice the slightest aberration, immediately caught the worry lines etching Sarah's brow.

"Look at her, Steven. She's... she's too quiet."

Sarah's fingers trembled as she pointed, her heart pounding a fierce rhythm against her ribs.

Steven knelt beside the bed, his nurse's hands deft and sure as he checked Victoria's pulse, his eyes scanning for signs only he could read.

"This isn't right," he murmured, more to himself than to Sarah. His touch was clinical yet caring, a paradox honed by countless hours in sterile hospital corridors.

"Is she..." Sarah couldn't finish the sentence, couldn't give voice to the terror that clawed at her throat.

Please, let her be okay.

"We need to get her to the hospital right now."

Steven's voice was a command, brooking no argument, but the undercurrent of urgency propelled Sarah into action.

As if in a dream, she watched herself gather Victoria into her arms—so tiny and fragile, a doll broken by an unseen hand. Her mind raced, thoughts disjointed and wild. This wasn't supposed to happen—not to them—not to their little girl who loved butterfly kisses and bedtime stories.

"Call 9-1-1 or drive ourselves?" Steven's question was weighty, speaking of life-altering decisions made in heartbeats.

"Drive. It'll be faster."

Sarah's decision was instinctual, the protective lioness within her rising. Every second mattered, every moment a precious commodity they couldn't afford to squander.

"Let's go." Steven's hand was on her back, guiding her even as she clutched Victoria closer. They moved together, a unit bound by shared purpose and unspoken vows; their world contracted to the tiny heartbeat between them.

As they hurried to the car, Sarah dared not look back at the home that was supposed to be a fortress against the world. She could only hope and pray that they weren't already too late.

Chapter 3

The salt-laden breeze from the nearby Atlantic wafted through the open door of the Cape Canaveral Police Station as I stepped inside, the sterile light reflecting off my polished FBI badge. The lobby was a muted tableau of beige and gray, punctuated by the occasional splash of color from "Wanted" posters and community announcements.

"I'm here to see the detective in charge of the Chapman case," I announced to the lady behind the counter.

"Agent Thomas," her voice cut through the formality like a knife through butter, her eyes not even glancing at the offered ID. "No need to show me your badge. I know who you are." Her fingers danced over the keyboard, pulling up information with an efficiency that spoke of years behind that desk. "That'll be Detective Ryan," she murmured, pressing the phone receiver to her ear. A beat passed before she motioned me forward. "Go right in."

The detective's office was a stark contrast to the antiseptic environment outside—papers strewn about, a whiteboard filled with scribbles and lines connecting various points of interest.

The man himself, Detective Ryan, looked up from his cluttered desk, his expression a mix of curiosity and caution.

"FBI Agent Thomas," he acknowledged, leaning back in his chair, sizing me up with a detective's practiced eye.

"Detective Ryan," I nodded.

"What can I do for you?" he asked.

"What can you tell me about the Chapman case?"

"Chapman?" He snorted, shuffling papers as if to emphasize the mundanity of it all. "Why the sudden interest in that case? It's not exactly FBI material. Wife shoots husband in bed. Open and shut. They had a fight. He had kicked her out. She was angry. Wait. Are you here to steal my case?" There was a defensive edge to his tone, the kind honed by too many years watching outsiders sweep in and claim the glory.

"Steal?" I echoed, feeling the weight of jurisdictional politics. "No, I just need to take a look at it."

"Look all you want from afar, Agent Thomas," he bristled, standing now, the energy in the room shifting to something akin to two rams butting heads. "But I do mind. I know how you people are. You can't just waltz in here, big-shot FBI agent, and snatch my case from under me."

"Detective Ryan," I began, trying to infuse my voice with calm reason, "I might be able to help—"

"No way," he cut across, stepping closer, his shadow falling over the paperwork between us, turning it into a landscape of grays. "Don't come in here all high and mighty thinking you can just steal my case. This is mine. Now, if you'd please leave."

"Of course," I said, but anger curled within me like smoke. The detective had made his stance clear; this was his turf, his victory or defeat to claim. But at what cost?

I turned and walked out, each step echoing my frustration. The door closed behind me with a click that sounded far too final, leaving me standing there, the taste of thwarted opportunity bitter on my tongue. But there was no way that was going to stop me. I would do this my own way. Sarah was my friend. I had to make sure justice was served in her case, and I had a distinct feeling that wasn't happening. I knew I had to take matters into my own hands, and that was something I wasn't afraid to do.

Chapter 4

Nicki's fingers danced across the rough surface of the chopping board, a rhythmic clack accompanying each slice through the carrots. The kitchen was awash with the warm glow of the setting sun, piercing through half-closed blinds and casting long stripes across the countertop. A pot simmered quietly on the stove, tendrils of steam curling up like delicate wisps of smoke.

The click of the front door announced Adam's arrival, and without missing a beat, she wiped her hands on her apron, turning to greet him.

"Hey," he said, his voice weary but warm as he leaned in, his lips finding hers in a brief sanctuary from the world outside. His kiss tasted of promises and long-shared comforts, an intimate ritual marking the end of another day.

"Rough day?" she asked, watching him as he loosened his tie with one hand, the other rifling absently through the stack of mail he'd scooped from the hallway table—bills, flyers, nothing that couldn't wait.

"Could say that," Adam replied, his eyes not meeting hers as they scanned the envelopes. "Did anything interesting happen here?"

Nicki hesitated, the carrot beneath her knife pausing mid-chop.

"Interesting isn't quite the word I'd use," she murmured. She stole a glance at him, gauging his attention before continuing.

"The police have been in and out of the house next door all day, parking their forensic vans on the grass that Steven always keeps so nice. And then all the people in their suits, trampling on those nice roses they just planted. I don't know how anyone can be so careless."

"Yeah, I noticed the police cars out front. I could barely get into the driveway." Adam's brow furrowed slightly, and he looked up now, concern knitting his features.

"I still can't believe that Sarah shot Steven," Nicki blurted out, the words tumbling over themselves in her haste. "They are our friends, our neighbors, Adam. They used to love one another; do you remember? When Victoria was younger. It's just... it's strange how something can go so wrong, don't you think? You think you know people. But I guess they say she was very drunk, which must have clouded her judgment. I just feel so awful, especially for Victoria. Don't you?" Her knife stilled, and she wrapped her arms around herself as though suddenly chilled.

"God, yeah. That's crazy." Adam ran a hand through his hair, a troubled expression etching itself deeper into his face. He was clearly barely listening anymore.

She chewed her lip, wrestling with the thought that had haunted her since she heard the news. "Could you ever consider... murdering me over a fight?" she asked, her voice barely a whisper.

Adam's head snapped up, his eyes wide with bewilderment. "Hm, what?" he asked, clearly caught off guard.

"Nothing," Nicki said quickly, too quickly perhaps, her heart pounding against her ribs. She forced a laugh, brittle and unconvincing even to her own ears. Turning back to her cooking, she focused on the carrots again, letting the rhythm of the knife restore a semblance of normalcy to the room. But inside, a coil of unease tightened. She wondered if normal would ever truly return or if it was just another casualty in a world where dinner conversations could turn so dark so quickly.

Chapter 5

The cold clink of my badge landing on the reception desk at Brevard County Jail resonated like an accusation. The woman behind the counter gave me a look.

"I need to speak with Sarah Chapman," I said, my voice steady despite the storm of emotions whirling inside me.

I was still cursing at Detective Ryan, who didn't want me to help on the case. Who did he think he was? Weren't two heads better than one? Wouldn't my expertise in solving murder cases benefit him? I knew he just wanted to take the honor for himself. I knew his type. And he definitely didn't want me around to question his evidence or conclusions.

"Right this way," the officer replied with a nod, leading me to a sterile room smelling faintly of bleach and despair. The walls were a stark white, and the furniture was bolted to the floor. It was hard to imagine Sarah in this place. She was such a sweet girl, around five or six years younger than me. She had lost her dad in the line of duty as a police officer, and that's why she was in the support group. She was also in AA. It was court-ordered after her last DUI, but they hadn't taken her driver's license just yet. I knew she could beat this addiction to alcohol. She had been so strong and so adamant about it. She was always so neatly dressed, matching her earrings with her shirts and sometimes even shoes. She had been doing so well and had not been drinking for months. What had happened? I wondered what had sent her over the edge.

I was left alone, seated on a hard plastic chair that chafed against my back—minutes stretched into what felt like hours, punctuated only by the distant echoes of clanging doors and muffled voices. My mind drifted, unbidden, to Matt—the sharp words we exchanged still hanging heavy in the air between us.

Guilt gnawed at me, the memory of his defeated eyes more than I could bear. Was I too harsh? I wondered, tracing patterns on the cool metal table before me. I should have been his solace, not another source of strife. But he seemed so lost, and I—I just wanted him to find that spark again, to kindle the fire that made him a great detective... that made him my Matt.

"Fight, damn it," I had urged him in the car on the way to rehabilitation this same morning, forcing cheer into my voice. "For yourself, for us."

My plea had sounded hollow, and now I felt awful. I wasn't doing enough to motivate him. But months had passed. Shouldn't he be getting better by now? Was it depression over the fact that he was injured and that he faced maybe never coming back to being a detective again? Why wouldn't he even try? Why not fight for it? I couldn't just let him lose hope, could I?

Suddenly, the door swung open, shattering my reverie. Two guards ushered in Sarah Chapman, her hands cuffed in front of her. Her hair was a mess, and it was the first time I had seen her without makeup, but when she lifted her head and our gazes locked, there was a flicker of recognition, a glint of the friend I knew and loved.

"Eva Rae," she breathed out, her voice cracking. Tears welled in her eyes, brimming with relief, remorse, and a thousand unsaid apologies. "I'm so glad to see you. You won't believe how glad I am."

Her words hung suspended, a fragile bridge across the chasm her actions had wrought.

"Sarah," I replied, my voice thick with a cocktail of empathy and duty. "Let's talk."

Chapter 6

THEN:

THE STERILE SCENT of the hospital mingled with the undercurrent of disinfectant and fear, wrapping around Sarah as she stood rooted in place by Victoria's bedside. Beeps and whirs from the machines formed a mechanical symphony that underscored the medical staff's urgent ballet. Their faces were masks of concentration, with occasionally furrowed brows betraying their confusion.

"Her pulse is there, but look at it—it's like a whisper," one doctor murmured, eyes fixed on the glowing monitor displaying Victoria's heartbeat.

"Have we run a toxicology screen? What about an MRI?" Steven asked, his voice cutting through the soft shuffle of nurses' shoes on linoleum. He was pacing, a creature caged by his own helplessness, every fiber of his being radiating the urgency of his training. Sarah didn't understand much of what was going on or why her daughter was suddenly so sick, and it frightened her so profoundly that it was hard to breathe.

Sarah turned to him, her eyes wide with worry, trying to decipher his rapid-fire jargon. "Steven, what... what are they looking for?"

"Anything, Sarah. A reason she won't wake up." His hands sliced through the air as if he could physically grab the answers from the space between them.

"Shouldn't they try...?" He cut himself off, rubbing his temples. It was clear he wanted to be on the other side—part of the team working to save his little girl.

A nurse adjusted a dial, and the steady beep of the heart monitor climbed an octave, pulling Sarah's gaze back to the small form lost in the tangle of white sheets.

"Come on, Victoria. Please, baby," she whispered, her mind a storm of silent pleas and bargaining prayers. The cold touch of the bed rail beneath her fingers felt like the only anchor in a world threatening to spiral out of control. Every beep was a lifeline, every hushed word from the medical team a potential harbinger of hope or despair.

"Have we considered encephalitis? Where are we with the lumbar puncture results?" Steven was relentless, each question a testament to his love and desperation.

"Steven..." Sarah's voice trembled, unable to articulate the dread pooling in her stomach—the terror that maybe this time, his knowledge wasn't enough.

"Hey." He stopped his pacing and took her hand, his own trembling slightly. "We've got to trust them. Okay?"

She nodded, squeezing his hand as though the pressure could somehow transfer her fears into him, where his clinical expertise might dissolve them. But deep down, both knew some fears were immune to even the most rational minds.

The room buzzed with activity, yet the silence within Sarah grew louder, a void where the sound of her daughter's laughter used to echo. She clung to Steven's hand, a lifeline amidst the uncertainty, her thoughts a mantra of hope that refused to be silenced by the ominous dance of the unknown. And that's when the machine monitoring her heartbeat flat-lined with a terrifying sound that cut through her bones.

"Victoria!" she screamed. "No!"

Chapter 7

The cold chill of the visiting room at the county prison seeped into my bones as I sat across from Sarah. Her hands trembled on the table, cuffs clinking softly with each uncontrolled movement. The fluorescent lights above cast a harsh glow on her pale features, deepening the dark circles under her eyes.

"Sarah," I began, my voice steady despite the cold, "tell me what happened."

She looked up, her gaze flickering with fragments of frustration and fear. "I don't know," she stammered, words choked by sobs that shook her slender frame. She buried her face in her hands, shoulders heaving as she tried to compose herself. Little rivers of tears escaped between her fingers, painting wet streaks on the tabletop.

"Sarah," I pressed gently but firmly, needing clarity amidst the chaos of her emotions. "You need to talk to me. I'm your friend in this. Tell me what happened last night."

"I didn't do it," she finally managed, peering up through moist eyelashes. "I... he must have killed himself."

"What do you mean?" My question hung in the air like the buzz of the overhead lights.

"He was already dead when I arrived at the house. He was on the bed, shot in the head."

I pulled out my notepad, flipping to the page where I'd scribbled notes from the police report. I had gone into the database and pulled it out myself since Detective Ryan refused to let me in on his investigation. I had read through his report and wasn't very impressed, to put it mildly. "According to this," I said, tapping the paper, "you were angry. You went to his house because you were mad, and then—you shot him."

Sarah's hands clenched into fists. "No! That's not...."

"The neighbor," I continued, relentless in pursuit of the truth, "found you with the gun still in your hand. How can you explain that?"

Her eyes darted away, then back to mine, filled with a desperate plea for understanding. "I was holding it between two fingers. I picked it up from the floor," she confessed, miming the action with a shaky hand. "I don't know why. It was just a reaction."

"Sarah," I sighed, closing my notepad with a soft thud, "the report also states that you were very intoxicated when it happened. How can anyone be expected to believe your story under those circumstances?"

"Because..." Her voice trailed off, and she swallowed hard before trying again. "My daughter was there."

"Victoria?" I asked, probing further.

"Yes." A small spark of maternal determination flickered in her eyes. "She was in her bed when it happened. She must have heard the gun go off before I entered the house. She must know the truth."

"Did you tell the detective this?"

"Of course I did!" Sarah's voice cracked with indignation. "But he wouldn't even talk to her. He just dismissed it."

I nodded slowly, absorbing the gravity of her claim. If Victoria had indeed witnessed something, it could change everything. Yet, whether it would exonerate her mother or condemn her further remained a mystery—one that I was now determined to unravel.

Chapter 8

Nicki's eyes bolted open, the muggy Florida air clinging to her skin despite the air conditioning running on high. She could hear the ceiling fan struggling to cool the room as she shifted in bed, trying to find a comfortable spot.

Beside her, Adam's snores grew louder and more obnoxious by the minute. She turned toward him, the moonlight casting silver shadows on his face, and couldn't help but glare at his peaceful obliviousness. With a heavy sigh, she closed her eyes and tried to drown out the sound of his snoring.

Hunger gnawed at her belly. She slid from the bed with a soft huff, careful not to wake him. Bare feet padded across the cool tile as she descended the stairs, craving a simple midnight snack—something, anything to help her sleep.

As Nicki stepped into the kitchen, her eyes adjusted to the dim lighting, and she reached for the switch. The sudden brightness made her squint, but it also revealed a familiar scene. She spotted a tray of freshly baked cookies on the counter, and a bottle of milk in the fridge caught her attention. Without hesitation, she poured herself a glass and indulged in a cookie, savoring each crumb that fell onto her fingers.

Beyond the window, palm trees swayed in the salty ocean air, their rustling leaves a comforting sound. But Sarah couldn't focus on their calming rhythm. The image of last night's events played over and over in her mind, each detail seared into her memory. She couldn't shake the feeling of disbelief as she thought about their neighbor, Sarah, being arrested for murder. It didn't make sense—sure, their marriage and separation had been messy, but could it have really led to such a heinous act? Killing the man she had once loved and had a child with?

"Victoria," she whispered, the name leaving a bitter taste. Poor kid. She'd been shipped off to an aging grandmother when she needed parents the most. It seemed unbelievable. Yes, Nicki knew that Sarah was a drunk. She had come to the house more than once after the split and yelled at him from outside the house, and once, they had to call the cops on her. It was Adam who wanted to do it, not Nicki. But she knew now it had been the right thing to do. Sarah needed to stop the drinking, and Nicki thought that she had. It had been months with no episodes, and when she met her at Publix one day, she was completely sober and told her she was in AA now and had been sober for three months.

So, what happened?

Nicki went outside. She sat on her porch swing, enjoying the warm breeze and the sounds of crickets chirping, when a loud rustling sound made her jump. She frantically looked toward her front door, scanning for any signs of movement. Her heart pounded in her chest as she imagined what could be causing the noise—was it a pesky raccoon or something more dangerous like a gator? She couldn't help but think of the videos she had seen online of wild animals invading people's homes in the middle of the night.

There it was again. That unmistakable sound of something meddling where it shouldn't.

"Okay, Nicki. Just a raccoon," she muttered to herself.

She walked inside and grabbed a pot and pan, the tools of suburban defense. Ready to make a racket, to send whatever critter scurrying, she crept to the door. Hand trembling, she reached for the knob, braced for chaos.

But there was no wild animal in the quiet shadow of the front porch. Instead, there was an envelope. Her name was etched on the front in sharp, deliberate letters. No raccoon wrote that.

She snatched the envelope and turned back inside, every nerve on edge.

Chapter 9

As I drove away from the prison, my tires kicked up a cloud of dirt, and my doubts followed me like unwelcome passengers. I couldn't shake the image of Sarah's glazed eyes as we spoke during the interview. A thick fog of confusion engulfed me as I tried to understand how she could still function on that fatal night with such a high level of alcohol in her system. Most people would have blacked out, but she seemed to have a remarkable tolerance. She was actually able to drive her car to his house.

I couldn't shake off the vivid images from the witness accounts. Her car careened down the lane, leaving a trail of debris in its wake before colliding with a trash can, the metallic thud echoing through the neighborhood. And then her body stumbling out and staggering toward his house. It was clear that she was severely intoxicated, an understatement to describe her condition.

How could I believe her when she told me what happened? But for some reason, I did. When my mind told me not to, my heart told me otherwise. Something wasn't right about this whole thing.

I believed her. I didn't know why, but I did.

Her rap sheet flashed through my mind. She had been in the hands of the police several times before. Once from being pulled over and getting a DUI, the second time when she showed up at her old house, wasted, and started to scream at and attack Steven, her estranged husband, and the neighbors had enough of her. That didn't bode well for her defense—not exactly a pristine record.

I fumbled for my phone; the number for the Cape Canaveral Police Station had already been pulled up. I pressed call and waited anxiously as the line rang. Finally, Detective Ryan answered with a heavy sigh, his voice sounding drained.

"Agent Thomas. Twice in one day? To what do I owe the honor this time?" he said with a mocking voice.

"The daughter," I said, gripping the steering wheel tighter. This guy rubbed me the wrong way. If it was his arrogance or his laziness, I didn't know—probably both.

“What about her?” His voice was flat, disinterested.

"Why didn't you interview her?" I asked. "She was in the house. She was a potential witness. If Sarah claims the gun went off before she entered the house, she could have heard it. Or at least she must have seen something. Didn't she run to her dad's bedroom when the shot was fired? Or even if she was too scared to, she might have peered through a crack in the door or at least heard her mother enter?"

Laughter crackled through the line. My grip on the phone tightened, knuckles whitening. What was it with this guy?

"What's so funny?" My voice was sharper than intended.

"Know anything about the daughter?" he shot back.

"No, why?" I felt tension coiling within me.

"Find out yourself if you're such a sharp FBI detective."

Click. The line went dead.

Fury bubbled up in my chest, sending a burst of heat through my body. My clenched fists slammed into the steering wheel, the sound reverberating in the small space of the car. Embarrassment flooded in next, making me feel small and foolish. I took deep breaths, trying to quell the tumultuous emotions raging inside me. But I knew this wasn't the end of it... not by a long shot.

Chapter 10

THEN:

THE HARSH, fluorescent lights of the emergency room illuminated Victoria's face in a pale, ghostly glow. Sarah's voice trembled with fear as she pleaded for help, her hands longing for something or someone to hold onto, to cling to, while the world crumbled beneath her.

Her daughter was lifeless; there was no heartbeat. The terror of the realization threatened to break her.

"Victoria, please... someone, anyone... you have to save her!" Her words echoed off the sterile walls, filling the air with desperation and hopelessness.

Steven was a crumpled figure on the cold tile floor, his face a mask of silent horror, hands pressed into the unforgiving surface as if trying to ground himself against the possibility of a world without his daughter.

"Charging to 200 joules," announced one of the doctors, a

steely note of determination threading her voice. "Everyone clear?"

"Clear!" echoed the medical team in unison, stepping back from the small form lying motionless on the gurney.

Sarah's eyes locked onto Victoria's chest as it arched in response to the defibrillator's pulse, a heart-wrenching mimicry of life that left her gasping for breath. The seconds stretched into eternities, each one an agonizing lifetime as they waited for a sign, any sign, of hope.

Then, a symphony of beeps erupted from the monitor—a chaotic yet beautiful melody that signaled the stubborn beat of Victoria's heart resuming its duty.

"Her rhythm's back!" shouted a nurse, relief washing over her features.

Sarah's knees buckled, and Steven caught her just in time. They clung to each other, their embrace a lifeline amidst the storm of fear and relief.

"She's back, Steven, she's back," Sarah sobbed, her words muffled against the fabric of his shirt.

The doctors busied themselves with stabilizing Victoria, connecting tubes and wires that would tether her to the machines now responsible for sustaining her fragile life. Steven, every line of his body speaking the language of protective vigilance, turned to Sarah, whose eyes were fixed on their daughter's pale face.

"Sarah, love, you should go home. Get some rest," he murmured, his voice a tender command. "You have that important meeting tomorrow, remember?"

"No, I can't leave her," Sarah protested weakly, her exhaustion written in the dark circles under her eyes and the tremble in her voice. "I don't care about the meeting."

"Shh, I'll be here," Steven assured her, his hand squeezing

hers with a strength that belied his own fear. "I won't leave her side. You need to sleep."

Reluctance warred with the knowledge that he was right; she was running on fumes, her body and soul pushed to the brink. With a final glance at Victoria, the rise and fall of her chest a metronome counting the precious seconds of her continued fight, Sarah nodded.

"Call me, any change—" she started to say.

"Immediately," Steven interjected, understanding the unsaid. "Now, go."

She leaned down, pressing a kiss to Victoria's forehead, a silent promise to return, before allowing Steven to usher her out of the room. As the door closed behind her, Sarah's steps faltered under the weight of the night's events, her mind echoing with the beeps of the monitors and the steadfast beating of her child's heart.

Chapter 11

I pulled into the parking lot, the familiar brick facade of the physiotherapist's office looming ahead. Stepping out of the car, I let the warm breeze from the beach on the other side of A1A ruffle through my jacket as I walked briskly toward the entrance. The glass door swooshed open, and the faint yet by now very familiar smell of antiseptic mingled with sweat greeted me.

"Hey," Dan called out from across the room, a clipboard in his hand. His eyes were serious, and his brows were creased with concern. "Can we talk for a sec?"

"Sure," I replied, following him down a narrow hallway to a vacant consultation room. The sounds of exertion and the clank of workout equipment dulled to a murmur. I felt like I was being called to the principal's office, and my kid had misbehaved.

Through the half-open blinds, I caught a glimpse of Matt, idle in his wheelchair, absorbed in something on his phone. Dan closed the door and leaned against it, shaking his head slowly. "I don't know what to do," he confessed, the frustration evident in his furrowed forehead.

"Matt is giving up."

"How do I help him?" I asked, my voice barely above a whisper, hoping for some kind of revelation.

Dan sighed, the sound heavy with helplessness. "He lacks the motivation to do the work."

"Is there anything that might give him that?" I pressed, thinking aloud. "His children? The prospect of him being able to play with them in the backyard again?"

I exhaled sharply, feeling the enormity of the situation press down on me. "I have tried," I said, the words tasting like defeat.

Dan rubbed the back of his neck, glancing back toward the window. "He has the prosthetic fitting coming up, and he's not even close to where he is supposed to be at this point. I fear he is giving up. Hope is his best bet right now, and he needs it."

A sigh followed by silence. I felt helpless.

"Maybe you could work on him this weekend?" Dan suggested tentatively. Could you try to get his motivation up a little before he comes back here on Monday?"

"I will try," I promised, though the assurance sounded hollow even to my own ears. "I will try my best."

With a nod to Dan, I left the quiet room and approached Matt. I mustered a smile that felt painted on and said, "Hi."

He barely looked up, his response flat and disinterested. "What took you so long?"

"I was working. Remember how I told you about what happened to Sarah Chapman? My friend from the support group?" I ventured, trying to pierce the bubble of his isolation with a tether to the outside world.

"I'm really not interested," he cut me off, his voice curt. "Can we just go home?"

The dismissal stung, a stark reminder of the abyss that had opened up between us. We left the facility in silence, my footsteps echoing my internal turmoil. Helpless and frustrated, I grabbed the handles of the wheelchair and pushed; he seemed to slip further away with each rotation of the wheels on his chair.

Chapter 12

Nicki's fingers trembled as the door clicked shut, the house's silence amplifying the pounding in her chest. The letter felt like lead in her hand, her name scrawled across the front in an unfamiliar hand. She traced the letters of her name, each stroke sending another shiver down her spine.

What is this? Her thoughts were a swirling maelstrom of confusion and fear.

She peered out the window, the fluttering police tape outside casting eerie shadows on the moonlit street.

Why now? In the dead of night? Nicki thought, her breath hitching. Who would do this?

Summoning courage she wasn't sure she had, Nicki tore open the envelope with shaky hands. The single piece of paper inside seemed to weigh more than it should as she unfolded it, her eyes flitting over the two stark words printed there:

YOU KNEW.

"Knew what?" she whispered to the empty room, turning the paper over in search of more, but there was nothing else.

Just those two accusatory words stared back at her and ignited a firestorm of questions in her mind.

A gust of wind rattled the windows, and Nicki jumped, her heart racing even faster. With an impulse to rid herself of the note's heavy presence, she crumpled it up and tossed it into the trash can. She needed distance from that ominous message.

Her feet carried her upstairs on autopilot, every creak of the steps echoing loudly in the stillness of the night. Nicki slipped into bed beside Adam, who lay sound asleep, oblivious to the turmoil within her. She pulled the covers up to her chin, trying to quell the tremors that refused to subside.

As the hours ticked by, Nicki lay wide-eyed, staring at the ceiling, feeling Adam's rhythmic breathing beside her. The darkness felt oppressive, filled with shadows and secrets. The cryptic message played on a loop in her head:

You knew. You knew.

But what did she know? What truth was lurking just beyond her grasp, taunting her? Did it have anything to do with what happened at the neighbor's house? With Sarah shooting Steven?

But what? How?

Her thoughts raced as she tried to piece together the truth that seemed just out of reach. The weight on her chest grew heavier with every passing moment, squeezing the air out of her lungs. She longed for morning to come and lift this suffocating darkness from her.

Each heartbeat was a reminder of the dread that had taken root in her chest, its tendrils wrapping tighter around her as the night dragged on.

As the first rays of sunlight peeked through the curtains, casting a soft glow across the room, Nicki realized she had spent the entire night tossing and turning, her mind a battleground between confusion and fear. As the light chased away the remnants of darkness, she sat up suddenly, her breathing quickening.

AT THAT MOMENT, the pieces clicked together like an unsolved puzzle, finally forming a clear picture. She clutched the bedsheet tightly, her knuckles turning white.

The realization hit her with the force of a tidal wave. The secret she had buried deep within her memory had been unearthed, thrust into her present in the most chilling way.

She realized at that moment her life was in great danger.

Chapter 13

The aroma of freshly brewed coffee filled the sunny kitchen as I took a moment to savor its warmth in my favorite mug. The steam curled up like a whispered secret, and I leaned back against the counter, watching Alex shovel another forkful of pancakes into his mouth. His eyes sparkled with anticipation.

"Mom, I'm going to score today. Just for you," he declared between bites, syrup smudging the corner of his lips.

I reached out and playfully tousled his sandy hair, my heart swelling with pride. "I can't wait to see that, champ."

The house was unusually tranquil. The teenager was still cocooned in her bed while little Angel sat on the floor, her chubby fingers stacking colorful bricks with determined concentration. It was a slice of domestic serenity I cherished on weekends like these.

The peace, however, was short-lived. The scrape and thud of crutches on hardwood announced Matt's arrival before he hobbled into view, a scowl etched deep across his features. He collapsed onto a chair with a heavy sigh, the lines of discomfort evident in the tight set of his jaw.

"Morning, Matt. Want some coffee?" I offered, hoping to ease some of the tension from his body. He was supposed to keep using his crutches while at home and not the wheelchair, and that made him angry.

"Thanks," he grunted, barely looking up as I poured the dark liquid into a cup and slid it across the table toward him.

"Would you like pancakes or eggs?" I asked, trying to maintain a cheerful tone despite the heaviness settling in the room.

"Neither looks good," he muttered, pushing the coffee around with a spoon.

"How did you sleep?" My voice wrapped around the question like a soft blanket, trying to comfort him.

"Awful, as usual. It's too darn hot in that bedroom downstairs." The words came out like gravel, and I sighed, wishing I could do more to alleviate his misery. It was just too hard for him to make it up the stairs, and he had chosen to sleep downstairs instead.

In her innocence, Angel toddled over to Matt, arms wide, a wordless plea to be lifted onto the safe harbor of his lap. But instead of opening his arms, Matt's hand went up, stopping her advance.

"Not now, Angel," he snapped, not unkindly but with a firmness that sent her retreating.

My heart clenched painfully. There was a time when Matt had been her hero, her playmate, her everything. Now, there was an invisible wall between them, one that seemed to grow higher by the day.

"Alex and I are heading out to his soccer game in Viera," I said, hoping to pull some reaction from him, but he only nodded absently, his attention elsewhere.

"What will you do all day?" The question lingered in the air, heavy with concern.

"Watch TV," he replied, already moving toward the living room, leaving me in a kitchen that suddenly felt too large and empty.

"Mommy, we need to go, or we'll be late!" Alex's urgency pulled me from my thoughts.

"Okay, love." I kissed his forehead, the promise of the game momentarily lifting the weight in my chest. "Go get your bag, and Angel and I will wait for you in the car."

As he bounded off, I turned back to Matt, now flicking through channels, lost in a world of flickering images. "Are you sure you don't want to come?" My voice was a mere whisper, almost drowned out by the TV.

He didn't even glance my way.

With a heavy heart, I scooped Angel into my arms, her tiny body a balm to my soul, and walked out to the car. As I strapped her into her seat, my mind wandered unbidden to the chilling case of Sarah Chapman. Her story was a somber reminder of the fragility within us all.

Could anyone reach a breaking point? I wondered silently, staring at the steering wheel but seeing nothing as the question echoed in the quiet space of the car. I had brought my laptop with the files to the game and was eager to get into the case details while my boy showed his skills on the soccer field.

“Hurry up, Mom; you’re so slow,” he urged me along as I started the car and took off down my quiet street. My mind was still fixed on the details of the case that didn’t seem to make sense to me. There were a lot of them, too many, in my opinion.

Chapter 14

THEN:

WITH EVERY BEAT of her heart, the clock's ticking grew louder. Sarah clicked through each slide, her voice rising and falling with her presentation's dramatic peaks and valleys. The graph on the final slide seemed to stretch toward the ceiling as if it held the company's future in its lines. She finished her speech with a flourish, holding her breath and waiting for her boss's reaction. And then came the nod of approval, sending a wave of relief and pride through her body.

Sarah's boss beamed with pride as he patted her shoulder, his strong, calloused hand a familiar weight.

"You did an exceptional job, Sarah," he said in a satisfied tone. His expression clearly indicated that the deal had been secured, and they were both relieved.

"Thank you," she managed, her eyes darting to her silent phone for the umpteenth time. There was no call from the hospital, no messages from Steven, and a cocktail of relief and anxiety churned in her stomach.

Guilt gnawed at her; she should have been there at Victoria's bedside, not here basking in corporate success. Yet, the rest had sharpened her mind and given her the edge she needed today—a mother's sacrifice, she reasoned, for the sake of her daughter's future.

"Sarah?" Her boss's voice sliced through her thoughts. "You did great."

"Thanks, I..." Her response faltered as her phone finally vibrated—just an email alert. False alarm.

"Go," he said, reading her turmoil like the spreadsheets they scrutinized daily. "Family first."

She didn't need to be told twice. Heels clacking with urgency, she burst through the revolving doors and got into her car. Traffic was mercifully sparse, allowing her thoughts to race ahead to the hospital.

Please, let her be okay. Please, dear God, let her not be sick.

She could still see her pale face as they had brought her in the night before. How quiet she had been, barely breathing, sometimes stopping completely. It was terrifying. Luckily, Steven was there and had been there all night. Being a nurse, he knew how to take care of her properly. He was the right choice, even though it hurt her to have to leave.

The sterile smell greeted her as she navigated the familiar corridors to Victoria's room, where she found Steven, his posture weary but his grip on their daughter's hand unyielding. He was talking to the doctor. Sarah's heart began to race. What was going on?

"Sarah, you're right on time," the doctor's voice cut through the hush, his face a canvas of professional neutrality.

"Is she...?" Her heart pounded, awaiting the verdict that hovered over them like a storm cloud.

"Steven has all the details," the doctor excused himself, glancing at his watch. "I must attend to another patient."

"Thank you, Doctor," she murmured, but her eyes were already pleading with Steven for answers.

"Steven," she whispered, her voice barely carrying. "What did the doctor say?"

Her heart raced as she looked into his tear-filled eyes. His lips trembled as he spoke, each word hitting her like a ton of bricks.

"It's not good," he said, his voice heavy with sorrow and regret. The weight of his words threatened to crush her, overshadowing any success she may have had in her professional life.

"It's not good at all."

Chapter 15

The shrill whistle pierced the air, and I glanced up from my laptop just in time to see Alex dart onto the field. The crowd's roar was a distant hum against my focused thoughts. He caught my eye and waved energetically, his face lit with the innocent pride of youth. I managed a smile and returned the gesture, but his moment was already slipping through my fingers as I sank back into the world of crime scene photos.

"Go, Alex!" I heard someone shout, and it might've been me in another life—one not entwined with murder and secrets.

Beside me, Angel had befriended a girl her size, their laughter mingling with the cheers. They played, oblivious to the weight of the world, creating their own out of sticks and sunshine on the sidelines.

With a sigh, I reopened the digital file, the glow of my computer screen painting cold light on solemn faces watching the game. Steven Chapman lay there, static and pale, eternally asleep on silken sheets. But something nagged at me—a gut feeling that screamed everything was wrong.

"Mom! Did you see? I scored!"

Alex's voice snapped me back to reality, but it was too late. The goal was a ghost; all I could do was wave, catching the tail end of his triumph. His eyes rolled theatrically before he jogged off, again absorbed by the game.

I couldn't shake the unease, so I grabbed my phone and dialed Detective Ryan. The ringtone was brief, an intrusion on his weekend calm.

"She couldn't have shot him," I blurted the moment he answered.

"Happy Saturday to you, too," Ryan's voice came through, tinged with resignation. In the background, splashes and giggles painted a vivid picture of his family day at the pool.

"Detective, it's about the positioning," I insisted, flicking back to the photo where Chapman lay too perfectly arranged. "That's not what a body looks like when it has just been shot."

"Okay, and?" There was the sound of water being displaced, a child's squeal.

"His legs, arms—all too straight. And the blood splatter, it doesn't match the angle." I swallowed, feeling the tension grip my throat.

"Maybe she moved him," he offered with an exasperated exhale.

"But the magazine, Ryan. It was under the bed, not in the gun." My finger hovered over the incriminating image, the magazine lying inert on the carpet, a puzzle piece fallen far from the board.

"Accidents happen. Maybe she dropped it." I could almost hear him rubbing the bridge of his nose.

"Or maybe someone else was there. Because how did it end up so far away? She couldn't have kicked it—not from where she was standing." I pressed, hoping he'd see reason.

"Look, I'm with my family. What do you want from me?" His patience was fraying at the edges.

"Consider the time. A passerby heard the gunshot at 10:45 pm, but the neighbors didn't see Sarah entering the house until 11:10 pm. How does that work, Detective?" I pushed, my voice steady despite the doubt creeping in.

"Times can be mistaken," he countered, but his tone lacked conviction.

"Or perhaps the killer is still out there, getting away with murder while we're talking." My words hung between us, heavy with implication.

Ryan's frustration echoed through the line, a tangible thing even amidst the din of playful shouts and splashing water.

"What's your point?"

"My point," I said, closing the files with a decisive click, "is that we're chasing shadows while the real murderer walks free."

“I don’t have time for this nonsense,” he said, then hung up. I stared at the phone, then lifted my gaze just in time to see Alex score again. I rose to my feet and clapped eagerly, making sure he noticed that I saw this one.

Chapter 16

The soles of Nicki's sneakers squeaked against the meticulously cleaned linoleum, causing her to flinch. The loud noise reverberated through the empty office space, sending chills down her spine. She nervously glanced around at the endless rows of identical cubicles, feeling like she was being watched. Despite no one lifting their gaze from their computer screens, a wave of paranoia washed over her, and her heart started racing.

Nicki's colleague barely looked up from their computer screen as she walked into the office.

"Morning, Nicki," they mumbled, their eyes glued to the monitor.

"Morning," she replied in a strained whisper, her voice betraying her tiredness and frustration.

At her desk, the click-clack of keyboards around her morphed into footsteps in her mind, following, always following. She forced a gulp of cold coffee down her throat, trying to ignore the tremors in her hands.

"Nicki, you okay?" a voice cut through her spiraling thoughts.

"Fine," she managed, her eyes darting to the clock. It was too early to leave, but the walls were closing in.

"Paranoid," she muttered to herself, glancing over her shoulder. There was nothing amiss, just colleagues immersed in their tasks. But her gut screamed danger, and she couldn't bear another second by lunchtime. Muttering an excuse about feeling unwell, she gathered her bag and fled.

Her heart raced with fear and relief as she turned the key in the rusty lock. The familiar scent of lavender greeted her as she stepped inside, flicking the lights on out of habit. She made a beeline for her bedroom, where a worn suitcase lay hidden under the bed. She pulled it out and laid it on the bed with a sigh of anxiety.

Clothes flew into the open case, not folded, just gone. She needed the essentials: cash, her passport, and her phone. Her hands trembled as she dialed the familiar number.

"Hey, it's Nicki... Can I crash for a few days?"

"Sure, but what's going—"

"Thanks." She cut off the questions she couldn't answer, not yet.

She ran her fingers along the cool metal zipper, pulling it closed with a satisfying slide. The suitcase's weight pressed against her chest, reminding her of everything she was leaving behind. She took one last glance around the room, taking in every picture on the wall, every knick-knack on the shelves. Her eyes glistened with unshed tears as she whispered, "Stay alive," to herself. With a grunt, she lifted the heavy suitcase and walked out the door.

She bounded down the stairs, her heart racing with urgency. The living room was shrouded in darkness, the heavy curtains pulled tightly shut. As she reached the bottom step, a figure stepped out of the shadows, startling her.

Nicki dropped her suitcase to the floor with a thud.

Her heart slammed against her ribs, cold sweat beading on her forehead. "I-I'm sorry," she stammered, the words dying in her throat. "I really am very, very sorry."

"Sorry doesn't cut it, Nicki," came the reply, low and devoid of warmth.

A metallic click and the world narrowed to the barrel of the gun. The trigger pulled, soundless over her own scream.

Chapter 17

The front door swung open as I drove up in the driveway, and there stood Mom, already with a disapproving tilt to her lips.

"Can you watch the kids for a few hours?" I blurted out, masking the urgency in my voice with a smile as I helped the little ones unbuckle their seat belts.

"Again, Eva Rae? You know I love them, but I had plans...." Her complaint trailed off into a sigh as she caught the look in my eye. "Fine, but you owe me."

"Thanks, Mom. You're a lifesaver," I said, planting a kiss on her cheek as the kids wrapped around her legs, already chattering about their day.

With a wave goodbye, I dashed back to my car and headed straight to the station. The weight of the Chapman case pressed down on me like the relentless, stifling Florida heat.

The police station was quiet, the usual bustle of weekday crime reduced to a sleepy hum. Chief Annie's door was closed, but light spilled from the crack beneath it, letting me know that my instincts were correct and she was there. I rapped softly, my heart thrumming against my ribs.

"Eva Rae?" Annie's voice held a mixture of surprise and mild annoyance. "Come on in."

"You have a minute?"

"Of course. What can I do for you on a Saturday?" she asked, her eyes scanning me over the rim of her glasses.

"I'm worried," I said, stepping inside and closing the door behind me. "About the Chapman case."

"The Chapman case?" Her eyebrows shot up. "But that's in the Cape Canaveral District. It's not even our case."

"I know," I admitted, shifting uncomfortably. "But I fear that the detective on the case is about to make a huge mistake—one that might end up sending the wrong person to prison for the rest of her life."

"And what are you building this upon?" Annie leaned back in her chair, the leather creaking under her weight. "We have enough cases of our own," she added with a weary rub of her temple.

I was about to speak when she interrupted me.

"And please don't say it's a hunch."

I met her gaze steadily, the certainty in my gut too strong to ignore. "It's a hunch," I answered.

She rolled her eyes, the ghost of a smirk pulling at the corner of her mouth despite herself. "You and your hunches...."

"Annie, I need to investigate further," I pleaded. "I need your permission."

"Okay," she sighed, her annoyance clear. "But no one can know, okay? It stays between the two of us. I don't want to get in trouble with our colleagues next town over."

"Of course not," I promised, already halfway out the door. "I'll be silent as a mouse."

"Uh-huh," she muttered, her skepticism ringing in the otherwise empty room. "Somehow, I doubt that, Eva Rae."

Part II

SUNDAY MORNING, CAPE CANAVERAL

Chapter 18

Sunlight spilled through the gauzy curtains, painting stripes of warmth across the hardwood floor. Pete Hancock sat at his kitchen table, a mug of freshly brewed coffee in one hand and his tablet in the other, scrolling through the latest headlines. The serenity of the morning wrapped around him like a well-worn robe, undisturbed but for the gentle hum of the refrigerator.

A rustle from the hallway broke the calm, and he didn't need to look up to know the source. She padded into the kitchen, hair tousled and eyes squinting against the light, remnants of last night's mascara framing her gaze with smudged shadows.

"Is there more coffee?" Her voice was raspy, hopeful.

"Sure," Pete replied, not lifting his eyes from the screen, "but pour it in a travel mug, will you? I've got plans today."

Her brows knitted together, a slight frown tugging at her lips. "Oh, I thought maybe we could—"

"Can't," he cut her off curtly, finally glancing up with a casual shrug. "Busy day ahead."

The air between them thickened, charged with unspoken words and expectations dashed. She crossed her arms, a defensive barrier that came too late. "You could've mentioned that last night."

He scoffed lightly, a smirk playing on his lips. "Last night was last night. Today's today." His tone was dismissive, indifferent to the sting he knew his words carried.

She huffed, grabbing her purse from the counter and shaking her head in disbelief. "You're an ass, Hancock."

"Never claimed otherwise," he retorted, watching as she poured the coffee with jerky movements, her irritation palpable.

"Whatever." The word was a venom-tipped arrow shot over her shoulder as she made her way to the door, heels clicking a staccato rhythm of frustration.

"Take care!" he called out, the mocking cheerfulness in his voice following her exit.

The door slammed with finality, its echo bouncing off the walls. Pete chuckled to himself, reveling in the silence that resettled over the room. He loved the chase and the conquest—each weekend a new game. But this one had been particularly dull, forgettable.

Just as he took another sip of coffee, a noise from the front door caught his attention. A muffled thump, like something soft colliding with wood. He frowned, setting down his mug. Perhaps she had forgotten her dignity along with her hair tie.

Annoyed, he stalked to the door and yanked it open, ready to dismiss her with a cutting remark. But the doorstep was empty, save for a solitary envelope lying there, a silent intruder in the stillness of the morning.

"Pete Hancock" was scrawled across the front in looping cursive. He scanned the street, searching for any sign of a messenger, but the neighborhood remained still as if holding its breath. Unease coiled in his stomach as he bent to pick up the envelope, the paper cool and impersonal in his hand.

"Who leaves letters anymore?" he muttered, turning the envelope over—no return address, no stamp, just his name, as though whoever sent it knew he'd be the one to find it.

With a last, wary glance outside, Pete stepped back into the sanctuary of his home, the door closing with a soft click behind him. He turned the envelope over in his hands, apprehension threading through his curiosity. This Sunday, it seemed, had just taken an unexpected turn.

Chapter 19

I raised my hand and knocked on the heavy, wooden door. The sound reverberated through the sticky air, mingling with the sweet aroma of magnolia blossoms. The house in front of me was a charming old Florida home, its exterior weathered by time yet still retaining its beauty. A perfectly manicured garden surrounded the house, adding to its idyllic charm.

The door's rusty hinges groaned as a petite woman in her early seventies appeared, her silver hair pulled back into a neat bun. She greeted me with a kind smile that crinkled the corners of her bright blue eyes.

"Are you Monica Chapman?" I attempted to soften my professional tone with a touch of warmth.

Her raspy, weathered voice echoed in the empty hallway. "Indeed," she said, her eyes locked on me standing before her. You must be Agent Thomas. You sound taller on the phone." She chuckled, revealing yellowing teeth as she extended a wrinkled hand for a handshake.

"Is Victoria here?" I inquired, stepping just inside the

threshold as Monica nodded and gestured for me to enter the living room.

The room grew heavy with tension as we avoided each other's gaze. I finally broke the silence, my voice shaking.

"Condolences on the death of your son. I can't imagine how hard this must be for Victoria. Her father gone and her mother... in jail."

Monica's eyes were filled with sadness, and there was a hint of regret in her voice. "It's a tragedy," she whispered, shaking her head, her hand reaching out to gently touch my arm. "But as her grandmother, it's my duty to do what I can."

She strode across the floor, her movements deliberate, and moved to a door at the end of the hall. My pulse quickened as she turned the handle and pushed it open.

"I think she's awake," she said, her voice barely above a whisper.

As I stepped in, my heart lodged in my throat. A small, frail figure lay in the bed, her skin almost translucent under the soft glow of the bedside lamp. Though she looked no older than nine, I knew the truth—Victoria was seventeen, a life measured in years but stolen in moments.

A wheelchair sat like a silent sentinel next to her bed.

"She doesn't talk much," Monica explained, her gaze lingering on her granddaughter. "The chemo sores in her mouth... they make it painful to speak. Her voice isn't what it used to be, either. Please, don't wear her out. She doesn't have a lot of strength."

I nodded, my throat tightening with emotion. I eased into the chair by her bed, careful not to bump the IV stand or disturb the oxygen tubes that fed into her nose. Her pale cheeks were sunken, and her eyes seemed to be searching for something in the dark room.

"Hello, Victoria," I said gently, taking her small hand in mine. "My name is Eva Rae Thomas."

Victoria's eyes flickered toward me, curiosity glinting within their depths. She blinked slowly as though she was processing the information. I could see the struggle in her gaze, the fight between wanting to retreat into herself and the desire to connect with the outside world.

I continued speaking softly, trying to bridge the gap between us. "I'm here to help, Victoria. I want to find out what happened to your parents—especially your dad. Do you remember anything from that night? Anything at all?"

A fleeting look of fear flashed across her face before she closed herself off again, retreating into a cocoon of silence. It was as if the weight of her past was too heavy for her to bear, locking her memories away within the confines of her fragile body.

Monica leaned against the doorway, her eyes filled with sorrow and determination. "She's been through so much," she murmured, her voice barely audible. "Please don't upset her."

I smiled reassuringly and nodded. "I understand, Mrs. Chapman. I'll be as gentle as I can. We just need to gather any information that could help us find out what happened to Victoria's parents."

Victoria kept her gaze fixed on me, her eyes filled with a mixture of curiosity and apprehension. I leaned closer, trying to convey empathy through my voice. "Victoria, I know this is difficult for you, but we need your help. Whatever you remember, no matter how small or insignificant, could be crucial to the investigation."

For a moment, it seemed like a spark of recognition flickered in Victoria's eyes. She hesitated, then for a minute looked like she would speak, but then gave up. Her eyes closed, and she was asleep.

"I'm sorry," Monica said. "The cancer is in her throat. It makes it difficult for her to talk. She has barely said anything to me since she got here."

I nodded, disappointed. "I understand. It must be hard."

Monica's eyes grew sad. "It is. I'm just praying I won't lose her as well and will do everything in my power to prevent that from happening."

I was about to leave when Victoria opened her eyes again and stared directly at me, and said:

"Wait."

Chapter 20

THEN:

SARAH'S TREMBLING fingers clutched the cold metal of the hospital bed where her daughter lay, a constellation of wires and beeping monitors surrounding her. Steven's words seemed to hang in the sterile air like a verdict.

"Leukemia?" Her voice cracked—a harsh whisper that didn't sound like her own. "But how? What?"

Tears gathered, blurring the edges of the room into a watery mirage, and she sank into the chair as if her legs could no longer bear the weight of the news. Steven moved closer, his presence a solid comfort in the chaos of her mind. He reached out, enveloping her shaking hands with his steady ones.

"Shh, it's okay," he murmured, his voice a soft but firm anchor. "I will take care of her. Don't worry. We need to be strong."

"Okay." The word was a fragile promise as Sarah willed her

tears to subside. She looked up at him, searching his face for certainty. "What does this mean? Will she—will she die?"

Steven's eyes held a well of compassion as he replied, "She will need to go through a lot of treatments—lots of time in the hospital. It was caught early on, so that's good. Treatments are very good, and most children survive it today."

Sarah's mind raced back to the small signs they had dismissed. "That's why she has been so tired lately?" She choked on the realization. "And pale, and she has hardly been eating?"

"Yes," he confirmed gently. "Those are all symptoms."

"Why didn't we see it earlier?" The terror in her voice clawed its way out, raw and exposed. Guilt gnawed at her insides.

This is all my fault. I'm her mother. I'm supposed to notice these things.

"Shh," he soothed, pulling her into an embrace that felt like safety. "We can't blame ourselves. We're doing everything we can, and that's enough."

Sarah found a sliver of solace in his arms, enough to find her voice again. "What kind of treatment will she need?" Her question was a whisper against the fabric of his scrubs.

"They don't know yet," Steven answered, his thumb rubbing soothing circles on her back. "They need to run more tests, many more tests, to determine what type it is and so on. But she will probably need chemo."

"Chemo?" The word was a specter that haunted Sarah's thoughts. "But... but she'll—oh, my poor baby. She's so small."

"I know," he said, his voice a mixture of empathy and resolve. "We will take care of her. I'm a nurse. I'll quit my job and take care of her full-time. That way, you can still take care of your job and career."

The enormity of his sacrifice hung between them, a testament to their shared love for their daughter.

"We can do this, Sarah," Steven asserted, his gaze locking onto hers, willing her to believe. "Together, we can."

At that moment, Sarah felt the steel of his determination meld with her own wavering strength. Together, they would face the uncertainty, the fear, and the love that bound them to their daughter and each other.

Chapter 21

The soft yellow light of the bedside lamp illuminated Victoria's room, creating a cozy atmosphere. Despite the warmth, I couldn't shake the coldness that had seeped into my bones. I sat on the edge of her flowery duvet, hunched forward with my elbows resting heavily on my knees.

"Victoria," I started softly, my words threading through the silence, "can you tell me about the night your dad died?"

Her shoulders tensed, and a visible shiver ran through her body, causing her chestnut hair to cascade over her face. She turned her head away from me as if trying to hide from my penetrating stare.

"Please," I urged, the weight of the investigation pressing on my tongue. "I know it's difficult, but we need to understand what happened."

Her grandmother stood like a guardian by the doorway, eyes sharp and protective. Victoria's hands fidgeted with the hem of the blanket, knuckles whitening. A tear breached the corner of her eye, trailing down her cheek like the first drop of a storm.

"Enough," her grandmother said in a stern voice. "Can't you see you're upsetting her?"

"Okay," I conceded, palms open in a gesture of peace. "I'm sorry, Victoria. I didn't mean to."

But the question gnawed at me, insistent as the ticking clock on the wall. "Just tell me about the shot."

"She doesn't remember," the grandmother said.

"I'll try anyway; she might remember something now that a couple of days have passed," I said, then turned to face her again. "Was it before or after your mother entered the house?"

Her breath hitched, caught between the need to speak and the desire to remain silent. She was in a lot of pain. It was visible. I knew this had to be awful for her—reliving that night when she couldn't do anything, being bedridden and unable to walk. It made me feel terrible and made me realize how fortunate I had been to have four healthy children. It was my biggest fear that one of them should get seriously ill someday. I guess it was the biggest fear for all parents.

Outside, a branch scraped against the window, a reminder of the world moving on, oblivious to the pain within these walls.

"Leave her be!" Her grandmother's words were a whip-crack, snapping the tense air between us.

"Please, Victoria," I pressed one last time, my voice barely above a whisper. "Please, this is important for your mother's fate."

Her lips parted, a quiver in her voice as fragile as a bird's wing. "First... I heard the shot," she breathed out. "Then my mom came inside the house and called my name." She paused, a shudder raking through her.

"Then, she screamed."

"Thank you, Victoria," I said, warmth seeping into my tone

as I reached for her hand, my fingers wrapping around hers in a tender squeeze.

"Thank you so much."

Feeling the weight of Victoria's words settle heavily on my shoulders, I rose from the edge of the bed and left the room, leaving Victoria and her grandmother in solemn silence. The house seemed to creak with a newfound eeriness as I made my way down the dimly lit hallway, each step echoing in the stillness.

As I reached the front door, my phone let out a shrill ring, jolting me from the somber atmosphere. I quickly glanced at the caller ID and saw it was Chief Annie. This couldn't be a coincidence. My heart quickened as I answered the call with trepidation.

"Hello, Chief," I greeted, trying to keep my voice steady despite my growing unease.

"Agent Thomas," Chief Annie's voice crackled through the line. "I just wanted to tell you that there was another incident in the neighborhood. The neighbor's wife was found shot this morning in their home. But you didn't hear it from me."

My breath caught in my throat, and my blood turned to ice. Another incident? It couldn't be a coincidence. My mind spun with possibilities, connecting the dots between Victoria's father's death and now this neighbor's wife. Something sinister lurked beneath the surface, something that tied these events together.

"Thank you, Chief," I managed to reply, my voice strained. "I'll look into it right away."

"Remember...."

"I didn't hear it from you."

"Exactly."

After ending the call, I rushed to my car and got in. The

puzzle pieces were slowly coming together, forming a picture that frightened me to my core.

Victoria's father had died from a gunshot wound, and now a neighbor's wife had suffered the same fate. Both incidents occurred near each other, raising suspicions of a serial killer on the loose. But why? What was their connection? I had to find out, and fast. If she really was innocent—and it seemed right now like she was—I couldn't let Sarah rot in jail for much longer.

Chapter 22

His fingers steady and precise, Pete Hancock sliced open the envelope with a letter opener. Within it, a single piece of paper folded neatly in half awaited his attention. He plucked it out, unfolding it to reveal just two words scrawled in a hasty hand:

YOU KNEW

His brow furrowed as he peered at the note, a bemused chuckle slipping out.

"What the heck is this?" His voice echoed faintly in the spacious, book-lined office. The note offered no answers, just the stark accusation printed on an otherwise blank canvas.

"Is this someone's idea of a joke?"

He shook his head dismissively, his mind racing through the roster of recent romantic entanglements. There had been a lot lately. Women came and went. He tired of them quickly and easily. They were fleeting and forgettable by design, connections that burned bright and fizzled fast. It was the way he preferred it—no strings, no complications. He liked it that way. But not all of them took it well when he broke it off or sent them home. Often, they called in the middle of the night, crying, telling him he was an idiot, or even sometimes they yelled and screamed at him. They all wanted the same thing—to drag him away from the life he enjoyed so profoundly, the single bachelor life, where another beauty always waited around any corner. They always wanted the same thing—to tie him down, to make him settle. But he never had—no wife, no children. Life was so much better without any of those complications. They knew what they were getting themselves into, as he was always upfront with them from the beginning—no strings attached. But most of them thought it was just because he hadn't yet met the right woman. And they were that perfect specimen that would make him change his mind. Except they never were. Not since Julie, the one who broke his heart when she ran off with his best friend. No one had ever been good enough since then and probably never would be.

"Typical," he muttered under his breath.

The women he entertained often mistook his charm for promises of something more profound. Tears were not uncommon, nor was the occasional melodramatic outburst when they realized their mistake.

"Ridiculous," he scoffed, reflecting on the emotional displays he had witnessed, each as predictable as the last. Now this—a cryptic message meant to... what? Spook him? Seduce him back into a dialogue?

"Two can play at that game," Hancock declared to the empty room. With a decisive movement, he retrieved his lighter from the mahogany desk—a silver piece engraved with his initials. The flame flickered to life at his command, dancing across the face of the note until the edges curled and blackened.

The paper crumbled. Unperturbed, Hancock used the dying ember to ignite the end of a waiting cigar.

He drew in deeply, the rich, earthy smoke filling his lungs before he exhaled a languid cloud that mingled with the lingering scent of charred paper as the remains ended in his ashtray.

"Game over," he smirked, settling back into his leather chair, the mystery of the note already retreating from his thoughts like the smoke dissipating into the air.

Chapter 23

As I drove down the streets of Cape Canaveral, the blazing midday sun beat down on my car. A knot formed in my stomach as I approached the scene—a feeling that something was not right. As I held up my badge to the uniformed officer stationed at the entrance, I couldn't help but notice how heavy it felt in my hand. It almost seemed to symbolize the weight of the truth that I knew awaited me inside. The officer's face remained stoic and emotionless as he allowed me to pass through.

"Detective Ryan," I called out as I ducked under the yellow tape, my shoes crunching on the gravel drive.

He turned, his eyes narrowing, not with suspicion but irritation. "What are you doing here? This isn't your case."

I could feel the impatience rolling off Detective Ryan in waves, but urgency threaded my words tight. "I've got new information. You need to hear me out."

"Listen," he said, crossing his arms, a clear barrier going up, "it's simple. A woman was shot. Looks like suicide. I suspect no foul play. The husband came home and found her. The gun was still in her hand."

"Simple?" My voice rose slightly, incredulously. "Her husband finds her with the gun still in her grip, and that's where the story ends for you?"

"Those are the facts," Ryan replied, unyielding.

"Except for the fact this happened right next door to another shooting that happened only days ago." My disbelief hung between us, a tangible thing. This guy was really getting on my nerves.

"Coincidence," he dismissed with a wave of his hand.

"Really? Because I don't believe in coincidences." My eyes met his, trying to ignite in him the same spark of curiosity, of doubt. "Let me have a look."

He sighed and shrugged. "Suit yourself," he muttered, gesturing toward the house.

As I moved past him, the crime scene came into focus—all sterile precision and hushed tones over the dull roar of the air conditioning. The forensics team worked methodically in the living room, documenting every detail of the grim tableau.

"Show me," I instructed, and they pointed to the body's position.

"Shot here," one of them indicated, motioning toward the bottom of the stairs, "straight through the head."

"Just like Steven Chapman."

I absorbed the scene, the room's stillness at odds with the chaos of death. Then, something out of place caught my eye. "And what's over there?" I asked, nodding toward a suitcase lying haphazardly on the floor.

"Found it just like that," one of the techs answered without looking up from their work.

I turned back to Ryan, who had followed me in. His skepticism was a physical presence in the room.

"Who packs a suitcase right before committing suicide?" I challenged.

Detective Ryan didn't answer, but the tightening of his jaw told me he was finally listening.

His eyes flickered from the suitcase to the floor, where the body had been before it was taken in, and I could see the gears in his mind turning. Yet he wouldn't admit it, even though it was staring him straight in the face. He was too stubborn.

"Can I at least talk to the husband?" I asked, leading the way out of the crime scene.

Chapter 24

THEN:

SARAH'S HANDS trembled as she stood in the nursery, carefully arranging stuffed animals on the shelves. The room felt empty without her daughter's presence, and the silence seemed to amplify her worries. She couldn't wait to bring her baby home, but the weight of responsibility settled heavily on her shoulders.

She glanced around the meticulously organized room, everything in its place, waiting for the joyful chaos that a child would undoubtedly bring. The soft glow of the nightlight cast a warm and comforting ambiance over the space. It was a haven, a sanctuary where they would nurture their daughter back to health.

As she folded a tiny shirt with trembling hands, Sarah's thoughts drifted to Steven. He had been at the hospital with their daughter for several nights, leaving her alone in this empty house. The distance had made her yearn for their family to be whole again.

Sarah flitted from corner to corner of Victoria's room, her hands smoothing over the freshly laundered sheets, fluffing pillows that hadn't been laid upon in days. The scent of disinfectant lingered in the air, a stark reminder of the hospital they were finally leaving behind. Her heart thrummed with anticipation, each tick of the clock a blessing and a curse. Steven had been their rock, steadfast by their daughter's bedside, while Sarah juggled the guilt of absence with the necessity of work and home.

A car engine hummed into the driveway, and her breath hitched. It was time. She peered through the window, watching Steven emerge, his strong arms cradling Victoria with a tenderness that brought tears to her eyes. She dashed outside, the breeze doing little to soothe her heated nerves.

"Let me help," she offered, reaching for her daughter.

Steven's gaze met hers, and there was a fierceness there that halted her mid-step.

"I got her," he said firmly, holding Victoria closer, denying Sarah the kiss she yearned to plant on her daughter's forehead. "Just grab the bag, please."

Sarah's fingers grazed the duffel bag, which was heavy with medications and care instructions. She felt an odd twinge in her chest, unspoken questions swirling in her mind, but she pressed them away and followed Steven inside.

In Victoria's room, the world seemed to shrink down to the three of them. Sarah hovered by the bed as Steven gently laid Victoria down. The little girl's eyelids fluttered, and her eyes opened, bright and clear.

"Hi, Mommy," Victoria's voice was a melody to Sarah's ears.

"Hi, sweetie," Sarah choked out, her smile trembling. "I'm so glad to have you home."

"Me too, Mommy."

Sarah brushed a stray lock of hair from Victoria's forehead. "I have missed you so much."

Victoria's brow furrowed with childlike innocence. "What's wrong with me, Mommy?"

Before Sarah could respond, Steven's voice cut through, steady and sure.

"You're sick," he said, tucking the blankets around Victoria's small frame. His words were gentle, but they carried the weight of their new reality. "You're very sick. But don't worry, I'll take care of you."

Sarah nodded, a silent sentinel at the foot of the bed, her worries multiplying like shadows at dusk. She forced a smile, willing it to be enough for both her daughter and herself. Somehow, it just didn't seem like she was enough.

Chapter 25

I stepped closer to Adam Andersson, his body tense and rigid as he stared off into the chaos of flashing lights and uniformed officers. Detective Ryan stood by my side, a silent presence amidst the chaos. The yellow police tape fluttered in the wind, creating a barrier around the scene of the tragedy. Adam stood still like a statue, unable to comprehend what had happened. He was obviously still in shock.

"Mr. Andersson?" I called out, breaking through Adam's dazed state. He turned toward me, his eyes bloodshot and empty. "I'm sorry for your loss. We just need to ask you a few questions."

He nodded numbly, running a hand through his disheveled hair before muttering, "Yes, of course."

My questioning gaze bore into him, searching for any sign of hesitation. "When did you get back?" I prodded.

Adam's shoulders slumped as he wearily replied, "Ten-thirty this morning. From work."

"Ten-thirty? That's an odd time to finish a shift," I raised an eyebrow in surprise.

"I work the graveyard shift at Ron Jon's," he explained with a monotone voice.

I leaned forward, my elbows resting on my knees. "Keep going," I urged.

His hands shook as he spoke. "I turned the knob and pushed open the door to the living room, only to find Nicki lying there, on the floor, a pool of... blood surrounding her head." His voice cracked, and he took a deep breath before continuing.

The strong odor of stale beer emanated from him, and I couldn't help but wrinkle my nose.

"Adam, have you been drinking?" He shifted his weight from foot to foot and avoided my gaze. "Just one beer with the guys after work," he mumbled.

"Can anyone confirm that?" I asked, crossing my arms. Adam hesitated before finally nodding. "Yeah, I can give you their names."

I wrote the names down, along with phone numbers, as he gave them to me.

"Am I under suspicion here? Do I need to get a lawyer?" His voice quivered with nervousness as he spoke, and I could see the fear in his eyes.

"Do you think you might need one?" I asked, trying to read his face.

"N-no," he stuttered. "But I just want to make sure I'm not being accused of anything," he blurted out.

I shifted my weight slightly on my feet, avoiding direct eye contact. "Let's focus on her state of mind," I replied, trying to deflect his question and move on with the conversation. "Was she depressed? Suicidal?"

"I-I... don't know," he stammered, shaking his head in bewilderment. "I really don't know."

"She never said anything to you? Never expressed that she wanted to end things?" I asked.

"N-not that I know of. Not to me, at least," he said.

I nodded and wrote it on my notepad. This guy was definitely hiding something from us. I could tell by his nervous sniffle. He was lying about something. I just didn't know what yet.

"Stay within the town limits, Adam. We may need to speak with you again," I said before turning away, feeling Ryan's glare boring into my back.

"Are we done here?" Ryan's tone held an edge as we stepped aside, away from Adam's earshot.

"Everyone is a suspect until proven otherwise," I stated, meeting Ryan's fiery gaze.

"Look, I've been on this case since the call came in," Ryan shot back, his stance confrontational. "And I don't appreciate you grilling him like that. He's grieving!"

"Suicide or not, I do my job, Ryan. And right now, my job is to question everything." My words were ice against the heat of his anger.

"Damn it! It's suicide!" Ryan's voice escalated, carrying across the lawn.

"Then, prove it," I called over my shoulder, walking away from the scene, Ryan's frustration, and Adam's quiet despair.

Chapter 26

Pete Hancock's strides were light and rhythmic, the leash in his hand slack as his golden retriever bounded ahead of him. The Florida sunshine draped over them like a warm blanket, and a grin spread across Hancock's face while he watched the dog's exuberant frolic in the sand—sand that was technically off-limits to four-legged beachgoers.

"Go on, Rufus! Have at it!" he cheered, the dog's name a bright note against the hush of waves. His chuckle rolled out, free and easy, as Rufus marked an abandoned towel with a carefree stream. "That's showing 'em, boy!"

The owner of the towel, a middle-aged man with skin the color of a well-oiled baseball mitt, bobbed in the water, blissfully unaware. Hancock whistled sharply, a signal honed through years of companionship, and Rufus came galloping back, spraying sand in his wake.

"Good boy," Hancock praised, but his eyes darted away as Rufus squatted, leaving a small indignity behind. He glanced around; no one seemed to notice. With a dismissive shrug, he hooked the leash onto Rufus's collar and set off toward home.

Whistling a tune from some old romantic movie, he made his way off the beach, the hot sand giving way to the firmer sidewalk. Mrs. Donnelly, who lived three houses down, was tending to her roses, the very picture of suburban dedication.

"Beautiful day, isn't it, Mrs. Donnelly?" Hancock called out, tipping an imaginary hat her way.

"Indeed it is," she replied, her smile genuine—if a tad strained.

As he passed her neatly trimmed hedges, Hancock allowed his smile to sour. "Nosy old bat," he muttered, sure she couldn't hear him.

A smug grin spread across Hancock's face, but suddenly, a tingling sensation shot up his spine, and he froze in place. He spun around, frantically scanning the empty street for any signs of danger. The rustling leaves and joyful cries of children playing were the only sounds that greeted him. He let out a nervous laugh and chided himself for being paranoid. He turned around and started to walk, then heard footsteps behind him.

He quickened his pace, the leash slipping through his fingers as Rufus struggled to keep up. The footsteps grew closer, echoing in his ears like a slow, ominous drumbeat.

Hancock felt a bead of sweat trickle down his temple as he debated whether to turn around. The instinctual fear gnawed at him, urging him to seek safety. But curiosity tugged at the corners of his mind, whispering that he needed to face whatever or whoever was following him.

He finally mustered the courage to pivot on his heel, heart pounding in his chest. But the street behind him was empty.

"Who's there?" he ventured, more to the wind than anyone in particular. Silence was his only answer.

"Probably nothing..." he mumbled, though he couldn't shake

the uneasy thought that one of his less-than-amicable flings had taken to stalking him. It would be just his luck that his cavalier love life had finally caught up with him.

"Come on, Rufus," he said, forcing cheer into his voice, "let's get you home."

But even as his feet moved, his mind raced, tallying names and faces, wondering which of his many dalliances might have turned into a stalker.

Chapter 27

The key turned smoothly in the lock, a routine gesture I had mastered over the years. With a gentle push, the door finally opened, and a burst of air-conditioned cool air greeted me. My children's lively chatter and laughter filled the room as they rushed past me into the living room. Angel ran to her dad, but he didn't want to talk to her and told her to go to her room and play. I walked closer, feeling the weight of the heaviness that had filled my house lately. Matt's form was unmoving on the couch, his eyes fixed on the TV screen. His crutches were leaning against the couch still, and I wondered if he had moved at all while I was gone.

"Matt?" My voice came out softer than intended, an involuntary reverence for the melancholy that seemed to drape over him like a shroud.

He didn't stir, his eyes fixed on some invisible point beyond the ceiling. Angel refused to go to her room and tried again to get her father's attention, whom she had missed so desperately these past few days. Angel's small arms wrapped around his leg in a burst of youthful exuberance, yet he barely registered her embrace. His world had shrunk to the cushions that cradled his brokenness.

"Did you manage to do your exercises today?" I prodded gently, setting down my purse and the weight of concern. "You know Dr. Dan told you to keep at it."

His voice was a low rumble, tired and edged with frustration. "I don't want to," he said, turning his head away just as I leaned in, aiming for a kiss that never landed.

Ouch. That hurt.

"Where were you all day?" The question held a note of accusation, or maybe it was just longing, thinly veiled.

"Trying to help Sarah," I answered, watching his expression for any sign of the man who used to devour intrigue. "Her neighbor was found murdered too."

"Really?" For a fleeting moment, a spark ignited in his dull eyes. Interest. It was slight but unmistakable and fanned the embers of hope within me.

"Do you have a suspect?" he asked, and I couldn't suppress the smile that curled my lips, even as it mingled with sorrow.

"Looking closely at the husband," I divulged, sidling closer to share this sliver of connection. "Do you want to help me go through the witness statements?"

The flicker of intrigue that had momentarily illuminated Matt's face wavered as a shadow of remembrance crossed his face. I had missed this. I had missed us taking on cases together, solving them side by side, and even arguing about them. At least we were together, and at least he showed an interest in something. A shadow rushed over his eyes and turned off the light in them. He remembered the bullet that had stolen his mobility, the prognosis that caged his aspirations, and the reality that he might never be a detective again.

With a heavy sigh, he slumped back into the couch, surrendering to the gravity of his despair. The remote control became an extension of his retreat, turning up the volume to fill the void between us.

And there I stood, the silence of our home shattered by the indifferent chatter of the TV, feeling the distance between us grow as vast as the chasm between who we once were and who we had become.

Chapter 28

THEN:

SARAH'S EYELIDS FLUTTERED OPEN, her consciousness surfacing like a diver breaking through a murky sea of sleep. She lay still for a moment, disoriented by the abrupt return to wakefulness without knowing what had summoned her from her dreams.

The room was shrouded in darkness, save for a thin sliver of light that sliced under the bedroom door, casting an amber glow across the foot of their bed where Steven's shape should have been.

Her heart thumped a slow, heavy beat; the other half of the bed was empty, the sheets cool to the touch. A thread of unease began to weave its way through her chest as she turned her head toward the source of the light: it was coming from Victoria's room.

The hospital had released Victoria weeks ago, but the battle scars of cancer treatments were still fresh, painting dark circles under her fragile eyes and sculpting her small frame even smaller. Steven had become her unwavering guardian, ferrying their daughter to the relentless chemo sessions that left Victoria listless, often retching into the early hours of the morning.

With a soft rustle of cotton sheets, Sarah pushed herself up, her feet finding the cold hardwood floor. Her movements were automatic, propelled by a mother's instinct that whispered of something amiss. She padded down the hallway, each step bringing her closer to the unusual light, her mind grappling with scenarios that might explain Steven's absence from their bed at this ungodly hour.

As she neared Victoria's bedroom, strange, disjointed sounds reached her ears—a symphony of distress that quickened her pulse. It was a guttural noise, interspersed with sharp gasps, unlike anything she had heard before. Her hand trembled slightly as it reached for the doorknob, her breath catching in her throat.

The door swung open with a soft creak, unveiling the scene within. There, in the dim glow of a bedside lamp, was Steven, his broad shoulders hunched protectively as he cradled their daughter in his arms. Victoria's body was convulsing, her limbs jerking uncontrollably as if pulled by invisible marionette strings.

"Call 911!" Steven's voice was raw, laced with panic as he locked eyes with Sarah, his plea slicing through the haze of terror that threatened to choke her.

In an instant, Sarah was sprinting back to their bedroom, her thoughts scattered like shards of glass. The phone seemed impossibly far away, her fingers fumbling over the digits as she punched them in with desperate haste. Her heart hammered against her ribs, a frantic drumbeat echoing the terror that seized her.

"Please, please hurry," she begged into the receiver, her voice barely more than a whisper strained with fear. The operator's calm, steady instructions were a lifeline in the chaos, grounding her enough to relay their address, to stutter out the words "seizure" and "cancer" and "daughter."

She dropped the phone as soon as they confirmed help was on the way, her legs carrying her back to Victoria's room, where time seemed to have slowed to a crawl. Steven's face was a mask of anguish, his strong arms now a fortress around their little girl, his whispers a litany of comfort and love.

"Shh, it's okay; Daddy's got you. Help is coming, my brave girl."

It tore through Sarah, seeing her husband, usually a pillar of strength and resolve, frayed at the edges with fear for their child. Dropping to her knees beside them, she reached out a shaking hand, brushing back the damp curls from Victoria's forehead, murmuring reassurances that felt brittle on her tongue.

"Mommy's here, baby. You're going to be okay," she said, though her gaze flickered to Steven's, seeking silent confirmation, shared hope amidst the dread that clawed at her insides.

They waited together, a family united by love and the shared helplessness of watching their daughter fight a battle neither of them could take on for her. Each second stretched into eternity, filled only with the sound of Victoria's labored breathing and the distant wail of sirens growing ever closer.

And in that quiet room, as the first hints of dawn began to seep through the blinds, Sarah held onto two things—the warmth of Steven's hand gripping hers and the fierce determination that somehow, someway, they would see their daughter through this night.

Chapter 29

The flickering glow of the laptop screen bathed the room in an eerie light as I leaned over the police report spread out on the kitchen table. The rest of the house was shrouded in darkness, save for the muted luminescence from the living room where Matt lay sprawled on the couch, the noise of the television seeping through the walls like a distant murmur.

I rubbed my temples, feeling the weight of fatigue pressing down on me. A glance at the clock confirmed it was well past midnight. Yet, there was no sleep for me—not with Nicki Andersson's case files splayed before me, demanding attention.

A residual scent of roasted garlic and thyme lingered in the air, remnants of the hastily assembled dinner I'd managed to cobble together for the kids. The younger ones had succumbed to sleep's embrace hours ago, their gentle breathing now part of the house's nighttime symphony.

Earlier in the evening, a call with Olivia had been a balm to my spirit. Brimming with collegiate excitement, her voice reminded me of life beyond these four walls and the grueling cases that occupied my mind. She spoke of new friends and the sprawling campus of UCF with such vivacity that I could almost forget the pang of her absence.

Now, with everyone settled and the house quiet, the reality of my solitude crept in. I turned back to the photographs, eyes scanning the graphic tableau of Nicki's final moments. The stark white of the coroner's marker stood out against the deep crimson that marred the scene.

Something felt wrong—off-kilter. Nicki's body position and the way her limbs were arranged were all too familiar. An uncomfortable chill traced its way up my spine as I shuffled through other images, hunting for the one that would confirm my suspicions.

There, amidst the chaos of papers, was Steven Chapman's death scene. My breath hitched as I placed the two side by side. The resemblance was uncanny—the same unnaturally twisted posture and deliberate placement of hands and feet.

The discrepancy that had nagged at me earlier now screamed for recognition. How her body was laid out didn't match the pattern of blood splatter on the wall and floor behind her. The angles were all wrong, like a jigsaw puzzle forced together without regard for the intended picture. The gun in her hand didn't seem natural. It was placed.

My gaze shifted between Nicki and Steven's photos, darting from one detail to the next. They weren't just similar—they were identical. The realization hit like a bucket of ice water; the implication of what lay before me was as undeniable as it was horrifying.

Goosebumps rose on my arms, each one a silent testament to the fear that now gripped me. A patterned killer was at large, moving among us with chilling precision. What dark motive drove them to replicate this morbid scene?

With a suddenness that startled even myself, I swept the

files into a neat stack, the sharp snap of paper echoing in the stillness. Determination hardened within me like steel. This killer relied on silence, on the shadows that hid their gruesome work. But I would be the light that exposed them, the relentless force that would bring an end to their macabre dance of death.

Matt's soft snore punctuated the quiet, a grounding reminder of the normalcy that lay just beyond this table. But for now, I was tethered to this world of secrets and shadows, bound by a promise to the silent victims whose voices cried out for justice.

There was work to be done, and I would not rest until the killer was found. Each photograph and report was now a piece of a larger, sinister puzzle, and I was determined to put it together, no matter the cost.

Chapter 30

Pete Hancock slumped into the worn leather of his living room armchair. With a forced chuckle that failed to mask his unease, he tried to dismiss the words in the letter as nothing more than a joke in poor taste. But the laughter died in his throat, strangled by the crawling dread that had taken residence in his gut since the moment he'd torn open the envelope.

The house creaked and groaned around him, a symphony of unsettling noises that kept his nerves frayed. He listened intently as branches, like skeletal fingers, scraped against the siding with every gust of wind. A sudden crash from outside jolted him upright; a trash can toppled over, its contents spilling onto the pavement. His heart raced, and he sprang to his feet, darting to the window to peer into the darkness.

His heart pounded as he scanned the darkness, anticipating what he might find. But there was nothing except the debris swirling around in the gusts of wind, creating a symphony of chaos and fury. No one was watching from the shadows; no faces peered through the windows above; it was just him and the storm's wild dance.

"Get a grip, Hancock," he muttered, pressing his forehead against the cool glass. "You're just being an idiot."

As he paced back and forth, his mind raced through memories of past relationships. Most had ended without any animosity, just the gradual fading of attraction or incompatible goals. But one face kept resurfacing in his thoughts—a woman with piercing green eyes and fiery red hair. What was her name again? Tiffany? Or was it Teresa? He didn't recall. But they had dated for a few weeks, more than what he usually did with anyone. He had liked her. The sex had been very good and intense, and she was so beautiful he decided to keep her around for a little while... until he got bored with her, which happened pretty quickly. Especially their arguments, oh, boy, there had been a lot of heated ones. He could still feel the intensity of their arguments and the passion that once drew them together. Yet now, it only brought up painful emotions and doubts about her true intentions. The idea nagged at him, refusing to be dismissed easily.

Tiffany, that was her name—definitely. He remembered clearly now. She was crazy as a bat.

Or was it Brittany?

She'd had that look. The one that could flip from adoration to something darker in a heartbeat. Even now, the memory of her gaze sent shivers down his spine. When they'd parted ways, her anger had been palpable, a storm much like the one raging outside his home. Could it really be her behind this twisted game?

A floorboard creaked upstairs, slicing through the cacophony of the wind. Pete's breath hitched, his pulse thundering in his ears. The primal instinct of fear drowned out rational thoughts. Was it just the house settling, or was someone else here with him?

He couldn't stand the uncertainty. Survival outweighed skepticism as he bolted across the room, not daring to look back. His movements were swift, fueled by adrenaline, as he reached the hidden compartment behind the bookshelf. With practiced ease, he retrieved the gun, the cold metal a familiar weight in his hand.

Now armed, Pete faced the shadows of his home, every sense heightened, ready for whatever—or whoever—might come.

Chapter 31

THEN:

SARAH'S FINGERS drummed a staccato rhythm on the leather armrest, her gaze never leaving Victoria. The little girl, with curls as wild as her spirit, was nestled among a fortress of colorful blocks on the carpet, her laughter the sweetest melody in the otherwise silent room.

"Look, Mommy, a castle!" Victoria's voice chimed, her small hands placing the last block atop her creation.

"Beautiful, just like you," Sarah responded, attempting a smile that didn't quite reach her eyes. The worry lines etched on her forehead betrayed her constant vigilance.

Suddenly, Victoria's laughter hitched—a sharp, jarring sound—and her body stiffened. Blocks clattered to the ground as she fell sideways, her tiny frame shaking uncontrollably.

"Victoria!" Sarah was on the floor instantly, her heart racing, her body trembling with fear. "Baby, stay with me."

"Mom-m-mmy..." Victoria's voice was a ghost of a whisper between convulsions.

"I'm here, darling. I'm here." Sarah cradled her daughter's head, her hands gentle yet firm, cushioning it from the hard floor. Memories of hospital corridors, white walls, and solemn nodding doctors flooded her mind. They had warned her—the seizures would come again.

"Shh... It's going to pass." Sarah's words were a mantra, a lifeline thrown into the chaotic sea of helplessness that threatened to drown her. She fought back tears, not knowing what to do but trying her best to remain calm.

The door hinges creaked, a soft murmur in the tense silence. Steven's shadow fell over them before he knelt, his presence a stark contrast against the chaos of moments ago. He reached out with steady hands, taking their daughter away from Sarah, cradling Victoria's shivering form.

"Hey, little warrior," he whispered, his voice a gentle balm. "Ride it out. You're doing great."

Sarah's fingers uncurled from Victoria's shirt, retreating as Steven took over. She watched, feeling a pang of helplessness as her husband's calm seemed to weave an invisible shield around their daughter.

"Is it easing up?" Sarah asked, her voice barely above a whisper.

"Almost there," Steven nodded, eyes locked on Victoria's face, reading every subtle shift of her features.

A heavy breath escaped Sarah as she observed Victoria's body relax, inch by inch. There was an art to Steven's touch, a silent communication that seemed to reach their daughter in depths Sarah longed to fathom.

"Mommy?" Victoria's voice was faint, laden with exhaustion.

"Right here, baby," Sarah leaned close, brushing a tissue across Victoria's sweat-dampened forehead. Her heart clenched at the sight of her daughter so fragile and spent. How she missed her daughter's hair and longed to take that bandana off.

"Did I do good?" Victoria's eyes fluttered open, a glimmer of her usual spark buried beneath the weariness.

"The best," Sarah smiled, the lie tasting sweet because it was for her.

"Can I sleep now?"

"Of course, sweetheart," Steven assured her, his arm secure beneath her head.

Sarah rose with them, her legs stiff, her mind whirring. Should they have adjusted her medication? Was there a specialist they hadn't consulted, a stone left unturned?

"Steven, should we—?"

"Let's get her comfortable first," he interjected, understanding the unsaid. "We'll talk after."

Sarah nodded, biting back the torrent of questions. She watched them go, Steven's strength carrying their daughter with ease she envied. The room felt emptier and quieter, leaving Sarah with nothing but the echoes of her own racing thoughts.

The door clicked shut, a soft seal on the silence that flooded the living room. Sarah's fingers twitched at her sides as she began to pace, each step a silent drumbeat in time with her heart. The scent of lavender from Victoria's clothes still lingered, a bittersweet note in the air.

Her mind careened from one possibility to another—genetics, diet, environmental factors? What demon had lodged itself into her daughter's life, turning bright days dark with its shadow? It was the treatments, Steven had said—the chemo that she was getting. But was there really nothing they could do to make it easier on her?

"Could be anything," she muttered, her voice barely a whisper against the stillness. "But there has to be something."

She halted, eyes drawn to the laptop perched on the coffee table like a beacon. With a decisive stride, she claimed her seat before it, the keys cool beneath her fingertips as she snapped the device to life.

"Okay, let's see what you've got," she whispered, her gaze fixed on the glowing screen.

"Seizures in children... cancer... chemo, how to treat...." She typed, her hands steady despite the tremor in her resolve. Links bloomed across the page, a garden of information and potential solutions.

"Come on; come on," she urged, clicking through medical journals filled with jargon that twisted her tongue, forums where other parents spilled their fears and findings. Sarah soaked up every word, every theory. Lots of children with cancer were getting chemo, but none of them spoke of seizures.

That's odd.

"Nothing?" she questioned the screen, frustration simmering. "There has to be more...."

She looked up seizures in children.

"Metabolic disorders, neurological conditions..." she read aloud, trying to find a foothold in the landslide of possibilities.

"Talk to me, Victoria," she whispered into the quiet, imagining her daughter's bright eyes and eager nod. "Tell me what's wrong."

The cursor blinked back at her, patient and unyielding, as she navigated the labyrinth of symptoms and syndromes, a digital detective hunting for the clue that would unlock this mystery.

"Genetic markers? No, that's not it." Her fingers churned through pages and pages, the click of the mouse a staccato against the silence. "Epilepsy? But the tests were inconclusive, Steven said."

She leaned closer to the screen as if proximity could wring clarity from chaos. "Environmental factors?" she murmured, squinting at a study on toxins. "But we live so clean."

"Contradictions everywhere," Sarah spat out, the words like acid. She pushed her hair back, a gesture of exasperation.

"Medication side effects?" Her voice rose, tinged with hope, then faltered.

"Damn it!" The laptop shook under the slam of her palm, a physical echo of her inner turmoil.

"Someone must know something." Her plea fell flat in the room, no one there to catch it.

"Could it be diet-related?" Her eyes darted through forums, each parent's account more varied than the last. "No gluten, dairy-free, sugarless... We've tried all that!"

"Useless!" She pushed away from the table, her chair grating on the floor. "It's like searching for a needle in a haystack made of needles."

"Victoria..." Her eyes welled up as she stared at the little girl's picture on the wall. "I'm trying, baby, I'm trying."

"Wait, what's this?" A new tab caught her eye, a glimmer of a different perspective. "An experimental trial?" Her pulse quickened; they weren't ready for that.

"Back to square one." She slumped forward, forehead resting against the cool surface of the desk. "I need answers, not riddles."

Steven came in with a deep sigh. "She's asleep now. I have the camera set up so we can keep an eye on her." He exhaled and rubbed his forehead. "That was a rough one. They seem to be getting worse."

"I can't find anything about seizures and chemo," Sarah said. "Are you sure it's not something else causing this?"

Steven grunted. "Look who's the expert now. I spoke to the doctor at the hospital when she had her first seizure, remember? The next day, when you had to go to work. I was in his office and talked to him. He said it was a side effect. I don't understand why you're suddenly questioning this?"

Sarah looked at her fingers. The comment about her going to work the next day hit her hard. She had to go in for the important meeting. Steven had even encouraged her to do so and told her he had this and that Victoria was in good hands. One of them had to make money, especially with the medical bills piling up.

"It's just... there are a lot of parents writing about this stuff, and no one is mentioning seizures, and if you Google it, then...."

"Different patients have different reactions to chemo; it's hard to generalize. There are always a few people who have very unusual reactions to any drug. Besides, I remember seeing it before when I was still working at the hospital. Trust me. I know what I'm doing. Didn't you have a meeting to prepare for? Some presentation?"

Sarah looked at him, then nodded. "Y-yeah. I guess I better get on that."

Chapter 32

The door creaked on its hinges as I stepped into the dimly lit Ellie Mae's bar, a place that seemed frozen in time with its worn leather stools and the soft hum of a neon sign flickering above the liquor shelf. The scent of stale beer lingered in the air, mingling with the faint trace of cigarette smoke from days long past when the laws were looser and the nights longer. It was the kind of place where secrets huddled in the corners and whispered across the polished wooden counter.

"Evening," I murmured, my eyes adjusting to the ambient glow cast by the lamps along the walls.

"First time?" The voice belonged to the bartender, a grizzled middle-aged man with hands that told stories of countless bottles opened and wiped down surfaces. His name tag read "Frank," and his eyes held the fatigue of one who'd seen too much yet never enough to dull the curiosity.

"Sort of," I replied, taking a seat at the bar. "I'm looking for someone who used to come here. Her name is Sarah. Sarah Chapman."

Frank's expression remained unreadable, but a twitch in his

jaw suggested recognition. He continued to dry a glass with a cloth that had seen better days. "Sarah, huh? You a friend of hers?"

"Something like that," I said, leaning in slightly. "I heard she would come here after her husband kicked her out?"

"Ah, Sarah," Frank let out a breath, setting the glass down with more care than necessary. "She came here for a while. What do you want to know?"

"Looking to understand her better," I ventured cautiously, "I get the sense her relationship with her husband wasn't all sunshine and rainbows."

Frank snorted softly, the sound almost lost in a low note from the jukebox starting up in the corner.

"You could say that."

“Did she tell you about it?”

“She would say stuff. Sometimes.”

He poured a drink, pushing it across the bar without being asked. "Passion's a funny thing. Burns hot until there's nothing left."

"Seems like it burned out for good this time," I mused, swirling the drink before taking a sip. Whiskey wasn’t my thing, but I did it just to be polite.

"Was it just passion, or was something else mixed in there?"

"Who's to say?" Frank shrugged, his gaze drifting over my shoulder, perhaps to a memory only he could see. "People are complicated. Love and hate are two sides of the same coin in a marriage like theirs. Having a sick kid like they did isn’t easy."

"Did she ever tell you anything... any details about their relationship?" I pressed, watching for any telltale shift in his demeanor. “Anything out of the ordinary?”

"Out of the ordinary is a relative term around here," he replied cryptically. "Why don't you tell me what you think 'ordinary' is, and I might be able to answer your question better?"

"Fair enough," I conceded, a smile tugging at the corner of my mouth despite the gravity of my inquiry. "Let's just say I'm interested in finding out what makes an ordinary couple turn extraordinary—for better or worse. They split up. He kicked her out. Did she tell you why? What happened?"

Frank exhaled a dry chuckle, his hands working on autopilot, wiping down glasses.

Then his eyes darkened. "Once...."

"Go on." I leaned in closer.

"Sarah came in, wild-eyed, on a tear about something Steven did—or didn't—do." He paused, setting a clean glass on the shelf with a soft thud. "She threw her ring at me and screamed so loud we heard it over the music. Said he could choke on it for all she cared."

"Her wedding ring?" I asked, picturing the scene.

"Yep," he confirmed.

"Did she take it back?"

"Didn't touch it. I picked it up and put it behind the bar, just in case." Frank gestured vaguely to the shelves lined with bottles, an unspoken history among them.

"Passion, hate, or desperation?" I murmured.

"Maybe all three," Frank replied, his voice a low rumble of brewing storms yet to come. A woman entered and sat at the bar. Frank poured her a drink. She didn't even have to ask. He knew what she wanted, and I guessed she, too, was a regular.

"Here you go, Lisa," he said, handing her the drink.

I edged my way through dim lighting, the murmur of hushed conversations acting as a backdrop to my purposeful strides.

"Mind if I join you?" I asked, pulling out the stool beside her without waiting for an answer.

She glanced up, her gaze sharp, then softened. "Free country," she said, though her voice was flat.

"Were you friends with Sarah?"

"Friends," Lisa echoed, swirling her drink. "Yeah, you could say that. We talked from time to time. Heard she got locked up, though. For killing Steven."

"Seems like she had a rough go."

"Rough," she scoffed, lips twisting wryly. "That's one word for it."

"Frank mentioned they fought."

"Ha!" The sound was bitter. "She was mad at the bastard. I can tell you that much. Drove her to the verge of insanity."

"Infidelity will do that." I watched her carefully, gauging her reaction.

Lisa's hand stopped mid-swirl, and she looked at me with new interest. "You know about all that?"

"Bits and pieces," I admitted. I was just guessing, but it worked. "Sounds complicated."

"Complicated doesn't even begin to cover it." Her tone suggested a labyrinth of secrets I was only beginning to uncover.

"Remember the night the glass shattered?" Frank asked, leaning closer to Lisa.

She paused, a distant look clouding her eyes as she drifted into the memory. "Loud and clear," she murmured, almost to herself. "Sarah was a storm that night. Threw the glass in anger, and it shattered behind him against the wall."

The clink of glasses and low hum of conversation faded as I pictured it: Sarah, wild-eyed and seething, her voice a serrated knife cutting through the bar's buzz.

"Did he ever...?" I didn't finish the sentence, but my hand mimicked a striking motion.

"Hit her? No." Lisa's gaze snapped back to the present. "Not that I know of, at least. But there was a rage. He drove her to the bottle, the poor thing. "

"Rage can be a motive," I muttered, thinking aloud.

"Sure can," she agreed, then leaned in. Her voice dropped to a conspiratorial whisper. "Sarah told me once about Steven's affair—said finding out about it nearly drove her mad."

"So, he was the one who had an affair?" The word hung between us, heavy with implications.

"Of course," Lisa said, eyes narrowing. "There was this one woman... it seemed serious. Sarah thought she might be the reason he threw her out. He told her not to come back. He was done with her. Nearly broke Sarah in pieces, the poor thing."

"Did she have a husband?" The question slipped out, laced with curiosity. "The woman he had an affair with?"

"Wouldn't be surprised." Lisa's mouth twisted into a wry smile. "That kind always does."

"Would give someone a hell of a reason to pull a trigger," I mused, my mind racing with the possibilities.

Lisa nodded, her lips sealed tight as if locking away secrets. Our conversation fell into a hush, the weight of our words sinking into the woodgrain of the bar.

That's when I felt it—eyes on me—a prickle on the back of my neck. I turned slightly, pretending to scan the shelves of liquor but really searching the dim reflections in the mirror behind the bar. There he was—a solitary figure obscured by shadow, a glass of something dark cradled between his hands. His gaze pierced through the gloom, fixed on us with an intensity that knotted my stomach.

"Excuse me for a sec," I murmured to Lisa, slipping off the stool.

I threaded through the tables, each step deliberate, casual. He didn't look away and didn't blink. The stranger's face was a mask of indifference, but something in his eyes betrayed him—a flicker of recognition or perhaps fear.

"Mind if I join you?" I asked, nodding toward the empty seat beside him.

He considered me, then gestured wordlessly to the chair. His fingers tapped a silent rhythm on the side of his glass.

"It seems you're interested in our little chat over there." I kept my tone light and non-threatening.

"Hard not to overhear." His voice was gravel, deep and rough around the edges.

"Sarah and Steven are quite the talk of the town," I prodded, watching for a tell, a twitch, anything.

"Are they now?" The corner of his mouth quirked up, but it wasn't a smile.

"Seems their story's got more layers than an onion."

"Layers can make your eyes water," he replied cryptically.

"Or they can hide a core rotten to the heart," I shot back, locking eyes with him.

His gaze held mine, unflinching, before he raised his glass to his lips, the golden liquid disappearing with a slow tilt of his head. When he set the glass down, it was empty, save for a ring of condensation clinging to the wood.

"Every story's got an end," he said, standing abruptly. "Just depends on who's writing it."

"Got a stake in how this one turns out?" I asked, but he was already turning away, melting into the shadows that seemed eager to swallow him whole.

"Maybe," he tossed over his shoulder, his footsteps a soft echo against the buzz of the bar.

"Hey," I said, stopping him as he tried to leave.

"Did Sarah ever talk to you about Steven's affair?"

"Maybe."

"Did she ever talk about the woman? Tell you who she was?"

"Her husband had his secrets," he said. "Of the female kind."

"Names," I pressed. "Did she mention a name?"

"Maybe." He looked away. "But names can be dangerous things."

"More dangerous than bullets?"

The stranger chuckled, a sound devoid of humor. "Sometimes."

"Do you know the name of the woman her husband was seeing on a regular basis?"

"Who's asking?" His gaze was steady, penetrating.

"Someone who doesn't want to see an innocent person take the fall."

"Is that right?" He took a step closer, his breath smelling like tobacco and beer. "Maybe I know something. Maybe I don't. But why should I trust you?"

"Because you're here," I said. "And you're talking to me instead of walking away."

"Observant," he acknowledged with a nod. "I'll give you this —Steven was playing with fire and not just with Sarah."

"Someone else got burned?"

"Seems likely." His eyes narrowed. "But motives are like ghosts; everyone believes in them until they try to find one."

"Help me find this ghost," I urged.

"They were neighbors," he said. "That's all I know. Sarah

told me one day, after a few drinks, that her husband was fooling around with the woman next door."

"Wait—" I began, but he was already striding away

"Neighbor," he repeated without turning around.

My mind raced, weaving possibilities, motives, and hidden truths. Who was this man? An ally or someone with a much darker agenda? Was he telling me the truth?

"Everything alright?" Lisa asked, her eyes searching mine.

"Maybe," I replied, glancing once more at the door. "Or maybe it's just beginning."

The stranger's words hung heavy in the air, a riddle wrapped in the smell of beer and cigarettes. As the bar's laughter and chatter swirled around me, a solitary thought echoed in my head:

What did Steven do, and who wanted him dead badly enough to murder him in cold blood in his own home? Sarah? And was the neighbor he had an affair with Nicki? The woman found shot to death in her home?

It was time to have a serious chat with the husband, Adam.

Chapter 33

With a charming smile pasted on his face, Pete moved graciously among his guests, ensuring everyone had a drink in hand and a smile on their faces. His friends admired the extravagant spread of food and drinks laid out before them, a testament to Pete's lavish lifestyle. Today was his birthday, so naturally, he hosted a big party, as he did every year.

Despite the glitz and glamour of the party, Pete's mind was consumed by fear. The threatening letter he had received gnawed at him from within, casting a shadow over the festivities. He tried to push aside his paranoia, convincing himself it was just a prank or perhaps one of his ex-lovers seeking attention.

As the evening progressed, Pete's smile faltered whenever he caught someone staring at him. The once welcoming gazes now felt like accusatory glares, and the laughter around him sounded like whispers of betrayal. His heart raced with anxiety, his mind racing with suspicions and doubts.

When Ben sidled up to him, his eyes gleaming with excitement, Pete couldn't help but feel a pang of unease.

"Hey, buddy, you've been acting a bit off tonight. Everything okay?" Ben asked with a knowing look in his eyes.

Pete forced a chuckle, the sound hollow in his own ears. "Just dealing with some work stress; you know how it is," he replied, trying to sound nonchalant.

Ben arched an eyebrow, his gaze piercing through Pete's facade. "Come on, Pete. You can tell me if something's wrong. You know I've got your back no matter what," Ben said in a low voice, a hint of concern underlying his words.

Pete hesitated, unsure if he could trust even his best friend with the weight of his fears.

"I appreciate that, Ben," Pete replied, his voice a little strained. "It's just some personal stuff I'm dealing with, nothing major."

Ben studied Pete for a moment, his expression unreadable. "You sure about that? You've been looking over your shoulder all night. Is everything really okay?"

Pete felt the familiar tendrils of paranoia creeping up his spine. Could Ben be involved? Did he know about the threatening letter?

"I'm fine, Ben. Just let me handle it my way," Pete said, trying to sound firm.

Ben nodded slowly, his gaze not leaving Pete's face. "Alright, but remember, I'm here for you no matter what. You don't have to face whatever it is alone."

As the party continued around them, Pete couldn't shake off the feeling of dread that clung to him like a second skin. Every laugh, every whisper felt like a threat, and he couldn't help but second-guess everyone's intentions.

The night stretched on, the music fading into a dull buzz in Pete's ears as his thoughts spiraled out of control. He excused himself from the crowd, needing a moment of solitude to collect his fraying nerves. The opulent mansion suddenly felt suffocating, each corner harboring unseen danger.

Alone in the dimly lit study, Pete sank into a plush armchair, his hands trembling slightly as he reached for the glass of whiskey on the mahogany table. The liquid burned down his throat, but it offered little solace against the turmoil brewing within him.

A soft knock on the door interrupted his inner turmoil, and Pete tensed, his gaze darting toward the entrance.

"Who is it?" he called out, his voice betraying a hint of apprehension.

"It's me, Ben," came the muffled reply from the other side.

Pete hesitated for a moment before unlocking the door, allowing Ben to step inside. His friend's concerned expression mirrored the turmoil within Pete, and for a brief moment, he considered confiding in him. But the fear that gripped his heart like a vise held him back.

Ben perched on the edge of the leather armchair opposite Pete, his eyes never leaving his friend's troubled face.

"Pete, I can sense something is really bothering you. You know you can trust me, right?"

Pete felt a flicker of desperation rise within him, a yearning to unburden himself of the heavy secret weighing him down. But just as he opened his mouth to speak, doubt crept in once more.

Taking a deep breath, Pete forced a smile he hoped looked convincing. "I appreciate your concern, Ben. It's nothing I can't handle. Just some work stress getting to me, that's all."

Ben's gaze bore into him, unwavering. "Pete, we've been through a lot together. If there's something more going on?"

Before Ben could finish his sentence, Pete's eyes darted toward the antique clock on the wall. The time seemed to mock him, each tick echoing in his ears like a drumbeat of impending doom.

"I think you should go back to the party, Ben. I just need some time alone," Pete said, his voice tinged with a newfound resolve.

Ben hesitated, studying Pete intently as if trying to unravel the depths of his turmoil. After a moment of silence, he nodded slowly and stood up. "Alright, but remember, I'm here for you whenever you're ready to talk," Ben said softly before turning to leave the room.

Alone once more in the dimly lit study, Pete felt the weight of his secret pressing down on him like a leaden shroud. The remains of the half-burnt threatening letter lay crumpled in the ashtray, taunting him with its insidious power. Pete's breath caught in his throat as he remembered the words, each syllable sending a shiver down his spine.

Just as panic threatened to consume him, a sudden noise outside the study door jolted Pete from his thoughts. His heart pounded in his chest, the sound echoing in his ears like a war drum. He cautiously approached the door, his hand hovering over the handle.

"Who's there?" Pete called out, his voice barely above a whisper.

Silence greeted him in response, thick and suffocating. Every nerve in his body screamed with tension, his senses heightened to a fever pitch.

Another noise, this time faint but unmistakable, came from behind him. Pete whirled around, his eyes wide with fear. In the dim light of the study, shadows seemed to morph and shift, taking on sinister shapes that threatened to engulf him. His own ragged breath seemed to mock him, echoing off the study's walls like a sinister whisper. The silence that followed was deafening, each passing second stretching into an eternity of dread.

Pete's hands trembled as he reached for the heavy book resting on the bookshelf beside him. With a shaky grip, he clutched it close to his chest, the weight offering a sliver of comfort in the face of the unknown threat that loomed around him.

As he stood there, his back pressed against the cool wood of the bookshelf, a figure materialized from the shadows before him. Pete's breath caught in his throat, his pulse thundering in his ears as he struggled to make out the features of the intruder.

The figure emerged from the shadows, and Pete's heart raced as he recognized the familiar features.

"You?" he whispered, his voice shaking in the tense stillness of the room. "No... it can't be...."

The ghost gave a haunting smile. "But it is."

A loud bang reverberated through the air as a gunshot echoed in the room.

Chapter 34

I pushed open the door, a gust of warm Florida wind nipping at my heels. Inside, shadows clung to the corners of the living room where Matt sat on the couch, a storm cloud of sulking silence around him. I greeted the void with a weary "hi" and set our daughter Angel on her feet, her tiny shoes pattering across the floor to her basket of toys.

"Matt?" My voice tiptoed around his brooding figure. No response. A sigh escaped his lips, a sound heavy with unspoken words. "Everything okay?"

"Does it look like everything's okay?" His words, sharp-edged, cut through the stillness.

"Your exercises..." I began, hope threading my tone, "did you manage to do them today?"

"Did them," he grunted, eyes fixed on a distant spot on the wall.

"Where have you been?" His question sliced into the air, abrupt and demanding.

"I told you," I replied, a defensive edge creeping in. "The Chapman case. Sarah needs me."

"Sarah again?" He turned now to face me, hurt etching his features. "Why haven't you told me more?"

"I did, Matt." My insistence felt frail against the weight of his stare.

"Did you?" Accusation wrapped around his words. "It doesn't feel like it. It feels like you don't trust me."

"Matt...."

"Stay home," he said, the plea soft but firm. "Help me instead. You're putting yourself in danger. The kids, too. For what? There's a detective on that case already."

"Sarah's innocent," I whispered, the truth of it burning clear in my chest. "She needs me." I perched on the armrest, my fingers coiling into fists. "I'm trying to help a friend, Matt. I'm close to solving this. I got some very important information today."

"Helping?" He scoffed, his gaze piercing through me. "You call this helping? You're obsessed!"

"Obsessed?" The word echoed in my chest, a hollow denial. "Steven Chapman is dead, Matt. And someone we know is being blamed for it—"

"Someone we know, or you?" His voice rose, laced with frustration. "Every waking moment, it's the case, the clues, Sarah's innocence. What about us?"

"Us?" My throat tightened. "I'm doing this for us, too, for justice. Detective Ryan believes the neighbor Nicki killed herself, but...."

"Justice," he spat out the word as though it burned him. "What about the justice of having a partner who's present, who's here with their family?"

"Matt—" I started, but his words steamrolled over mine.

"Present. Not just physically, but really here," he continued, his hands gesturing wildly, animating his anguish.

"When was the last time we had a day without... without all this?"

"Without the truth? Without fairness?" I leaned in, my resolve hardening. "That's not a world I can accept sitting down."

"Fairness?" He laughed, hollow and short. "Tell me about fairness when you miss another dinner, another bedtime story, because of 'the case.'"

"Because it matters!" I snapped, standing now, feeling the space between us stretch and strain.

"Does it? More than your own boyfriend? The father of your child?" He locked eyes with me, the hurt unmistakable. "I'm hurt. I need you. We all need you here. It's like you're running away from us because it's too much for you to handle."

"Matt, that's not fair." My voice cracked, betraying my mounting desperation.

"Fair...." He shook his head, looking away. "You keep using that word, but I don't think it means what you think it means. Not anymore."

I reached for his hand, the one lying dormant on the armrest. He flinched but didn't pull away.

"Matt," I said gently, watching the conflict play across his face.

"Every time you walk out that door...." His voice trailed off, a haunted look in his eyes that I knew all too well. "It's like I'm back on that floor, bleeding out, not knowing if I'd ever see you or Angel again. I'm scared, dang it. Don't you understand that? I'm terrified of losing you. This job... our line of work. It's... I'm scared, Eva Rae. Heck, I'm terrified even to go outside anymore."

My heart clenched. The memory of his broken body

sprawled on the cold tiles flashed before me, a stark reminder of the risks we once took daily.

"Hey." I squeezed his hand tighter. "I'm here, Matt. I'm not going anywhere."

"Physically, maybe." He met my gaze, his eyes shimmering with unshed tears. "But emotionally? You're miles away, lost in a case that's chipping away at the edges of our lives. I got hurt doing what you're doing now. And it terrifies me, every day, that history will repeat itself."

"Matt...."

"Promise me." His plea cut deep. "Promise me you won't let this... obsession become more important than coming home to me. To us."

I searched his face, seeing the raw vulnerability of the man who had faced down criminals yet stood defenseless against his own fears.

"I promise," I whispered, feeling the weight of my words, the gravity of their meaning. "You, Angel, and all my kids are my world. I can't lose you either."

"Then be here with us," he implored. "Really here."

"More balancing, less... tunnel vision. I can do that." I leaned in, pressing a kiss to his forehead, lingering in the comfort of his presence. "We'll get through this together. I love you."

"I love you too." His voice was soft, and a tentative smile touched his lips as he wrapped an arm around me, pulling me closer. "Just... stay safe, okay?"

"Always."

The tension in the room thickened, pressing against my skin like a physical force. Matt's gaze strayed to Angel, now curled up with her favorite stuffed bear on the other end of the couch.

"Look at her," he said, his voice barely above a whisper. "She's so small, so vulnerable."

Angel's tiny fingers twitched, clutching at the soft fur as if holding onto a lifeline. A concern grew inside me that I couldn't let go. Was Matt asking me to stop the investigation completely? Or just to stay safe?

"Matt, what are you saying?" My voice caught in my throat, the question emerging as an anxious croak. "I mean, what are you really saying?"

"Your work...." He paused, struggling to find the words. "It's dangerous. And after... what happened to me, it's not just your safety I worry about. It's hers. It's all of our kids' safety. What if something you're tangled up in comes back here? Comes back to them?"

His fear was palpable, a living thing that crept into the corners of the room, wrapping around us like a cold fog. The memory of his shooting, the blood, the hospital beeps, they played in my head on a vicious loop.

"Matt, I'm sorry." The apology tumbled out, quick and sincere. "I didn't mean to...."

"Sorry doesn't cut it!" His hand balled into a fist, the knuckles whitening. "Not when it comes to their lives, to your life."

"I'm not gonna stop. I can't give up now. Sarah needs me." My voice was firm despite the quiver I fought to suppress. "She's sitting in a cell for a crime I believe she didn't commit. I can't turn my back on her, not when she has no one else."

"Even if it means you're risking everything?" His eyes searched mine, pleading for understanding.

"Everything I do is to make sure we keep everything." My hand reached out, hovering before settling on his. "But I hear you, Matt. I'll be more careful than ever. I can't lose you or the kids either. Sarah's innocence won't mean much if I let my family fall apart."

"Promise?" His voice broke on the word, the single syllable heavy with unspoken dread.

"That I can promise." I squeezed his hand, a silent vow passing between us.

"Look at me, Matt." I waited until his eyes met mine, the shadows of fear still lingering. "I need you to understand something. Our family," my gaze flickered toward where Angel sat peacefully, "you are my world."

He watched me, a silent sentinel, waiting.

"But being a detective... it's not just what I do. It's part of who I am." The words hung between us, heavy with truth. "But I can—"

"Will," he interjected.

"Will," I corrected, nodding. "Find a way to balance them better. Our relationship, our kids, they'll come first. That's my promise to you."

"Involve me," he said after a moment, his voice steadier than before. "Not just as your partner, but as someone who knows the dangers. Who's lived them."

"Involve you?" I repeated, surprised.

"Information, updates, decisions—don't shut me out. Maybe I can keep you safer if I'm in the loop." His hand gripped mine tighter. "I don't want to lose you."

"Okay." It was a simple word, but it sealed an unspoken pact. "Together, then. We tackle this together."

"Exactly." Matt exhaled, the tension in his shoulders easing. "We're a team, right?"

"Right." I smiled, letting his strength seep into me. "Team us."

"Team us," he echoed, a faint smile touching the corners of his lips.

Leaning in, I brushed a kiss against Matt's forehead. His eyes, once clouded with doubt and fear, softened under the warmth of my lips.

"Thank you," I whispered, tracing the line of his jaw with my fingertips, feeling the stubble that spoke of days spent worrying.

"For what?" he murmured, his hand finding its way to the small of my back,. pulling me closer on the couch.

"Listening. Understanding."

He chuckled quietly, a sound that danced against the tension that had surrounded us. "I think I should be thanking you."

"Matt...."

"Shh." He pressed a finger to my lips, silencing me. "Let me speak, okay?"

"Okay," I conceded, my voice a mere breath as I settled into the crook of his arm.

"I am trying to fight it, you know?" His admission was raw and vulnerable. "But ever since the shooting, everything feels... fragile."

"Life is fragile," I said, tilting my head to meet his gaze.

"Exactly. Which is why—" Matt paused, searching my face, "—I can't bear the thought of losing you—not to the job, not to anything."

"Hey, look at me." I cupped his cheek, urging him to understand. "You won't lose me. I'm right here."

"Promise?" The word hung between us, a plea for reassurance.

"Promise." I sealed it with a kiss, gentle and lingering, a testament to the depth of our bond.

"Okay," he breathed out as we parted, his thumb caressing my cheek. "Okay."

"Team us, remember?" I repeated, then smiled, nudging his nose with mine.

"Always, team us." His smile matched mine, a mirror of relief and love.

As the weight of our promises hung in the air between us, a sense of unity settled over the room, wrapping around us like a shield against the dangers lurking outside. Matt's hand found mine, fingers intertwining in a silent vow to face whatever came our way together.

"I love you," he said, his voice a soft declaration that filled the space with warmth.

"I love you too," I replied, my heart swelling with gratitude for having him by my side.

Chapter 35

THEN:

SARAH'S FINGERS clenched the fabric of the curtains, her knuckles white as she peered through the window. The red and blue lights from the ambulance painted the night in urgent strokes, casting an eerie glow over Steven's hunched figure as he carried Victoria's limp body outside. Victoria's arm dangled lifelessly, her head rolling against Steven's chest with each hurried step he took. He told her he would take Victoria. Sarah wasn't good at handling these situations of crisis. She would only be in the way.

"Be safe," Sarah whispered, her voice a fragile thread in the vast silence of the room.

The ambulance doors slammed shut, muffling the distant wail of the siren that soon faded into the night. Alone now, the house's quiet pressed in around her, amplifying the rapid beat of her heart—a drumbeat of fear and helplessness.

She turned away from the window, her reflection in the glass a ghostly specter shadowed by doubt and worry. Her breath came in short bursts, her mind replaying the convulsions that had seized Victoria's small frame, the terror in her eyes before they rolled back.

"God, not again," she murmured to the empty room.

Her gaze fell on the wine rack, its contents glinting seductively in the dim lighting. One bottle stood slightly askew as if beckoning. With a trembling hand, Sarah reached for it, pulling the cork free with a practiced twist. The pop resonated, oddly loud in the stillness.

"Please, just one glass," she bargained with herself, though she knew the lie for what it was.

The wine poured, a deep crimson river flowing into the glass, the sound of it hitting the bottom oddly soothing. She wrapped her fingers around the stem, the coolness of the glass a stark contrast to her feverish skin. Raising it to her lips, she drank deeply, the rich liquid a bittersweet balm to her fraying nerves.

"Help her," she whispered into the empty glass, a silent prayer for Victoria as the alcohol began its familiar dance through her bloodstream, promising oblivion but delivering only more shadows.

The last drop fell, a final crimson tear. Sarah tilted the bottle, coaxing it out. The bottles stood like sentinels, guardians of her secret pain, each label a testament to a night spent drowning in vineyard graves.

She eyed the empty vessel, its hollow echoing back at her—accusatory. Her fingers traced the curve of the glass, cool and smooth, like her daughter's cheek in slumber. The urge to reach for another was there, a whisper in her mind growing louder with each heartbeat.

"Stop," she breathed out, a command more to herself than the silence around her. Her hands shook as she pulled her cell phone from the pocket of her jeans. It felt heavy—like it was made of lead rather than silicone and glass.

"Come on; come on," she muttered, thumbing through the contacts until Steven's name appeared. She tapped the call button, her heart thudding against her ribs.

"Hello?" His voice came through, strained but clear.

"Steven, how... how is she?" Her words tripped over her tongue, a clumsy dance of vowels and consonants.

There was a pause, a stretch of time where she could hear the beeping of machines, the distant murmur of hospital life.

"Stable," he said finally. "They're running tests."

"Tests," she echoed, the word a stone sinking in her gut.

"Sarah, are you—" He began, but she couldn't bear the weight of his unspoken question.

"Thank you," she interjected, the words sharp, a blade cutting the line that tethered them. She ended the call, the screen going dark, reflecting back a woman frayed at the edges —a mother coming undone. He called her back.

"Sarah? Are you... have you been drinking?" Steven's sharp and accusatory voice cut through the static of the phone line.

She could feel the heat rising in her cheeks, a wildfire burning away any pretense. "I just needed...." She couldn't finish the sentence, couldn't find a lie that would sound like truth in her own ears.

"Needed what? To be drunk while our daughter is lying in a hospital bed?" There was an edge to his words, a disappointment that sliced deeper than anger.

"It's not like that," she said quickly, the words tumbling out in a jumble. But they were slurred, her tongue heavy and uncooperative in her mouth.

"Isn't it, Sarah?"

The room spun slightly, or maybe it was her head, filled with too much wine and too little courage. She glanced at the phone, its glowing screen a beacon of her failure.

"Steven, I—" The apology choked in her throat, strangled by shame.

"Sarah, this—"

"Goodbye, Steven." She pressed "End Call," the beep punctuating her humiliation. Her hand trembled as she set down the phone, the silence in the room now complete, oppressive, and all-consuming.

Sarah's hands shook, the clatter of glass against glass as she collected the empty bottles. Each one was a memory, a moment of frailty, a time when the wine had whispered false promises of peace into her ear. She gripped them tighter, the knuckles on her fingers whitening.

"Enough," she muttered to herself, the word a blade severing the threads of her denial. Gathering the last of the bottles, she marched to the door, her steps unsteady but determined.

The humid evening air clung to her face as she stepped outside, the pile of glass in her arms. The recycling bin loomed before her, a confessional waiting for her sins. With a heavy heart and an arm weighed down by her habit, she tilted the bottles and let them fall. They cascaded into the bin with a cacophony of crashes that seemed to echo around the quiet street.

"Out of sight, out of mind," she whispered, but her voice held no conviction.

Back inside, the house was still; the only sound was her breathing—too quick, too shallow. As she turned to lock the door behind her, her gaze fell on the counter where the unopened bottles of wine stood, calling her back.

"Damn it." The words hissed between her clenched teeth.

She reached out, her fingertips brushing the cool surface of the bottle. Her reflection stared back through the darkened glass, distorted and wavering.

"Sarah, stop!" she commanded herself. "This isn't helping."

But the wine promised solace, a balm for her fraying nerves. She thought of Victoria, of Steven's disappointed voice, and felt the pull grow stronger. The seal cracked under her twisting hand, the sound a betrayal of her earlier resolve.

"Only a glass," she bargained, pouring the deep red liquid and watching it swirl in the goblet. "Just one."

She brought the glass to her lips, the familiar aroma wrapping around her senses, pulling her further from the edge of reason.

"Victoria needs you sober," she reminded herself, the wine hovering, untouched. But her worries screamed louder than her conscience.

"Tomorrow," she vowed weakly. "I'll start tomorrow."

The first sip was both a defeat and a reprieve, the taste of surrender bittersweet on her tongue.

The glass tipped and drained. Another poured. Then another. The room began its languid tilt, the corners blurring into shadows. Sarah's thoughts muddied with each gulp, and her resolve drowned to a whisper beneath the wine's seductive tide. The world spun, and she spun with it until the floor rose to meet her in an unforgiving embrace.

"Sarah!"

Her name cracked through the fog. She blinked against the harsh light, the room coming back into sharp, unkind focus.

Steven towered above her, his face contorted with anger and disgust.

"Look at you," he spat, "Drunk again."

She tried to rise, but her limbs were heavy and uncooperative. The room swayed, and she slumped back down. Her head pounded in time with her quickening pulse.

"Go to bed," Steven commanded, his voice cold and distant. "You're useless like this."

"Steven...." Her tongue felt thick, words slurred and distant. “It’s not like you don’t drink.”

“I don’t drink like this. And certainly not anymore. I have a sick daughter to attend to. But you have apparently forgotten that?”

“But....”

"Bed," he repeated, turning away. His steps thudded across the floor, each one echoing her shame.

Dragging herself up, Sarah stumbled toward the staircase, the weight of her body immense. Each step creaked underfoot, a mournful chorus to accompany her retreat. Her hands shook on the railing, the last of the day's wine sour on her breath.

"Victoria?" she tried again, her voice barely a whisper.

"Sleep it off, Sarah," came the reply, devoid of warmth.

"Steven," Sarah croaked, her voice steadier than she felt. "Victoria—how is she?"

He paused at the doorway, his silhouette rigid against the hallway light. "She's very sick." His words were clipped, heavy with unspoken accusations.

"Did they... did they say what's wrong?" Her heart stumbled over each beat, aching for her daughter.

"Tests," he muttered. "More tests. The cancer might have spread. They don't know yet." He faced her now, his eyes searching and dissecting. "But really, Sarah, when did you last care? You can't even stay sober."

"Steven, please—" She reached out, fingers trembling, grasping for understanding amidst the wreckage of their conversation.

"Your concern is convenient," he scoffed, stepping away from her outstretched hand. "Always after the fact. After another bottle."

"Steven, I...."

The weight of his judgment bore down on her, crushing her resolve.

"Save it, Sarah." His voice cut through the tension, sharp and final. "I just came home to grab some things in a bag. I'm going back to the hospital and sleeping there with our daughter."

He left, footsteps retreating down the hall, each step a gavel sentencing her to guilt. Alone in the gloom, Sarah's hands clenched into fists, the fight to prove her love for Victoria burning beneath her ribcage.

She fumbled with the hem of her shirt, the fabric twisted in her unsteady grip.

"Bed," she whispered to herself, a mantra to keep the world from spinning out of control. "Just go to bed."

The mattress accepted her without judgment, cool sheets embracing her exhausted frame. She sank into its depths, a solitary island in a sea of turmoil. Her breath hitched, a silent sob catching in her throat as she turned her face into the pillow.

"Victoria...." The name was a prayer, a plea for forgiveness.

The room spun gently, cradling her in its indifferent arms. Shadows danced on the walls, whispers of memories and better days. A tear escaped, hot against her skin, the dam breaking in the quiet of the night.

"Stupid," she murmured, chastising herself as another tear followed, carving a path of sorrow. "So stupid."

Her hand reached out, the space beside her empty and cold. She imagined Steven's warmth, the steadying presence she had pushed away with every clink of glass.

"You need to be strong," she told the emptiness.

But strength was a stranger, an elusive specter that fled at the scent of alcohol. Her eyelids grew heavy, weighted down by the gravity of her own failings. She surrendered to their insistence, letting the darkness pull her under.

"Tomorrow," she breathed out, a promise or a lie, it didn't matter which.

Sleep claimed her, but peace eluded her grasp. Tears continued their silent journey, mapping the contours of her face, each one a testament to a mother's love entangled in the vines of her vices.

The next morning dawned in a wash of pale light, filtering through the curtains to paint the room in soft hues. Sarah stirred, her body a canvas of ache and regret, limbs heavy with the weight of her choices. The remnants of the night clung to her like a shroud, a reminder of her weaknesses and failings.

Rising with reluctance, she pushed back the covers, revealing the world beyond her cocoon of solitude. The house lay still, quiet in its judgment, as she navigated the halls with cautious steps. Memories of the previous night prickled at her consciousness, each one a thorn in her side.

In the kitchen, she paused, confronted by the detritus of her undoing. Empty bottles stood sentry on the counter, a silent testament to her descent into darkness. The sight soured her stomach, a bitter cocktail of shame and self-loathing.

With trembling hands, she swept them into a bag, their clinks muffled against the plastic cradle she offered them. The weight of her actions pressed down, a heavy burden she carried alone. She tied the bag tightly, sealing away her transgressions, but the memories remained unyielding in their presence.

A glint caught her eye—a new bottle of wine by the sink, its label pristine, untouched by guilt or remorse. Her resolve wavered, teetering on the precipice of temptation. The cork beckoned a siren call that promised oblivion in its ruby depths.

Fingers hovered over the bottle, indecision painting her features in shades of uncertainty. One glass wouldn't hurt, she reasoned, her voice a fragile thread in the silence of the room.

"Just one glass."

Chapter 36

The gravel crunched under my shoes as I approached the faded green door of Adam Andersson's house. It was a modest dwelling, the kind that held secrets behind the dark windows. I rapped sharply, the sound echoing, betraying my resolve.

There was a moment's shuffle, and then the door swung open. Adam stood there, his features tight, eyes wary.

"Agent Thomas? Can I help you?" His voice had an edge like a knife carefully sheathed.

"Hi, Adam."

I kept my tone level. "I'm looking deeper into Steven's... situation. As well as Nicki's. Mind if I step in?"

He hesitated, a muscle ticking in his jaw, then stepped aside. The living room was dim, curtains drawn against the intruding gaze of the sun. I scanned the room, noting that you could still see the blood on the ground where Nicki had died. Adam had been living with a friend for a few days while the forensic department had taken what they needed. When they were done, he had tried to clean the floor, but it was still visible. How anyone could live in a house after something like that happened was beyond my understanding.

"Steven," I started, easing onto an armchair with rough upholstery. "How well did you two know each other?"

"We were neighbors." Adam remained standing, arms crossed. "You know how it is."

"Neighbors can mean a lot of things. Were you friends, acquaintances...?"

"Acquaintances," he clipped out the word. We'd nod and say hello, and that's about it."

"Must be tough," I said, watching his reaction closely, "with everything going on."

"Life's full of surprises," Adam replied, but his voice betrayed nothing.

"Indeed, it is."

"Their daughter," I said, shifting in the chair to face him more directly. "I heard she's ill."

Adam's gaze dropped to the floor, his posture sagging slightly. "Yeah, leukemia. It's been... rough on them." The words seemed to weigh heavily on him.

"They must have changed their routines quite a bit," I ventured carefully.

He nodded, the movement barely perceptible. "They didn't get out much after it started. Hospital visits, treatments...." His voice trailed off, lost in the sea of unspoken hardships.

"Before that," I pressed on, leaning forward with feigned casualness. "They had more time for themselves, no?"

"Sure," Adam replied, a touch of defensiveness slipping into his tone. "But I really don't know a lot about them."

"Of course not," I conceded with a quick, placating smile. "Just trying to paint a clearer picture of their relationship."

"Sarah liked to unwind—a glass of wine, a night out with the girls," Adam said, his fingers drumming an irregular beat on the armrest. It got worse over the years, and she came home drunk many times. We saw her drive up in the car, swerving down the street. It was tragic. Steven? He preferred a quiet night in."

"Sounds like they had different ways of dealing with their daughter's illness," I said, eyeing Adam for any telltale signs of discomfort.

"Opposites attract, right?" He forced a chuckle that didn't quite mask the strain in his voice.

"Sometimes," I agreed, keeping my tone light. "And Steven never joined her on her evenings out, even just to keep her company?"

Adam shook his head. "Not after Victoria got sick. But even before that, he wasn't much of a drinker. They would go out, but she was the one who liked to drink. And when Victoria got sick, he stayed home with her or spent his nights at the hospital."

"Interesting." I tapped my finger on my knee, feigning contemplation. "With Sarah out, it must've given Steven some... opportunities. Not only did she go out at night from time to time, she also worked a lot and was a career woman."

"Opportunities?" His brow furrowed, and he leaned back, arms crossing defensively.

"Sure," I continued as if stating the obvious. "Time alone can lead to new friendships... maybe more intimate ones."

"Are you suggesting—?" Adam began, his voice rising before he caught himself. "No. Steven wasn't like that."

"Wasn't like what, Adam?" I probed, locking eyes with him. "Seeing someone else?"

"Absolutely not," he snapped. There was a flash of anger in

his eyes, quickly doused. "I would've known. He was devoted to his daughter. It was really hard for him."

"Would you have known?" I asked softly, almost sympathetically. "It's easy to miss the signs, especially when life's so hectic."

"Look," Adam said, his hands unclasping and reclasping, "Steven had his faults, but he was loyal to Sarah. Especially after...." His voice cracked, and he looked away.

"Especially after his daughter got sick," I finished for him. The room filled with a tense silence, and Adam's jaw tightened as he fought back emotions.

"Right," he whispered, almost to himself.

"Because that's when people show their true colors, isn't it, Adam?" I pressed on, my voice barely above a whisper.

Adam met my gaze again, his eyes wells of unshed tears, but there was something else there—fear, perhaps, or guilt. "You have no idea what they went through," he said, his voice barely audible.

"I'm trying to understand," I assured him. But understanding was only part of the game. The other part was unraveling the truth.

Adam's posture stiffened, the tendons in his neck standing out like steel cables. His hands, once restless, were now planted firmly on the arms of his chair, gripping with white-knuckled force.

"Am I under arrest?" The words sliced through the thick air between us, sharp and sudden.

I leaned back slightly, giving him space, though the distance did little to soften the intensity of our exchange.

"No, Adam," I said evenly. "You're not under arrest."

"Because if I'm not," he continued, a hard edge cutting into his tone, "I'd like you to leave. Now."

"Understood," I replied, my voice steady, betraying none of the curiosity that buzzed in my veins like electricity. "But we both know something isn't right here. You feel it too, don't you?"

His eyes darted away for a fraction of a second before locking back onto mine, a silent battle raging behind them.

"I don't have to listen to this," he muttered, but there was a tremor in his voice, a crack in the armor.

"Of course," I conceded with a slight nod, rising from my seat. My movements were calm and deliberate, a counterpoint to the tension that thrummed through the room. "Just doing my job, Adam."

Adam watched me, the lines of his face etched with a mixture of anger and something that looked suspiciously like fear.

"Adam," I said, my voice cutting through the charged silence. "We both know you're holding back."

He stood rigid, his fists clenched at his sides, a vein throbbing visibly in his neck. The room felt smaller, the air thicker.

"My wife, Nicki, was... she had someone else," Adam's voice broke, shattering the facade of indifference he'd been clinging to. "I found texts on her phone, late-night calls. I confronted her, and she admitted it—said it was Steven."

"Steven?" My question hung between us like an accusation. "Did you confront him too?"

Adam shook his head, a bitter laugh escaping him. "No. What was the point? It was already over, all of it."

"Did you think about revenge?" I probed, watching his face closely.

"Revenge?" He spat out the word like it was poison. His eyes flared with a raw, untamed emotion. "I loved Nicki. Despite everything. But Steven...."

"Did you kill them, Adam?" I asked sharply, seizing the crack in his composure. "Was that your idea of justice?"

His face contorted with rage; his body tensed as if preparing to lunge. "You think I'm a murderer?"

"Someone killed them," I pressed on, unrelenting. "And you just told me you had every reason to hate the man who was with your wife."

"Get out!" Adam's voice was a roar, his hands shaking with the effort to control himself. "I didn't kill anyone!"

"Good motive, though," I murmured, locking eyes with him, letting the implication hang heavy in the air.

Adam's breath was ragged, his chest heaving. "You have nothing on me."

"Maybe," I conceded, maintaining my ground. "But motives matter, Adam. And yours is as clear as day."

I quickly stood up from the couch, feeling my heart racing. Adam's face twisted with anger as he took a step toward me.

"Get out," he growled, his voice low and menacing.

"Okay, okay," I said, holding my hands up in surrender. "I'm going."

But as I made my way to the door, Adam lunged at me, his arms outstretched. I dodged him, stumbling toward the wall. He tried to grab me again, but I managed to slip past him and run to the exit.

"Stay away from me!" I yelled, my voice shaking with adrenaline.

Adam let out a frustrated scream and slammed the door shut behind me. I took a deep breath, trying to calm myself, and started walking to my car.

As I drove home, my mind was racing with thoughts about what had just happened. Was Matt right? Was I putting myself in harm's way by investigating this case?

I couldn't deny that the possibility of danger scared me, but I also knew I couldn't give up now. There were too many unanswered questions and too many loose ends. And if I didn't find out the truth, who would?

Part III

CAPE CANAVERAL

Chapter 37

The steam from the bowl curled into the air, a fragrant dance of herbs and warmth. Monica sat rigidly, her posture a disciplined arc over the table where the colors of the kitchen—pale blues and sunlight—played upon the surfaces.

"Come on, Victoria," she said, her voice soft but firm, "you need to eat."

Victoria, draped in the shadows of her wheelchair, seemed so small, her presence diminished to the space she occupied beside the table. Monica dipped the spoon into the soup, cradling a careful amount, and lifted it toward Victoria's lips.

"For strength," Monica coaxed, "just a little."

The spoon hovered with an unspoken promise, trembling slightly as if it bore not just sustenance but hope.

Victoria's lips parted, and the spoon's tepid offering brushed against her tongue. "Ugh," she sputtered, recoiling as though the taste had physical form. "It's awful."

"Shhh...." Monica's brow furrowed in concern. She set the spoon down, reaching across to pat Victoria's hand.

"You know I'm not much of a cook," she said with a half-hearted chuckle. "But it's nutritious. Your body needs this."

"Why does it have to taste so bad?" Victoria muttered, turning her head away.

"I'm doing my best here. Your father," Monica began, the tone of her voice shifting, now edged with a solemn duty, "he asked me to look after you should anything ever happen to him." She locked eyes with Victoria, ensuring the gravity of her words settled between them. "I promised him."

"My mom would've made it taste better," Victoria whispered almost to herself, a tear betraying her stoicism.

"Sarah," Monica scoffed quietly, her hands tightening around the bowl. "She didn't have your best interests at heart. I do, Victoria. I always have." The spoon clinked against the china as Monica gathered another mouthful. "Let's try again, for strength, for your father."

"I don't want to."

"But you have to. Open up," Monica said, her voice soft but firm as the spoon approached Victoria's lips once more.

"I can't," Victoria murmured, a hand weakly pushing Monica's away. "It makes me feel sick."

"Victoria, you need to eat." The spoon was insistent, edging closer.

"Please, no more." Her voice was a thin whisper, eyes glistening with the effort of defiance.

Monica paused, her expression hardening. "If you don't eat, we'll have to use the tube."

At the mention of the feeding tube, a shudder coursed through Victoria's frail frame. She looked at Monica, the plea in her eyes raw and unguarded—a tear shaped in the corner of her eye.

"Please, I'll try. Just... not the tube."

"Then, eat," Monica insisted, her tone leaving no room for further protest.

"Okay," Victoria relented, tears spilling over as she opened her mouth to accept another spoonful.

With a spoon poised like a sculptor over marble, Monica waited for the moment of surrender.

"Good girl," Monica praised as if speaking to a young child rather than a teenager confined to the bindings of a wheelchair. With practiced care, she slid the spoon past Victoria's reluctant lips, the warmth of the broth preceding the taste.

Victoria's face contorted, a dance of muscles weaving expressions of disgust and defeat. Her tongue betrayed her, recoiling against the flavor that invaded her mouth.

"Swallow," Monica commanded gently, yet her eyes sparkled with a sense of triumph that belied the softness in her voice.

The soup made its reluctant journey down Victoria's throat, each spoonful an unspoken battle. Her face remained pinched in distaste, a silent testament to her inner loathing for the meal and, perhaps, for the hands that fed it to her.

"Every spoonful is a step toward recovery," Monica said, offering Victoria the brimming utensil. "Strength comes with nourishment."

Victoria's mouth opened mechanically, a trace of resolve flickering in her eyes as she accepted the tepid liquid once again. She swallowed, wincing subtly.

"See? You're doing well," Monica coaxed, her words clipped with urgency.

"Feels like swallowing needles," Victoria muttered after another spoonful, her voice barely above a whisper.

"Your body needs it," Monica replied, dismissing the

complaint with a wave of her hand. She scooped up more soup, watching as Victoria steeled herself for the next bite.

"Can't we try something else?" Victoria asked, her plea soft but firm.

"Soup's what the doctor ordered." Monica's response was automatic, her focus unyielding. "Finish it."

Victoria nodded, the corners of her mouth downturned. She took another spoonful, determination etched into the lines of her face, a silent acknowledgment of the ordeal. Monica's gaze never wavered, capturing each moment of Victoria's reluctant compliance.

"Good girl," Monica murmured, the pride in her voice failing to mask its commanding edge. The spoon clinked against the bowl as she scooped another portion of the murky broth.

Victoria's lips parted, accepting yet another mouthful. Her face twisted, a silent scream etched into the lines around her mouth. She gagged slightly but managed to swallow, her body convulsing with distaste.

"Nearly there," Monica said, peering into the bowl. Only a few spoonfuls remained in the watery grave of vegetables. "See, you can do this."

"Can I stop now?" Victoria's voice quivered, each word laced with the hope of reprieve.

"Almost done," Monica assured, the finality in her tone brooking no argument. She watched, almost clinically, as Victoria forced down the last of the soup, the grimace clinging stubbornly to her features like ivy to ancient brickwork.

"Every bit," Monica instructed, her voice a firm whisper. She held the spoon just inches from Victoria's mouth.

Victoria's eyes locked onto the quivering surface, her throat working to muster saliva for the task.

"I can't—"

"Shh." Monica cut her off, tender yet unyielding. "It's for your own good. Strength comes with nourishment."

The spoon hovered, waiting. Victoria willed her lips to part, her body yielding to the command more than the plea within her. The warmth of the liquid did nothing to comfort the chills that danced up her spine.

"Swallow," Monica coaxed, her eye tracking the painful journey of the broth down Victoria's throat.

Gulping down the bitterness, Victoria's face contorted once more, a battle of revulsion and obedience. The empty bowl clattered lightly as Monica set it down, a hollow victory on the wooden table.

"See?" Monica's voice softened fractionally. "All done."

Victoria nodded, her eyes glistening not with gratitude but with the effort it took to keep everything down. The promise of no more forced her into submission; the taste lingered like a threat.

Chapter 38

The key turned with a reluctant twist, the click of the lock thunderously loud in my ears. I pushed the door open; my entry was a stagger more than a step. The familiar scent of home did nothing to soothe the panic that clung to me like the clammy sweat on my skin. My heart hadn't ceased its wild thrumming since I'd left Adam Andersson, his words still lodged in my mind.

My hand trembled as I reached back to shut the door, the fine tremors betraying the adrenaline that still coursed through my veins. A shaky breath escaped my lips, but it brought no relief. The safety of the walls around me felt like a facade, a thin veil that could be torn away at any moment by the truth of what had transpired.

I leaned against the cool wood for a moment, willing myself to regain composure. In the mirror by the entrance, I caught sight of my reflection—eyes wide and reflecting a terror that clawed at my gut, forehead glistening with the effort of keeping my fear at bay. The vulnerability was stark, naked in the harsh light of the foyer.

"Are you okay?" Coming from the living room, Matt's voice cut through my reverie, a thread of concern woven into the simple question.

I glanced up, meeting my own gaze in the mirror once more before turning away. My response was a whisper, tangled up with the remnants of dread, "Yeah, just... tired."

"Sure?" Skepticism laced the single word, an invitation for the truth I wasn't sure I could afford to give.

"Positive," I lied, forcing a smile that didn't reach my eyes, a smile I hoped would be enough to mask the storm raging within.

Matt couldn't know what had happened.

I pulled off my coat, the fabric sliding against my clammy skin. Matt was in the living room, his torso leaning back against the couch, arms folded across his chest.

"Hey," he said, eyes scanning my face with a precision that felt almost invasive as I walked in. "How did it go with Andersson?"

I swallowed, my throat dry. The words seemed to stick somewhere between my mind and mouth, refusing to form.

"Eva Rae?" His brow knitted together in concern as I walked into the living room, and he glanced at my face. "You're shaking. What happened?"

"Nothing—nothing I didn't expect." My voice betrayed me with a slight quiver, an audible crack in my facade.

"Doesn't look like nothing." Matt's voice rose slightly, a crescendo of worry and frustration. "I see your hands, Eva Rae. They're trembling. And your eyes—they're not just tired, they're scared."

I inhaled sharply, a failed attempt to steady myself. "It's just been a long day, Matt."

"Cut the crap." He was raising his voice now, his anger

seeping into the space around us. "You think I can't tell when you're terrified? Talk to me."

I averted my gaze, fixating on a nonexistent point past his shoulder. "I'm fine," I lied once more, the words hollow as they hung in the air between us.

There was no way I could tell him, not after the conversation we had just had about him fearing for my safety.

I turned away, a shaky breath betraying my resolve. Matt's presence was a balm and a curse. To tell him was to drag him into the darkness that clung to my every step since I started this investigation. Not to tell him was to build a wall of secrets between us.

"Eva Rae?" Matt's voice was a low rumble, his concern palpable.

"Can we not do this now?" I closed my eyes, fighting the images flashing through my mind. If Adam was the killer, then he had almost gotten me today. I had played it too risky. He could have killed me.

"Something's wrong." His statement was a command demanding truth.

"Matt...." The name felt like a plea on my lips—a plea for understanding without confession.

"Whatever it is, I'm here. You know that."

I nodded, the gesture empty. Thoughts clashed: Tell him. Don't. Trust him. Protect him. Each argument warred for dominance.

"Hey." His hand reached out, fingers gently reaching mine. I lifted my chin up to meet his gaze. "I've got you."

"Have you?" My heart pounded, the question more for myself than for him.

"Always." Conviction burned in his eyes, a silent promise.

My secret teetered on the edge of revelation. But revealing

the truth meant exposing him to danger—a danger I wasn't sure I could shield him from. Unspoken words crowded my throat.

"Eva Rae, please." His voice cracked with worry.

"Matt, I...." My words faltered, fear wrapping around my tongue.

"Talk to me."

"Nothing—I mean, it's nothing new," I whispered, each word laced with guilt.

"Doesn't feel like nothing." His grip tightened, a lifeline offered in the wake of my internal storm. "Please, let's just... sit down, Eva Rae." He gestured toward the space next to him on the couch. I went to sit down, my eyes desperate to escape his searching eyes.

"Okay." He followed, but his confusion hung in the air, a thick fog of unasked questions.

I sank into the couch, the cushions swallowing my body.

"Eva Rae?" His voice hovered, waiting for an anchor in the silence.

Could you please stop saying my name like I have done something wrong?

I exhaled, a shaky breath betraying my calm facade.

"I got it, Matt."

My voice wobbled like a poorly set table, ready to collapse at the slightest touch.

"Got what?" His brow furrowed, his hands tentatively reaching out as if to grasp the elusive truth.

"The information," I said quickly, too quickly. "The information I needed."

Matt paused, processing my words with a skeptic's ear. "And? What was it?" He leaned forward, his eyes searching mine for clarity. "Did you find out about the affair?"

“Yes, he admitted they had an affair,” I said. “And that he knew about it.”

“Well, that’s a big step. It gives him a pretty good motive. How did he react when you confronted him?”

"He... he wouldn’t admit to it." I avoided his gaze, focusing on an invisible spot on the wall. My heart thumped a guilty rhythm.

“Of course not,” Matt said. “But how did he react? How was his demeanor?”

“It was pretty... normal.”

"Eva Rae, this doesn't add up." Disappointment laced his voice, mingling with an edge of frustration. "You're shaking, you look— tell me what happened."

"Please, Matt." The plea cut through the room, sharp and clear. "It was all fine. Nothing happened. Just trust me on this."

"Trust works both ways." He leaned back, arms once again crossing over his chest. "I'm trying here, but you have to give me something. You promised, remember?"

I swallowed hard, the lie heavy on my tongue. "It's just another piece of the puzzle," I managed to say. "We're closer now, that's all."

Matt's shoulders slumped, the weight of unanswered questions bowing his frame. "Closer to what, Eva Rae? You're scaring me."

"Nothing dangerous," I lied again, my voice threadbare.

"Right." He nodded, though his eyes betrayed his skepticism. "Because none of this has been dangerous so far."

"Matt—"

"Save it." He held up a hand, silencing my next falsehood. "I can see there's no point in pushing."

"Thank you," I murmured, relief mingling with the sour taste of deceit.

"Doesn't mean I'm okay with this, Eva Rae." His voice faded.

"Are you hungry?" My voice quivered slightly, betraying my nerves as I turned toward the kitchen, avoiding Matt's probing stare. "I could make us something to eat."

Matt's eyes followed me as I rose to my feet, his presence like a shadow trailing my every move. "Eva Rae, food is the last thing on my mind right now."

"Right." I forced a brittle laugh. "Silly question. Well, I'm hungry, and I bet the kids are too."

I walked to the kitchen and fumbled with pots and pans, clanging them louder than necessary to fill the silence that expanded between us. I didn't dare look at him; his gaze was too penetrating, too knowing. Then he got up with much effort, and, using his crutches, he approached me.

"Talk to me," he implored from the doorway, his voice softened, but the underlying urgency unmistakable.

"Nothing to say." Short, curt. A wall of words to keep him out.

"Eva Rae...." His sigh whispered across the room.

"Really, I'm fine." The lie stung my throat.

"Fine doesn't shake like a leaf or jump at shadows." His words were gentle but firm.

"Please, Matt." My plea was half-hearted and hollow.

"All right," he conceded, though it sounded more like defeat than agreement.

"Sit down," I insisted, gesturing to the table. "Let me do this for you."

"Okay." But he didn't move, watching me instead.

My hands shook as I sliced vegetables, the knife tapping a morse code of guilt on the cutting board. Each chop fractured the air, mirroring the fissures in my resolve.

"Stop." Matt's voice sliced through my actions.

"Stop what?" I didn't turn; I couldn't face the concern I'd see etched on his face.

"Stop pretending." His words echoed, bouncing off the kitchen tiles.

"Matt, really, let's just eat." My tone was sharp, final.

"Eva Rae...."

"Please." The word hung between us, a barrier, a wish.

"Okay."

Guilt clawed at my insides as I watched him sit with much trouble. Fear gnawed at me as I braced myself against the counter, taking a moment to breathe. Silence wrapped around me, heavy and charged with the things left unsaid.

"Food will be ready soon," I called over my shoulder, my voice nearly steady.

"Take your time." His reply was distant; the space between us was more than just physical now.

I glanced back. Matt sat, head bowed, hands clasped—a statue of patience and pain. I turned away, a tear escaping, tracing a path down my cheek. I hated doing this to him. I wiped it away angrily, knowing the cost of my secrets, feeling their weight.

"Almost done," I lied again, the words hollow, as I continued to cook.

The steam rose from the pot, wrapping tendrils around my face. I stirred mechanically, the spoon circling, grazing the bottom. My mind was a battlefield, thoughts clashing, each one sharp as shrapnel. Guilt. Duty. The need to protect.

"Food's almost ready," I called out, the lie sticking in my throat.

"Can't wait," he replied, a hint of resignation in his voice.

My heart thrummed, a drumbeat of dread. Would he see through me? Would my facade crumble like stale bread?

I called the children.

"Dinner is ready!"

"Looks delicious," Matt said, though his eyes searched for more than what was on the table.

"Let's eat," I urged, avoiding his gaze.

The kids came running and sat down. I helped Angel with her food, and she laughed happily. Forks scraped plates in a symphony of normalcy. But nothing was normal. Not now. I didn't know how to get it back.

Dinner ended. Alex and Christine cleared the dishes while Matt got up on his crutches and moved toward the living room, his movements slow and weighted. My heart sank with them.

As I cleaned up the last of everything and let the kids go, the lie sat heavily on my chest, a stone pressing against my ribs. I closed my eyes, saw Adam Andersson's face, and felt his threat coil around my neck. I could almost feel his fingers grab me; that's how close he had been.

What had I done? I was suddenly lying to Matt, hiding things. What would this do to us? Was it worth it?

Chapter 39

Mary's heels clicked on the polished floor, a staccato counterpoint to the thumping bass that vibrated through the mansion's walls. She wove through clusters of laughing guests, each adorned in shimmering fabrics and expensive colognes, their faces illuminated by the soft glow of strategically placed lighting. She scanned each exuberant face, searching for the one man who had ignited her fury.

"Pete!" she called out, but her voice was swallowed by a new wave of music. He was nowhere in the thrumming sea of bodies. Her jaw set, she stormed past the living room, her eyes raking over the revelers. The kitchen proved just as fruitless—no sign of him amid the clinking glasses and bursts of laughter.

"Damn it," she muttered, pushing a strand of hair from her eyes. With a determined pivot, she made her way to the grand staircase, the click of her heels now muffled by the plush carpet runner.

Ascending the stairs, a flicker of memory teased at the edges of her thoughts. It was here, on these very steps, where

Pete had charmed her with his mischievous grin and an offer of a private tour during another of his lavish parties.

"Quite a view from the top, isn't it?" he had whispered, his breath warm against her ear, his hand lightly grazing hers as they reached the landing. That night, under a canopy of stars, their laughter had given way to stolen kisses in the shadows, each touch more daring than the last.

"Your eyes," he'd murmured, tracing the line of her jaw, "They hold secrets and fire."

"Maybe I'll let you in on them," she teased back, her heart racing as his hands found the small of her back and pulled her close.

Now, as she continued to climb, the ghost of that passion lingered, the heat of his skin, the urgency of his lips pressing into hers, the sensation of being wanted so completely. The memory hung in the air like the faintest scent of cologne, tempting her resolve, promising more forbidden pleasures. But tonight, anger laced her veins, not desire.

"Where are you, Pete?" she whispered to herself, reaching the upper hallway. Her pulse quickened, not from desire but from the frustration boiling within her. Why hadn't he called her afterward? She needed answers, and she would get them.

Mary paused at the top of the stairs, the vibration of music from below softening to a dull pulse. She closed her eyes and inhaled deeply, an attempt to steady herself—to fortify her will against the memories that threatened to undo her. In the darkness behind her lids, she saw Pete's face and heard his laughter mixing with the clink of champagne flutes... the taste of bubbles tickling her throat, sweet yet sharp. One glass, two glasses.... Her resolve wavered like a flame in a gentle breeze.

"Damn it," she muttered, her eyelids snapping open. The

plush carpet felt cool under her heels as she took a determined step forward. "I'm stronger than this."

"Pete!" Her voice sliced through the muffled beats, wielding frustration like a weapon. Yet beneath the edge of vexation, a note of something softer played—a melody that sang of silk sheets and whispered promises.

"Pete Hancock!" she called again louder, her tone mingling reprimand with a hushed plea. It was a strange duet of emotions: wanting him to hear her anger but also her need. She hated herself for the latter.

"Where are you?" Her voice echoed down the corridor, seeking him out, demanding he face her. Each word was a dance of shadows and light, conveying more than mere annoyance. It was the sound of a woman scorned yet still perilously close to succumbing to the very source of her anger.

"Pete!" She changed her tone. Her voice became a blend of seduction and fury that cut through the bass that throbbed from below. Mary's hand trembled as she nudged the door wider, the soft glow of the study beckoning her in. "Are you hiding from me?"

The door creaked, protesting her intrusion. She stepped inside, her high heels clicking on the hardwood floor, an insistent staccato against the distant rhythm of the party.

"Playing games now, are we?" A smirk danced on her lips though her heart hammered with a cocktail of emotions.

Her eyes adjusted to the dim light, scanning the room for any sign of Pete. "I know you're here," she cooed, her voice draping each word in velvet.

Silence greeted her, starkly contrasting the revelry seeping through the walls.

"Pete, this is no time—" Her words caught in her throat as her gaze landed on the figure sprawled across the Persian rug.

"Pete?" The name escaped as a whisper, a ghost of sound.

There he was, motionless, a crimson halo seeping into the intricate patterns beneath him. Mary's breath hitched, her body rooted to the spot. The world seemed to tilt, reality skewing as she took in the horror before her.

"Pete!" Desperation laced her cry now, raw and ragged. But there was no answer, not even the slightest twitch from the man who had consumed her thoughts.

"Please." It was a plea, a prayer to break the nightmare's hold. But the silence was unyielding, the truth undeniable.

Tears blurred her vision, fear and disbelief warring within her. Pete, the charmer, the rogue who had stolen her resolve, lay lifeless before her. And Mary stood alone with the echo of a party that suddenly felt worlds away.

Mary's heart thundered, a drumbeat syncing with the pulse of panic. She whirled, eyes darting across the expanse of Pete's study. The air thickened, each breath a struggle against the weight of dread pressing on her chest.

"Who's there?" Her voice was barely a thread in the vastness of silence, betraying her fear.

The room remained undisturbed except for the macabre scene at its center. Books were aligned perfectly on shelves, and pens were laid out in an orderly fashion. There were no overturned chairs or scuffs on the floor, and not a single paper was out of place—an eerie order that screamed wrongness.

"Think, Mary, think," she muttered, words like lifelines to her own sanity. "What now?"

Her gaze caught on the phone on Pete's mahogany desk. But no, calling from here could taint evidence. She couldn't risk it. Her phone was downstairs in her purse.

"Help...." The whisper was for herself, a reminder that she wasn't helpless. She needed to move, to find safety, to alert others. Yet her feet felt rooted in place as if the plush carpet held her captive.

"Get out," she commanded herself, voice strengthening with resolve. "You need to get help."

She glanced back once more, a silent vow to Pete that she would unravel this nightmare. Then, turning on her heel, she fled the study; every step away from the horror was a mix of terror and determination.

Mary's heels clicked a hasty retreat from the study. She kept her palms raised, wary of brushing against the walls, her eyes scanning for unseen obstacles. The blare of the party grew louder, a siren call back to a world ignorant of the death that lay silently above.

"Easy," she whispered to herself. "Don't touch anything."

She reached the thrumming energy of the party. Faces blurred before her, laughter and clinking glasses a grotesque soundtrack to the tragedy unfolding.

"Need to find someone... anyone," she muttered, her voice lost in the cacophony.

Her gaze latched onto a cluster of familiar faces by the fireplace, people she'd laughed with and shared secrets with. Trust was a luxury she couldn't afford, yet necessity demanded it.

"Michael!" Her voice cut through the noise, sharp and urgent. A tall man with a shock of sandy hair turned, concern etching his features at the sight of her pallor.

"Mary? What's—"

"Upstairs," she gasped, each word punctuated with the beat of her heart. "Pete... he's dead."

"Dead?" Michael's eyes widened, his drink forgotten in his hand. "What do you mean?"

"Dead." The finality of the word hung between them, heavy and undeniable. "I think he's been... shot."

"Shot?" He echoed, disbelief shading his tone. "Are you sure?"

"There's blood everywhere," she said, her voice trembling as the image flashed again before her eyes. "We need to call the police. Now."

"Okay, okay." Michael set his jaw, determination replacing the shock. He reached into his pocket, pulling out his phone with steady hands. "I'll make the call. You stay with me, alright?"

"Thank you," Mary managed, her relief mingled with sorrow. She leaned slightly toward him, seeking the solace of his presence, her mind still spinning with the night's grim revelation. "I don't know who would do this," she confessed in a near-whisper.

Mary's breath came in short, sharp gasps as she stared at the sea of bodies surrounding them. The laughter and clinking glasses starkly contrasted the horror etched into her every feature.

Was the killer still here? Among these people?

"Call the police, now!" Mary's command sliced through the haze of her shock.

Michael's fingers flew over the phone screen, his professionalism surfacing amidst the chaos. "I'm dialing," he assured, glancing at Mary with eyes that demanded facts. "Details, Mary. I need details for them."

"His study. A pool of blood. He's not moving. Not breathing. I'm pretty sure I saw a gunshot wound." The words tumbled out, raw and unfiltered.

"Stay with me, Mary. Focus." Michael's voice held steady, a counterpoint to the thumping bass. He relayed the information into the phone with practiced precision.

Mary fought to anchor herself in the present, away from

the haunting image of Pete's lifeless form. Her hands fisted at her sides as she drew a deep breath, trying to still the tremor in her limbs.

"Officers are on their way," Michael reported, pocketing his phone. The weight of urgency hovered between them.

"Good, good." Mary nodded, repeating the word like a mantra. Her mind raced, scanning through every interaction, every passerby who might have crossed Pete's path tonight. Was it the killer?

"Anything you remember could be crucial," Michael coaxed, guiding Mary to a secluded corner. "Think."

"Guests, so many faces," Mary murmured, her gaze distant. "Laughter, dancing, drinks... nothing strange. Until...."

"Until?" Michael prompted, his hand a reassuring presence on Mary's arm.

"Until I found him," Mary finished, the reality settling like lead in her stomach. "Upstairs, alone."

"Okay, we'll start there." Michael's assurance was a lifeline in the storm of Mary's thoughts. "The police will sort this out. You're safe with me until they get here."

"Safe..." Mary echoed, but the word felt foreign on her lips. She leaned on Michael's unwavering strength, finding solace in her friend's resolve as the party's gleeful ignorance continued.

Blue and red lights soon bled through the curtains, casting a surreal glow over the throngs of unsuspecting partygoers. A heavy knock resonated above the music, the sound sobering.

They were here.

Chapter 40

I stared at the empty coffee mug, tracing a finger around its rim, the ceramic cool against my skin. Detective Ryan's words from our last meeting played on a loop in my mind—curt, dismissive, a barricade of finality in his tone when he said, "Case closed." But cases don't close with questions still clawing for answers, and Nicki's case had too many to be silenced by a simple suicide verdict.

My phone buzzed against the tabletop, an abrupt snarl of vibration that made me jolt. "Ryan" flashed across the screen; the name was a challenge I couldn't ignore.

"Detective," I answered, voice steady despite the pulse quickening at my throat.

"Listen, I don't know what you think you're doing, but you need to back off," Ryan's gruff voice cut through the line like a blade, no pleasantries to blunt its edge.

"Back off?" I echoed, feigning ignorance.

"Adam Andersson. He's been through enough without you showing up at his doorstep, asking questions, and stirring things up. You've got some nerve."

The accusation hung between us, a heavy cloud waiting to burst. It was clear; the lines were drawn, and I was on the outside looking in. But the truth had a way of blurring boundaries, and I wasn't about to let it slip through the cracks.

I squared my shoulders, pressing the phone closer. "I thought I was helping."

"Helping?" His scoff crackled over the line. "By chasing ghosts?"

"Nicki wouldn't—"

"Stop." The word was a command, sharp and absolute. "I've got the autopsy report right here. It's suicide. End of story."

"Reports can be wrong," I countered, thumb tracing the rim of my coffee mug, feeling the rough edge where a chip was missing.

"Are you a pathologist now? You think you know better than the professionals?"

"Then help me understand because it doesn't add up."

Silence threaded through the line, taut and suffocating. Then, a sigh.

"Listen, you're out of your depth. It's not what you want to hear, but it's what the evidence says. Let it go."

The words "let it go" hung between us, a mantra of futility. But acquiescence was a language I never learned to speak.

"Adam Andersson," I breathed into the receiver, my voice steady despite the storm brewing on the other end. "He's the link, Ryan. Steven's death wasn't an isolated incident. Steven and Nicki had an affair."

A crackle of static answered me before Detective Ryan's anger filled the space. "You have no right—"

"Two deaths, same circle. It's more than coincidence." I stared out the window, watching the palm trees sway in the warm wind.

"Christ, you're relentless," he snapped. "And you're crossing lines. Adam is a grieving man, and you're pointing fingers with nothing to back it up!"

"Patterns speak, Ryan. They're screaming," I insisted, feeling the heat of conviction in my veins. "I can't ignore them."

"Patterns?" His laugh was bitter, edged with frustration. "You think this is some kind of game? You think you can just waltz in and solve the puzzle?"

"Someone has to," I shot back, my grip on the phone tightening until the plastic groaned in protest. "Because there's a killer out there, and I'm not content sitting back while they're free to strike again."

"Damn it, this isn't your job!" The detective's voice was a whip, each word lashing out. "You're tampering with evidence, harassing witnesses. You're lucky I don't haul you in for obstruction."

"Then, do it," I challenged, heart thudding with fear and determination. "If that's what it takes to get you to see beyond your report—"

"See what? Your delusions?" Ryan's anger was palpable, a force that threatened to crush through the phone line. "I'm warning you; back off, or there will be consequences."

"Consequences," I repeated softly, almost to myself. "Like the ultimate consequence Nicki and Steven faced?"

There was a sharp intake of breath from the other end, a momentary break in his assault. But I knew, even as we hung on the precipice of understanding, that the divide between us had never been more pronounced.

"Adam's not grieving. He's hiding something," I said, each word a bullet of conviction.

"Enough!" Ryan's voice cracked like thunder, a storm unleashed. "What do you know about grief? About loss?"

"More than you think."

"Your theories—wild accusations! You're stepping into quicksand."

"Maybe," I conceded, "but at least I'm not blinded by procedure."

"Blinded?" The detective's snarl was almost visible. "You have the audacity to question my competence?"

"Questioning isn't a crime, Detective. Not yet."

"Your 'investigation' is a joke. What are you really after? You want your name remembered? Some twisted sense of justice?"

"Justice doesn't twist," I shot back, "people do. Let's talk evidence, then," I said, the cool edge in my voice a stark contrast to his heated barbs. Sarah's phone records show calls to Steven at all hours—pleas for help."

"Harassment," Ryan countered. "He was looking to move on. She couldn't let go."

My fingers drummed on the kitchen counter, keeping time with my racing heart. "And Adam's financials? I had a good look at them earlier. Lots of transactions that don't add up. Money flowing like a river between accounts."

"Coincidences. You're building castles in the sky!" Ryan spat out the words. "I've already talked to him about that; he owes some people money."

"Am I?" I leaned forward, my shadow stretching across the pile of photographs and notes littering the table. Or am I the only one willing to dive deep enough to see the murky truths below?"

"Deep? You're drowning in your obsession!" His voice rose, a crescendo of fury.

"Perhaps," I admitted, "but even in the depths, patterns

emerge. Patterns you're ignoring. He has a motive. A pretty good one."

"Patterns? Motives?" The scoff in his voice was bitter. "You think you've got it all figured out from behind your desk? This is my case."

"Better than ignoring what's right in front of me."

"Right in front—?" he sputtered, incredulous. "You have no idea what you're meddling with!"

"Meddling?" I echoed sharply.

"Fantasies!" he yelled. "You latch onto fantasies because you can't handle reality!"

"Reality?" I pressed the phone closer to my ear, my voice steady despite the storm raging through the line. This hit me hard. Was I really just trying to avoid having to deal with my boyfriend being in a wheelchair? With the guilt I felt for him being in this situation? "The reality is that someone is dead. Two people are dead. And we owe it to them to look at every angle."

"Every angle?" His laugh was harsh and humorless. "You mean your angle."

"Nicki was scared, Ryan. She packed a bag. She called a friend up north and said she was coming to visit. That was her last call, remember? She was scared enough to reach out to anyone who'd listen. That fear—it wasn't just paranoia. It was real."

"Real?" There was a venomous bite to his question. "How do you know? You weren't there. You didn't see her—"

"Did you?" I interrupted, firm and unyielding. "Or are you just choosing to see what you want to see?"

"Dammit!" The sound of something—a fist, perhaps—striking wood reverberated through the receiver. "Sarah was holding the gun in her hand when Adam came into the bedroom. Her fingerprints were all over the weapon! Nicky felt overwhelmed and wanted to get away. Her lover had just been killed."

"Overwhelmed," I agreed softly. "By secrets. By lies. By someone who wanted her silent."

"Silent..." he trailed off, his anger momentarily diffused by doubt.

"Adam had motive, means, and opportunity," I continued relentlessly. "Look at it, Ryan. Really look."

"Look?" His voice hardened once more. "I have looked. What I see is someone trying to make sense of a senseless tragedy."

"Senseless?" I countered. "Or meticulously planned?"

"Stop!" The word was a command, an explosion of frustration.

"Stop?" My gaze fell upon the photo of Nicki, her smile haunted now by the knowledge of her fate. "No, Detective. We can't stop. Not until this is resolved. Not until justice is served."

"Justice..." Ryan's voice faded into a murmur, wrestling with the weight of my words.

"Justice," I affirmed, knowing the risks but bound to the pursuit of truth. "And I intend to find it, with or without your blessing."

My hand slid across the cluttered surface of my desk, fingers brushing the edges of papers scrawled with timelines and connections. "A man being murdered in his home and soon after the woman next door is shot too? And they were involved with one another? It's not rocket science. Besides, I don't believe in coincidences."

"Coincidences?" Ryan's voice crackled over the line, a sure sign of his patience fraying. "Or are you just seeing what you want to see? Because you're bored or need an escape."

"Am I?" The question lingered between us, challenging and demanding introspection. "Am I the one blinded by what I want, or is it you who can't afford to see the truth? Because then you'd actually have to do your job."

Silence followed—a stretched, brittle thing ready to snap.

"Nicki's death, Steven's—it's all connected, and you know it deep down. Adam isn't just mourning; he's hiding something. Can't you see that?" I wasn't pleading; I was stating a fact—one I wished he could acknowledge.

"Enough!" The shout from Detective Ryan was like a gunshot in the quiet. "You have no right—"

"Rights?" I cut in sharply. "What about Nicki's rights? Steven's? Don't they deserve someone to dig deeper, to fight for the truth?"

"Truth...." There it was again—that hesitation, the softening at the edges of his resolve.

Detective Ryan's sigh crackled like static, a sound of surrender mixed with anger. "You're out of line," he ground out, the words heavy with a threat he had yet to voice.

"Perhaps," I conceded, "but I'm also on the right track. And you're letting your protocol blind you to possibilities. Need I remind you that Steven's body had been moved? How did Sarah move him when she was still holding the gun? And the magazine was under the bed?"

"Protocol keeps order, keeps wild theories from clouding judgment," he retorted, but the conviction behind his words had begun to wane.

"Does it? Or does it keep us from asking the questions we're afraid to answer?" I asked.

"Damn you," he muttered after a prolonged quiet, his voice a low growl of defeat and exasperation. "Damn you for making me doubt."

"Good," I whispered, almost to myself. "Doubt is the first step toward finding the truth."

"Find your own damn truth," he spat out before the line went dead, a click echoing the finality of doors slamming shut in the corridors of justice.

The line's dead hum was a stark reminder that I was on my own. I let out a breath I didn't realize I'd been holding and felt the cool air snake around me, ruffling the papers strewn across the desk. They were scribbled with notes, leads, and connections—all pointing to a truth that seemed to slip through my fingers like water.

"Risks," I murmured, tracing a finger over Nicki's last photo. Her smile, once radiant, was now a haunting question. It was a risk worth taking, I assured myself. The shadows in the room deepened as the day bled into twilight, my only audience to the silent vow I made.

"Uncover what's hidden," I continued, my voice steady, even though it quivered inside. "No matter what." The weight of those words settled in the room, heavy, unyielding. A promise to Nicki, to Steven, to the faint echo of justice that still rang somewhere in the back of my mind.

I stood up, stretching muscles tight from tension and too many hours hunched over clues that led in circles. The lamp on my desk flickered slightly, casting long, dancing shadows on the walls.

"Truth," I whispered, stepping into the living room where Matt was sleeping on the couch. "I'm coming for you."

I changed the channel to watch the evening news and almost dropped the glass of wine I had just poured.

A man had been shot tonight in the office of his house while hosting a party. And it was in Cape Canaveral, on the same street where the two other bodies had been found.

Coincidence? I think not.

Chapter 41

THEN:

THE SOFT GLOW of the table lamp threw shadows across Sarah's face as she perched on the edge of her sofa, a glass of red wine cradled in her hand. Her thumb brushed against the stem, tracing circles that mirrored the turmoil swirling within her. Victoria's laughter, once the soundtrack of this room, now felt like a haunting melody from a distant past. The silence was oppressive, punctuated only by the faint ticking of the wall clock—each second a stark reminder of her daughter's fragility.

Victoria was back in the hospital, and Steven was with her, spending the night, never leaving her side. Every time she went in, Sarah worried she would never return home.

"Come on, Sarah," she murmured to herself, a half-hearted attempt to break the spell of anxiety that had woven itself around her heart. Her voice sounded alien in the quiet.

She pushed herself up with reluctant resolve, the cushion

springing back into place. With its dimmed lights and the lingering scent of vanilla candles, the living room held too many ghosts tonight. She needed something else, something tangible to tether her to a time less complicated and less heavy with dread.

The office seemed like a refuge in comparison, the moonlight spilling through the open blinds casting a checkerboard pattern across the floor. Sarah moved toward the antique desk nestled in the corner.

"Old memories," she whispered, almost a prayer, as she slid open the stubborn drawer that always stuck a little on the left side.

Inside were the remnants of a life before illness, hospitals, and hushed conversations behind closed doors. A life where the biggest worries were scraped knees and monsters under the bed, not test results and treatment plans.

"Let's see what you've got for me," she said, the words meant to inject some semblance of lightness into the task at hand. Her fingers danced over envelopes and faded concert tickets, each touch a balm for her aching soul.

Underneath a pile of discarded papers, Sarah's hand brushed against the cool surface of glossed photographs. She drew them out slowly, spreading them across the mahogany desk like a mosaic of memories frozen in time. Each image was a captured echo of Victoria's life—her first steps, toothless grin, and the way her laughter seemed to fill the room even in stillness.

"Look at you," Sarah murmured, tracing the outline of her daughter's face in a photo where Victoria wore a bright yellow sundress, the garden behind her blooming with promise. The next few pictures showed the same vibrant scenes, but with each passing year, the girl in the images remained unchanged, as if time itself had become an unreliable narrator.

Her fingers lingered on a particular photograph taken on Victoria's twelfth birthday. Balloons framed the tiny figure seated at the head of the table, her smile hesitant between the candles' glow. Yet the child in the picture bore the delicate features of someone much younger, her illness casting a shadow that no amount of light could dispel. She couldn't even walk anymore and was confined to that darn wheelchair all day long. At twelve years of age, she looked like she was eight.

"God, why?" The words escaped Sarah's lips, a whispered accusation against the cruelty of fate. Her vision blurred as tears welled up, spilling over and dotting the picture with translucent spots. The paper curled slightly at the corners, absorbing her sorrow in silence.

"Twelve years old," she choked out, her voice cracking with the weight of realization. "You should be outgrowing clothes faster than I can buy them, not... not this." The edges of the photo became jagged through the watery veil of her eyes, and Sarah felt a pang deep within her chest—a mother's grief, raw and untamed.

"Little bird, it's not fair," she sobbed, clutching the photos to her heart as if by holding them close, she could somehow shield Victoria from the harsh truth of her stunted youth. "You've flown so high on such fragile wings."

The silence of the room wrapped around her like a cold embrace, heavy with the unspoken fears that flickered in her mind like shadows. In the quiet, the only sound was the soft patter of her tears marking the passage of time on glossy paper—moments captured, growth denied, a childhood overshadowed by the specter of illness.

Gently putting the photos back, Sarah's hand paused

midway to the drawer. A sliver of brown peeked from the shadowed recesses, a silent siren amidst the sea of forgotten trinkets and papers. It was a folder, worn at the edges, the material creased by the pressure of many hands, or perhaps merely the weight of time itself.

With the tips of her fingers, she coaxed the folder forward. The pull of curiosity drew her gaze to the faded label, its once-bold letters now soft and yielding to the touch. "Victoria—Medical," it read—a simple title that carried the gravity of their shared past.

Sarah's breath hitched, her heart momentarily caught in the trap of nostalgia. Opening the cover released a faint scent of antiseptic, a ghost of hospital corridors and sterile rooms. The first page crackled under her trembling fingers, yellowed with age but still holding the meticulous notes of doctors who had once been stewards of hope.

Her eyes flitted across the lines—dates, measurements, medical terms that had become an unwanted part of her vocabulary. Each entry was a stepping stone in Victoria's daunting journey, reminders of battles fought and small victories celebrated in hushed tones so as not to tempt fate.

"Little bird," Sarah whispered again, the endearment mingling with the mustiness of the paper. How many times had she prayed for a miracle? And still, the answers seemed as elusive as the cure that danced just beyond their reach.

Absorbed in the journal's contents, Sarah found herself traveling back to those early days of uncertainty when every cough or fever sent them hurtling toward the emergency room, hearts thrumming with fear. The past clung to her, a tapestry of memories woven through with threads of sorrow and resilience.

In the dim light of the office, with shadows encroaching upon her solitude, Sarah continued to leaf through her daughter's medical history—a chronicle of struggle and strength that was both intimately familiar and unfathomably distant.

Sarah's fingertips traced the date, her pulse quickening. The entry was dated just after Victoria's third birthday, a time stamped in her memory by relentless hospital visits and the sterile scent of antiseptic that seemed to cling to their clothes long after they returned home.

"Patient in remission," the words leaped from the page, stark against the backdrop of clinical jargon. Her breath hitched, eyes darting over the subsequent lines, seeking an anchor in the sea of medical terminology. That term had never been uttered by any of the doctors or Steven.

"Remission..." she muttered, the syllables tasting foreign on her tongue.

This entry spoke of something spontaneous, a sudden shift in the tide of Victoria's illness that should have sparked hope and been celebrated with more than just a clinical note buried within a forgotten journal.

Sarah's gaze flickered to the author of the note, a doctor whose name was unfamiliar, one that Steven had never mentioned. A chill ran down her spine as she realized the gravity of the omission.

"Steven, what didn't you tell me?" Her voice was a whisper lost in the silence of the room. The shadows seemed to press closer, and Sarah could feel the weight of deception heavy in the air. She closed the journal slowly, the soft thud of the cover marking the end of one chapter and the ominous beginning of another.

"Victoria," she breathed, the name a vow. The revelation was a crack in the foundation of their life, a single strand unraveling with the potential to undo everything they knew.

Sarah's hand trembled as she held the journal in front of

her, eyes darting back and forth across the name, her mind twirling. Her pulse hammered in her ears, a cacophony that drowned out the soft ticking of the grandfather clock in the corner. The room seemed to tilt, reality warping around the edges as her mind struggled to align these new pieces with the puzzle of Victoria's illness.

"Impossible," she murmured, tracing the name on the front with a shaky finger. Then she opened it and read it again. The entry blurred as fear glazed her vision, thick and suffocating.

She reached for the wine glass, its stem cool beneath her fingertips. She took a sip, the rich red swirling down her throat like liquid fire, stinging and acrid. It provided no comfort, only a momentary distraction from the spiral of confusion.

"Steven, what is this?" she said to the empty room, the question hanging heavy in the air. Each syllable was laced with betrayal, the name she had whispered countless times with love now tainted with suspicion.

The wine failed to soothe the raw edges of her thoughts, each one a razor slicing through the fabric of trust she had woven around her husband. Victoria's face, so often bright with a smile despite the pain, haunted the corners of Sarah's vision, a silent plea for the truth.

"Answers," she whispered, setting the glass down with care. "I need answers."

The bottle tilted, a steady stream of crimson flowing into the waiting glass. Sarah watched the liquid dance and shimmer under the lamp's glow, her hand unsteady. The scent of oak and berries mingled with the dust motes that floated lazily in the half-light.

"Enough," she muttered, cutting off the pour. Her voice was a stranger's—hard and resolute. The wine lapped at the rim, a hair's breadth from spilling over.

Her gaze fixed on the glass, but she saw Victoria's face instead, her small frame shadowed by years of illness and unanswered questions. The journal lay open beside her, accusing and mocking. It promised answers that only birthed more secrets.

"Steven," she said, the name now a splinter under her skin. The taste of betrayal soured on her tongue. Why hadn't he spoken of this?

She lifted the bottle again, this time foregoing the glass altogether, her lips meeting the cold glass edge. The wine flowed freely, too freely, a river seeking escape. It was warmth and numbness, a fleeting sanctuary from the storm of emotions that raged within her chest.

"Answers," she repeated, words slurred. "I deserve answers."

The final drops fell, a hollow echo as they hit the bottom of the empty bottle. She placed it on the table with a dull thud, its weight mirroring her own heavy heart.

"I have to confront him," she told herself, her thoughts sharpening to a point. Victoria's eyes, wide and trusting, seared into her memory. "For her."

Fear and anxiety hit her hard. How deep did the deception go? What would it cost to unravel it?

"Tomorrow," she breathed, the promise a whisper in the silence. "Tomorrow, we face this."

Her hands clenched into fists, a warrior preparing for battle, even as her pulse hammered a frantic rhythm against her temples. The truth waited, sinister and elusive, just beyond the horizon, and Sarah knew she had no choice but to chase it down.

Sarah's fingers trembled as they relinquished their grip on the empty wine bottle. With a heavy sigh, she pushed it aside, its hollow sound against the wooden table echoing the emptiness she felt inside. The room was still; the only movement was the gentle rise and fall of her chest as she inhaled deeply, trying to steady herself.

Her mind, once foggy with alcohol, was now sharpened to an agonizing clarity. She had to speak with Steven; there was no turning back from what she had uncovered. But the thought of confronting him twisted her stomach into knots. Would he deny everything? Accuse her of overreacting? The possibilities spun around her head like vultures circling their prey.

"Get it together, Sarah," she muttered, her voice barely audible. Her hands clasped together, seeking stability in one another as if holding herself together by sheer force of will.

She rose unsteadily to her feet, each step toward the kitchen heavy with dread. Reaching the countertop, she paused, staring at the array of bottles. Just one more, she convinced herself... to take the edge off.

Pulling the cork from a new bottle with a practiced motion, she didn't bother with a glass this time. The liquid crimson, darker than blood, sloshed into her mouth, coating her tongue with its acrid sweetness. She drank, each gulp a futile attempt to drown the rising tide of questions that threatened to consume her.

The room began to spin, the edges of her vision blurring as the wine took hold. Doubts swirled in her mind, intermingling with images of Victoria's pale face, Steven's evasive eyes, and the words from the medical journal that had set her world tilting.

"Victoria," she whispered, her voice breaking. "What have we done to you?"

But there was no answer, just the echo of her fears bouncing back at her from the walls of the lonely house. Her hand wavered as she took another drink, the bottle slipping slightly. Sarah caught it, her grip iron-tight, fueled by a mother's desperation.

Her worried expression, a mask of uncertainty and fear, reflected in the darkened windowpane—a silent witness to her unraveling. She didn't see it, though; her eyes were lost in the past, fixated on memories that now seemed tainted with lies.

Drink followed drink until the room slipped away entirely and, with it, her consciousness. Sarah collapsed onto the couch, the uncorked bottle slipping from her grasp and rolling onto the floor, forgotten. Her last coherent thought was a prayer for strength; tomorrow, she would have to face the truth, whatever it may be.

Then, darkness took her, granting a temporary reprieve from the nightmare that awaited her in the waking world.

Chapter 42

The air crackled with panic as I shouldered open the front door and stepped into the chaotic house, filled with scared faces and the echoes of a party that had ended abruptly.

"FBI Agent Eva Rae Thomas," I announced to the officer at the door, my voice a calm contrast to the bedlam, badge outstretched like a shield parting a sea of wide-eyed onlookers.

"Ma'am, you can't just—" a uniformed officer started, reaching for my arm.

"Can and will," I cut him off, not breaking stride, my gaze locked on the staircase rising above the foyer, an artery to the heart of this chaos. The badge glinted in the dim light, an unequivocal statement of purpose. I was here for answers; boundaries be damned.

The foyer convulsed with frenzied whispers and stifled sobs. An officer's pen scratched rapidly over a notepad as he hunched over, coaxing fragmented tales from shell-shocked partygoers. A woman in a sequined dress clutched a tissue, her mascara bleeding down her cheeks like dark rivulets of regret.

"Where's the body?" I barked out, my question slicing through the murmurs.

"Upstairs, Agent Thomas," said a voice tinged with solemnity. I knew this guy. It was Officer Edwards with Cape Canaveral PD. His eyes were heavy with the night's weight. He gestured toward the grand staircase where shadows danced on the wall, cast by the flashing lights outside.

"Lead on," I commanded, brushing past a cluster of guests who recoiled at my approach, their faces a gallery of ghoulish masks painted with fear and confusion. Edwards nodded, his steps sure but slow as if each one took effort in the gravity of dread that filled the house. “What have we got?”

“A Male, living alone, was hosting a party for his friends when it happened. His name is Pete Hancock.”

"Was he alone when it happened?" My voice rose above the dissonance of grief and disbelief that echoed off the walls.

"Seems so," Edwards replied without looking back, "the rest were downstairs, oblivious, until someone walked up there and found him, a woman."

"Oblivious..." I mused, the word lingering in the air between us like a specter. We walked up the stairs, leaving behind the chaos.

The office door was open, and I saw him right away. Pete Hancock lay sprawled across an ornate rug, his once-charming features frozen around the indignity of a single gunshot wound that marred his forehead. The blood had pooled in a dark halo on the Persian weave, his eyes staring up at a ceiling he would never see again.

"Handsome devil," I muttered, kneeling beside him, my gaze taking in the designer suit that now served as his death shroud. "Too young for this to end."

"Mid-thirties," Officer Edwards confirmed from over my shoulder. "Could charm the stars from the sky, they said."

"Stars aren't what's falling tonight," I replied, standing back up. A chill ran through me as I looked around the room. Three shots, three victims, all within a stone's throw of each other. My mind raced, connecting invisible dots that floated in the air like the remnants of a spider's web.

"Nicki and Steven," I said aloud, turning to Edwards. "They were shot too, and both lived with their spouses just down the street. Random violence doesn't usually stick so close to home."

Edwards crossed his arms, his brow furrowed. "You think there's a connection?"

"Maybe." My voice trailed off as I peered into Pete Hancock's lifeless eyes. "What did you three know?" I looked up at Edwards. “Bring me the woman who found him, please.”

A WOMAN'S tear-streaked face turned to me, her hands trembling. "We were just... I was just looking for him, I swear."

I glanced at the bubbles fizzing out their last bit of life in the half-empty flute on the desk.

"No one actually heard the shot," her voice piped up. “I guess the music was so loud, we just... even if we did hear it, we probably just didn’t think it was anything. I don’t know.”

"Did anyone leave the party early? Slip away?" I pressed, scanning the faces for a flicker of guilt or fear.

"I didn’t notice," the woman whispered. "We were having a good time, and then... it was too late."

"Agent Thomas," a uniformed officer beckoned me with a nod. His gloved hand extended toward me. In his palm lay a crumpled, half-burnt piece of paper.

"Where did you find this?" I asked, stepping closer, my senses heightening.

"Right there, on his desk, inside the ashtray," he said, nodding toward the mahogany behemoth that loomed over the chaotic scene. I pulled a pair of latex gloves from my jacket pocket, snapping them against my wrists.

I tried to read what the paper said, but all I could make out was one word.

...KNEW

The word hung heavily in the air, an accusation or a warning—I couldn't tell which. But it bore down on me, sinking hooks deep into my curiosity. What deadly truth had Pete Hancock stumbled upon? And more importantly, who else knew that he knew? Nicki? Steven?

"Anything else with it?" I asked, voice low, as I lifted the remains of the letter closer to my eyes.

"Nothing," the officer replied, watching me intently. "Just that."

"One word," I murmured, "yet it's screaming volumes." My mind raced, piecing together a puzzle with too many missing parts.

"Knew what, Pete?" The question slipped out, though I knew better than to expect an answer from beyond the grave. My gaze shifted between the letter and the stillness of his form, searching for a whisper of the secret that cost him his life.

I stepped closer, the scent of iron and gunpowder invading my senses as I approached Pete's body. His once-charming features were now etched in eternal shock, the finality of a bullet's kiss apparent on his brow.

The room was still, the only sound the distant murmur of sirens bleeding through the walls. Shadows clung to the corners like silent spectators to our grim tableau.

"Steven... Nicki... and now you," I continued, half-expecting him to sit up and explain it all away with a hearty laugh. But death had claimed its due, and Pete Hancock would speak no more.

A chill brushed against me from the realization that I was missing something crucial—a hidden thread that could unravel this entire mystery. But one thing was certain: if this was the same killer, it couldn't be Sarah. But how could I prove these murders were linked?

"Who else knows what you knew, Pete?" The question lingered, unanswered.

Then, from the desk, a glint caught my eye. I reached out, the latex of my gloves creaking softly, and picked it up.

A flash drive.

"Hello, what's this?" My voice was a murmur of intrigue, the device cold and heavy in my palm. What secrets did it hold? Was this the knowledge Pete died for?

"Agent Thomas?" a voice called from the doorway, but I barely registered it.

"Later," I replied, pocketing the flash drive without breaking my gaze from Pete's face. "We've got work to do."

Chapter 43

Adam's hands shook as he grabbed a handful of shirts from the drawer, not bothering to fold them before they landed in the open suitcase. Socks and underwear followed, tossed in with the same disregard for order. The urgency in his movements was palpable; every second seemed to hammer against his temples, a relentless tick-tock reminding him that time was a luxury he could no longer afford.

"Come on; come on," he muttered under his breath, zipping open another compartment to shove in a toothbrush still damp from use.

Wild with fear and determination, his eyes darted around the room, ensuring nothing essential was left behind. They paused as they caught sight of the picture frame sitting innocently on the bedside table. It was Nicki, smiling in that carefree way she had, her eyes alight with joy. Adam's frantic activity ceased for a heartbeat, his chest constricting as if caught in a vise.

"Nicki...." The word was a whisper, a ghost of sound that carried the weight of a thousand confessions.

He reached out, fingertips grazing the cool glass that protected her image. At that moment, the chaos of his escape attempt faded into the background, leaving only the piercing clarity of her absence. Regret gnawed at him, etching sorrow deep into the lines of his face.

"God, I'm so sorry." The apology hung in the air, unheard by anyone but the shadows.

"Nicki, this isn't how it was supposed to go," Adam muttered, his voice barely above a breath as he groped through the drawer for socks. The fabric felt like sandpaper against his skin, starkly contrasting the smooth silk of their bed sheets that Nicki had picked out.

He shoved the socks into the suitcase's side pocket, his hands moving on autopilot while his mind spiraled with images of his wife. Each apology that spilled from his lips seemed to echo around the empty room, a testament to his solitude.

"Forgive me, Nicki, please." His throat tightened around the words, the plea suffused with a desperation that he knew would remain unanswered.

Adam's gaze fell upon the nightstand again, where his gun lay hidden. He had tucked it there, always within reach. Now, its reality beckoned him with a grim necessity. With hands that betrayed a tremor, he reached for the weapon.

The metal was cold, an unforgiving chill that seeped into his bones. Adam's fingers wrapped around the grip, the familiar contour a grotesque comfort. He hesitated, the weight of the gun heavy in more ways than one.

"Damn it," he exhaled, a shuddering breath that carried his resolve.

The gun, once a symbol of protection, now felt like a harbinger of his downfall. Still, he slid it into the suitcase, nestling it between a pair of jeans and a shirt. It was a decision made from the instinct to survive, though every fiber of his being screamed in protest.

"Sorry," he whispered once more, a silent vow to the woman in the photograph as if the act of including the gun was another betrayal in itself.

The suitcase's teeth meshed in a hurried zip, finality ringing through the action. Adam's fingers were firm on the slider, his grip betraying none of the tremors that had shaken him just moments before. He hefted the bag, its weight grounding him to the present—this was real, this was happening.

"Okay, okay," he muttered, a mantra against the panic that threatened to claw its way up his throat.

He strode to the front door, the fabric of the suitcase handle digging into his palm. The police cars down the street were ominous shadows beneath the streetlights, their presence a silent accusation. His pulse hammered, a staccato rhythm syncing with the tick of the living room clock that used to belong to his mother.

"Come on; come on," he urged under his breath as if he could will away their prying eyes and suspicious minds.

Adam's hand found the doorknob, the cool metal a stark contrast to the warmth pooling at the base of his spine. He peeked through the curtains again, scanning for any movement or sign they knew he was there. The cruisers sat idle, their engines purring like dozing predators.

"Almost out," he whispered, a promise or perhaps a plea. His heart felt like it might burst through his ribs, a frantic bird caged by bone and sinew.

Every second was a thief, stealing time he didn't have. With a deep breath, he cracked open the door, ready to slip through the night's dark embrace.

The door eased shut behind Adam, a silent sentinel to his

escape. Florida's night air clung to him, humid and heavy, an unspoken reminder of the world he was about to leave behind.

He didn't allow himself a backward glance; instead, his eyes darted from shadow to shadow, seeking any hint of movement, any glimmer that might betray an observer's presence. Nothing stirred except for the distant rustle of palm fronds in the gentle coastal breeze.

"Clear," he breathed, the word barely escaping his lips.

His feet moved before his mind fully caught up, propelling him with urgency down the path. He could almost feel the seconds slipping through his fingers, each one precious, each one possibly his last as a free man. The usually quiet street lay before him, houses bathed in the soft glow of porch lights, people watching the commotion from their porches or from behind curtains drawn against the late hour.

"Got to move; got to move," he chanted silently, his mantra now one of motion.

He reached the car, his heart racing, his hands trembling like leaves in a storm. The keys jingled loudly in the silence, the sound magnified to a cacophonous din in his ears. Fingers slick with sweat fumbled once... twice until they found the button. He willed his shaking hand steady, opening the lock with a click that felt like a gunshot in the stillness.

"Come on, come on," he urged, the door swinging open, a gateway to his fleeting chance at freedom. His frantic pace belied the cool exterior he attempted to project; every muscle tensed for flight, every sense alert for the whine of sirens or the shout of discovery.

But the night remained still, the street empty. For now, Adam was just a man, a suitcase, a car—and a hope that the road ahead could outrun the mistakes snapping at his heels.

Adam slumped into the driver's seat, his body a tangle of

nerves. With hands that shook like he was in an earthquake, he stabbed the key into the ignition. The engine turned over with a rumble he felt sure could wake the dead—or worse, alert the cops. He held his breath, listening. One Mississippi... Two Mississippi... Silence. Relief was short-lived; it wouldn't last if he didn't move.

"Quiet. Stay quiet," he whispered to the car as if it had ears and cared about his predicament. His foot eased onto the gas pedal, the motion gentle, coaxing the vehicle into a soft purr as it rolled down the driveway.

The headlights cut through the darkness, twin beams dancing over familiar roads now turned foreign by fear. He squinted against the harshness, acutely aware of the vulnerability the light brought with it. Every shadow seemed a hiding spot, every rustling leaf a signal of pursuit.

"Easy, easy," he murmured, guiding the car with more care than he'd ever shown anything in his life.

His eyes flicked to the rearview mirror, catching his pale reflection staring back—a ghost haunted by what-ifs and should-haves. Adam forced his gaze away, locking it on the road ahead. The street behind remained empty, a void where danger lurked unseen.

"Keep it together," he told himself. He couldn't afford the luxury of panic. Not now. Not when every second counted.

Adam's grip tightened on the steering wheel, knuckles whitening as he navigated through the labyrinth of his own making.

"How did it come to this?" The whisper tore from his lips, a plea for understanding from an audience that wasn't there. He flinched at every shadow, every flicker in his peripheral vision—a hunted animal too scared to acknowledge its own scent.

"Dammit, not like this." His voice broke, a jagged edge sawing through the thick tension in the car. The rearview mirror held his accusatory gaze; the man looking back was a stranger, a doppelganger wearing his fear like a second skin. "Nicki, I'm sorry," he choked out, the words a mantra against the chaos.

"Running is for cowards," he spat into the silence. But the echo that returned bore a different message: survival. Adam shook his head, trying to dislodge the truth that burrowed deep. "I am no coward," he insisted to the darkness that pressed against the windows. Yet with each mile marker he passed, the label seemed to stick, a post-it note on his conscience.

"Get a grip!" he snarled, slamming his palm against the dashboard. The car responded with a slight jolt as though startled by his sudden ferocity. Ahead, the road stretched endlessly, a black ribbon unfurling beneath the stars. "You can do this. You have to."

The engine hummed a steady rhythm, a counterpoint to the erratic drumming of his heart. Adam leaned into the speed, allowing the rush of air through the cracked window to cleanse the stifling dread. He could outrun the sirens and the flashing lights but not the persistent specter of regret tailing him.

"Focus," he commanded himself, his resolve hardening. The past was a shackle he'd left behind in that hastily packed suitcase, the future a path he carved with each turn of the wheels. "I'll get through this," he promised the night sky.

"Keep moving. Don't look back."

The car surged forward, a metallic beast spurred by Adam's will. With each passing second, the city lights dimmed, his old life receding into a memory too painful to hold onto. Ahead lay obscurity and uncertainty but also the faintest glimmer of hope.

"Whatever it takes," he whispered.

Fear and regret might be his passengers, but determination took the wheel, driving Adam deeper into the night.

Chapter 44

Pete Hancock lay sprawled on the carpet, a lifeless marionette with strings cut. His eyes, wide and startled even in death, stared blankly at the ceiling fan circling above like a lazy vulture.

"Who did this to you, Pete?" My voice, barely a whisper, frosted in the chill air as I knelt beside him. The scent of iron tinged my nostrils; it was strong and recent.

A shiver crawled up my spine, not from being cold but from the crawling realization that someone had stood here, in front of Pete, with the intent of ending his life right here and now. My heart thrummed a staccato rhythm against my ribs; each beat spelling out the silent question: Why?

I scanned the room, hunting for a clue, an anomaly in the mundane.

"Who hated you enough to do this or feared you enough to want silence?" I murmured more to myself than to Pete. My mind raced through the possibilities, each more unnerving than the last.

Each tick of the clock overhead punctuated the silence, a countdown to an answer I wasn't sure I wanted to find.

"Hey! What the heck do you think you're doing here?"

The sudden yell ripped through the silence, jarring me from my internal inquisition. I spun around to see Detective Ryan barreling into the room, his face a mask of barely contained fury.

"Ryan," I started, but he cut me off with a wave of his hand, his eyes never leaving mine as he closed the distance between us in a few ground-eating strides.

"Answer me!" His voice was a growl, aggressive and demanding. "Why are you contaminating my crime scene?"

I took a step back. It was clear he saw my presence here as a personal affront, a disruption in his domain.

"Detective, I—" My words were calm and measured, but he wasn't looking for calm.

"Save it!" He was close now, the heat of his anger palpable. "You shouldn't be here. This is my scene, my case!"

His hands balled into fists at his sides, and I could see the tension coiling in him like a spring. Ryan was a storm personified, a man who believed control was akin to law, and I had just broken his cardinal rule.

"Because, Detective," I said, my voice a stark contrast to his rage, "there's a pattern you're missing."

"Pattern? What pattern?" He was inches away now, close enough that I could see the vein pulsing in his temple.

"Every crime scene," I continued, unwavering. "A note with the same words: 'You Knew.'"

His eyes narrowed, suspicion and interest warring within them. "What are you talking about?"

"Three victims, three notes. They were all found by the techs at the scene of the crimes. Steven's was found on his desk,

Nicki's in the trash, and Pete Hancock's half burnt in the ashtray. " My heart raced, but my tone remained steady. "I noticed them when going through the case files myself. You didn't seem to take notice of them, so I did. They're identical messages. That's not a coincidence."

"Coincidence or not—" he started, but I cut him off.

"Detective, someone is playing a game with us."

"Us?" His laugh was harsh, dismissive. "There is no us. This is my city, my responsibility."

"Then why are they all dead?" I shot back.

"Because—" Ryan faltered for a moment, his certainty wavering.

"Because we're dealing with a calculated killer," I said, filling the silence he left. "And unless we work together, there will be more bodies."

"More grandstanding," he sneered. "I've heard enough. You're out of your depth here."

"Am I?" I countered. "Or are you just afraid to admit that you need help?"

"Help?" The word seemed to strike a nerve, his posture stiffening.

"Look at the facts, Ryan. The notes, the methodical planning—it screams serial."

"Serial...." The fight seemed to drain out of him, replaced by a reluctant consideration. "If you're wrong—"

"But what if I'm right?" I pressed, holding his gaze.

He stared at me, the storm in his eyes churning into something else—a grudging respect, maybe even the dawning realization that I wasn't just an interloper. I was here because I needed to be—because Pete Hancock, lying cold and still on the floor, wouldn't be the last unless we put our heads together.

“I don’t want you here.” He turned to face his officers. “Please, make sure she leaves.”

"Wait," I said, my voice slicing through the buzz of radio static and murmured orders. Two uniformed officers halted mid-step, their hands firm on my arms. Detective Ryan's glare could have cut glass, but I met it without flinching.

"Let her speak," Ryan barked, curiosity overcoming irritation.

I reached slowly into my jacket, watching the officers tense, and pulled out my badge, flipping it open with a practiced flick. "I’m a special agent with the FBI, and I’m allowed to be here."

The room stilled, the weight of my declaration hanging heavy in the air. I saw the shift in their eyes—from dismissal to reluctant respect.

"We know that, but this is not an FBI investigation," Ryan repeated.

"It’s about to be. Look at the pattern, Ryan." I stepped closer, lowering my voice to a compelling timbre. "Three victims, three notes, identical words. Three murders make a serial killer.”

"Local cases," he countered, but his stance had softened somewhat. “There’s no proof they’re connected.”

"Think bigger," I urged. "These aren't isolated incidents. They're pieces of a larger puzzle, and right now, you're missing the box."

"Convince me," Ryan challenged, crossing his arms.

"Each victim knew something, something critical enough to get them killed. We need to find the connection before there's another 'You Knew' note sitting on your desk."

"Dammit." Ryan's curse was more resignation than anger.

"This is a serial killer, Ryan. Without a doubt." My gaze didn't waver. "And that means FBI jurisdiction."

"Special Agent or not, you've no right to come here and mess with my case!" Ryan's voice cracked like a whip through the stillness of the crime scene. He advanced on me, his jaw set and eyes blazing with a fury that was hard to ignore.

"Ryan," I started, keeping my tone level, "you need to listen."

"Listen?" His laugh was hollow and bitter. "To you?"

"Sarah didn't kill Steven." My words came out crisp and confident in the charged silence.

"Based on what? Your gut?" Sarcasm dripped from every syllable as he glowered at me.

"Based on evidence and patterns that don't fit her profile." I unflinchingly met his glare.

"Patterns and profiles?" he scoffed, stepping closer—so close that I could see the reddening in his cheeks. "You're seeing ghosts, Agent."

"Three dead, Ryan. Three notes. One message. This isn't Sarah's doing." My finger jabbed toward the body, Pete Hancock's lifeless form.

"And you're so sure because?" His stance was confrontational, hands on hips, challenging me to convince him.

"Because she was locked up when Pete and Nicki were both killed. It's impossible unless she can be in two places at once." The logic was sound, undeniable.

"Nicki was a suicide," he shot back, but there was a flicker of doubt in his eyes.

"I'm telling you. This is the work of someone else. Someone calculating. And they're still out there." I kept my voice steady despite the adrenaline coursing through my veins.

"Damn you and your FBI profiling." Ryan's anger seemed to wrestle with the notion, his brow furrowed.

"Think about it," I pressed on. "The killer is playing a game, and Sarah is just another pawn."

"Or maybe you're playing me." But now his accusation held less venom, more searching.

"The truth isn't always comfortable, Ryan. But it's necessary." I locked eyes with him, willing him to see past his resistance.

"Comfortable?" He snorted, shaking his head. "Nothing about this damn case has been comfortable."

"Then, let's make it right. Together." My offer hung between us, a bridge over tumultuous waters.

"Sarah's not our killer," I reiterated. "But the one we want is laughing at us right now, thinking they've outsmarted the entire department."

"Outsmarted...." His words trailed off, and for a moment, he seemed lost in thought.

Ryan's jaw clenched, the muscle ticking like a time bomb. "If there is a serial killer...."

"Then we're wasting precious time," I cut in, urgency sharpening my words.

“This is still my city, my case." His finger jabbed the air between us, a clear boundary. “Until otherwise is told to me, I'm in charge. And I want you to leave this scene. Now.”

“You'll regret not accepting my help more,” I said. “Gonna make you look like a fool.”

“I'll take that chance. Now, please leave.”

“As you wish.”

The sound of my sneakers echoed through the silent corridor as I made for the exit, the tension from our confrontation still crackling in the air behind me. A shiver ran down my spine—not from fear, but anger. Why was this guy so thick-headed? Why was he so set on Sarah being Steven's killer?

Outside, the sky hung heavy, clouds like dark smudges against the night. A storm was brewing, both in the atmosphere and in the case that lay sprawled out like a twisted puzzle before me. I could feel it in my bones.

"Watch your back, Agent," Ryan called out just as I reached the door.

"Always do," I replied without turning, stepping into the darkness, our unfinished business whispering in the wind.

Chapter 45

THEN:

SARAH'S SENSES clawed their way back through the fog of sleep, tugging her into a reluctant wakefulness. The living room swirled into view, a hazy blend of shadows and muffled sounds. Her head felt heavy, an anchor trying to pull her back down into the depths of unconsciousness.

"Sarah?" The voice cut through the silence, more piercing than the slivers of morning light that snuck past the half-drawn curtains.

Her eyelids, stubborn and weighted, lifted at last. Steven stood there, his presence grounding yet charged with an unspoken urgency. His silhouette was sharp against the soft glow that filtered into the room.

"Sarah, can you hear me?" he persisted, his tone threading the space between concern and impatience.

She tried to reply, to acknowledge him, but her throat was a desert, words lost in the barren expanse. She nodded instead, a slight dip of her chin that took monumental effort. Her gaze found his, locking onto her husband's familiar yet distant eyes.

Sarah's focus drifted to the side, where a half-empty wine bottle lay on its side, a silent testament to the night before. A pang of shame knotted in her gut as she lifted a hand to her face, brushing away the trace of drool that had escaped the corner of her mouth. Her thoughts scrambled for coherence, clinging to the remnants of dreams quickly dissolving in the harsh light of reality.

"Victoria's home," Steven said, his voice breaking through her haze.

She blinked, trying to process the words. "Home?" Her voice was raspy, barely above a whisper, as she tried to sit up straighter on the couch, her limbs protesting with stiffness.

"From the hospital," he clarified, his eyes softening for a moment with a mixture of relief and something else—weariness, perhaps. "I put her to bed."

"Already?" The question came out muddled, her brain lagging behind the conversation. The room swayed slightly as she attempted to ground herself in the present, in the gravity of Steven's news.

"Yes, Sarah. They allowed her to come home. She's resting now."

He watched her closely, his gaze searching for signs of the woman he knew beneath the veneer of confusion and alcohol.

Sarah nodded slowly, absorbing this new piece of reality. Victoria was here, not in a sterile hospital room with machines beeping and nurses bustling. She was here, where she belonged —with them.

"Okay," she murmured, a resolve beginning to form amidst the chaos of her thoughts. "Okay. That's good."

Sarah sat for a few seconds until she suddenly remembered. “The medical journal,” she said.

“What medical journal?” Steven asked.

She reached out and grabbed it from the coffee table.

"Steven, what is this?" Sarah's fingers trembled as she held up the medical journal, its pages dog-eared. "Have you been lying to me about Victoria?"

"Sarah, now is not the time," Steven's words were sharp, a stark contrast to the softness from moments before. “I'm tired.”

"Tell me!" Her demand cut through the air, a jagged edge to her voice that even the wine couldn't dull. “It says here she was in remission? Years ago?”

"Dammit, Sarah!" His outburst was sudden, like a thunderclap in the room's silence. "You think I wanted any of this? You think I enjoy watching our daughter suffer while you—"

"While I, what?" she challenged, pushing off the couch, her body still swaying slightly from the alcohol.

"Focus on your career! Drown yourself in bottles every night!" He was pacing back and forth, a caged animal with frayed nerves. "Who do you think has been here, huh? Who takes her to all her appointments?"

"Stop it, Steven." She put a hand to her temple, willing the room to stop spinning.

"No, I'm tired, Sarah. Tired of making excuses for you and trying to protect you from this!" His finger jabbed toward the journal in her hand, his eyes blazing with resentment.

"Protect me?" Her voice broke, a small crack in her resolve. "Is that what you call lying?"

"Taking care of our daughter; that's what I call it." The fury in Steven's voice subsided into weary resignation. "Someone had to, Sarah. Someone had to."

"Remission," Sarah's voice was a husky whisper, "what does

that even mean in Victoria's case? Why didn't you tell me the truth?"

Steven's face contorted with frustration as he let out a heavy sigh. "It was a mistake, okay?" His hands gestured wildly, words tumbling out. "The previous doctor got it wrong. This was years ago."

"Wrong?" she echoed, her mind grappling with fragments of reality.

"Yes, wrong!" Steven's annoyance was palpable as he paced the room, his footsteps a dull thud against the carpet. "That's why we changed doctors; don't you remember? We had to be sure."

"Sure of what?" The question hung between them, dense and unyielding.

"Sure that..." he hesitated, rubbing the bridge of his nose, "Victoria was still sick. She wasn't getting better, Sarah." His eyes found hers, pleading for understanding. "Don't you remember any of this?"

"Remember..." Her voice trailed off, the word feeling foreign on her tongue. She sifted through hazy memories, trying to latch onto something solid.

Steven collapsed into the armchair opposite Sarah, the weight of his body sending a soft puff of air from the cushion. He leaned forward, reaching for her hands, and she felt his grip firm and warm against her cold fingers. His eyes fixed on hers, the intensity of his gaze unwavering.

"Sarah," he said, his voice barely above a whisper but laced with urgency. "We need to talk about... this." His free hand gestured vaguely at the wine bottle.

Her vision swam as she struggled to focus on his face, to anchor herself to the moment.

"I'm trying, Steven," she murmured, her words slurred around the edges.

"Trying isn't enough anymore." Concern etched deep lines across his forehead. "You're slipping away from us, from Victoria."

She winced at the mention of their daughter's name, a stab of guilt sharper than any hangover.

"I remember... something about a new doctor," she stammered, her mind grappling with the slippery threads of her memory. "You told me not to worry."

"Because worrying is all you do when you're like this," he retorted, his tone softening as he squeezed her hands. "Drinking yourself into oblivion isn't going to help her or you."

"Help...." The word echoed in her head, hollow and distant. She knew she should understand and connect the dots, but they skittered away and were just out of reach.

"Sarah, please." Steven's voice cracked, a hint of desperation bleeding through. You have to stop this—for Victoria, for us."

"Us...." There was a world contained within that tiny word, a world she felt herself drifting away from with every bottle she finished. She wanted to reach out, to pull herself back, but the current of her own habits was too strong.

"Remember, Sarah," Steven coaxed, his thumbs rubbing circles on the back of her hands. "Try to remember for Victoria."

"Yes, of course for Victoria...." Her voice was a breath, a prayer. She would try—she had to try for her daughter.

Steven's gaze bore into her, searching for a flicker of the woman he once knew. "I'll show you the journals," he said quietly, yet there was an edge to his voice that demanded sobriety. "But when you're sober. You need to see things clearly."

"Okay," Sarah whispered, nodding slowly. Her mind clung

to the clarity in his eyes, a lifeline amidst the fog. "I'll be... I'll be sober."

"Good." He paused, uncertainty flickering across his features. "And you should come with me to Victoria's next appointment. But Sarah, I mean it—"

"I know, sober." She cut him off, the word foreign but necessary on her tongue.

"Sarah...." His voice trailed off, waiting for her resolve to solidify.

Her pulse thrummed with a mix of fear and determination. "I want to understand what's happening to her, Steven. Really understand." Her fingers twitched, aching to grasp at the knowledge she'd avoided.

"Then, it's settled." He offered a short nod, the unspoken promise hanging between them like a fragile truce.

The silence stretched between them. Sarah's gaze found their linked hands, Steven's fingers a vise around hers, grounding her trembling resolve.

"Steven," she began, her voice barely above a whisper, "we've... we've been through so much."

He turned to her, eyes weary yet resolute. "Yes, we have. But we'll face what's next together."

She searched his face for the certainty she felt slipping from her grasp. "How did we get here? How did I let...?" Her words trailed off, choked by regrets too numerous to voice.

"Sarah." His firm voice pulled her back from the edge of despair. “We can't change the past. We focus on Victoria now, on getting better—for her."

"Getting better," she echoed, the phrase laden with ambiguity. Better health for Victoria, sobriety for herself. The path ahead loomed daunting, steeped in accountability.

"Tomorrow," she said, more to herself than to him. "Tomorrow is a new day." A promise, a plea.

"Tomorrow," he agreed, squeezing her hand in affirmation. "We'll start fresh. You'll see the journals and understand everything. And you'll be at that appointment sober and clear-headed."

"Clear-headed," she murmured.

The concept seemed alien, yet vital. She needed clarity, not just for Victoria, but to salvage her own fragmented self.

"Sarah." His tone softened, threads of old warmth weaving through his concern. "You're stronger than you know. We both are. We'll get through this."

"Thank you," she mused. It felt distant, but his belief in her sparked a fragile hope. Could she find that strength within herself?

Their hands remained clasped, a physical manifestation of their tentative unity. Outside, the sun grew high in the sky, indifferent to the frailty of human plans. Inside, two parents sat in quiet resolve.

"Victoria needs us," Steven whispered into the hush. "And we need each other."

"Yes," Sarah affirmed, the word a vow. "For Victoria. For us."

Chapter 46

The front door creaked, a shiver skating down my spine as I stepped into the dimly lit kitchen.

"Mom?" Alex's voice cut through the silence, small and uncertain.

"Hey, sweetheart." I forced a smile, crossing the room to plant a kiss on his damp forehead. His eyes, wide and dark with something he shouldn't know at his age, met mine.

"Mom, a man... when I got off the school bus. He said...." Alex hesitated, his small hands fidgeting with the hem of his shirt.

"What is it, honey?" I urged, my heart throbbing in my chest.

"He said that we're all in danger." The words spilled out, and the room spun. "Because of you."

I froze. I bent down in front of him, forcing him to look into my eyes.

"Who said that, Alex?"

He shrugged. "I don't know who he was. Just some man."

"Have you seen him before?"

"No." He shook his head, the fear palpable in his voice. "I've never seen him. He just told me to tell you."

"That we're in danger? Because of me?"

"Yes."

"Matt!" My voice was sharper than I intended, panic clawing at my throat.

"What's wrong?" Matt hobbled in, his crutches clicking against the tile floor. He saw the fear on my face immediately. "What's going on, Eva Rae?"

"Someone threatened Alex. They said...." The words choked me. "He said that we are in danger...."

"Damn it!" Matt's face flushed red, the veins in his neck bulging with anger. "I told you this would happen!"

"You really think we're in danger? He might just be some lunatic," I said, trying to calm myself.

"And what if he's not?" Matt said. "Is that a risk you're willing to take?"

"I'm sure he's just someone trying to...." I paused, unable to believe my own words. "I mean, who would...?"

"We can't take that chance," Matt said. "I, for one, am not prepared to."

"Do you want me to call the station? Have them put a patrol outside?" I asked.

I saw the fear on Matt's face. It was somehow deeper than anything I had ever seen in him before, fueled by his PTSD from the incident. It was getting serious.

"What do we do?" Desperation laced his tone. "This man must know where we live. The bus stops right outside. He knows Alex is your child. Are we even safe here tonight?"

"Calm down," I said. "I'm sure we're okay here. I'll get the chief to have a patrol come by and"

"God, I don't know!" Matt slammed his crutch down. "It

might not be enough. I don't like this. We have to keep the kids safe, but how?"

"Safe... yes. We will." My mind raced, fear turning to steel inside me. I had to calm him down somehow. I didn't want him scaring the kids. "We'll figure this out. Together."

"We should go somewhere," Matt said with a deep sigh. "Somewhere safe. Just for tonight, and then we'll see."

"Okay, we can do that for one night if that makes you feel better. My mother's?" I asked.

Matt sighed. "Too obvious."

"Hotel?" I asked.

He nodded, eyes on fire. "Has to be."

"Okay, let's pack light. Just the essentials." My voice was steady, but inside, my heart raced like a trapped bird. I was worried about Matt's state of mind and about the children. Would this scare them? Going away was the right solution for us all.

I dashed to the kids' rooms, tossing clothes into backpacks. "A hotel is good. That's definitely somewhere they wouldn't look. Whoever they are."

"Got it." The frustration was evident in his voice, but beneath that was a current of resolve.

"Christine! Alex! Angel!" I called out, my throat dry. They appeared, confusion etched on their innocent faces. "We're going to spend the night at a hotel, okay?"

"Why, Mom?" Christine's eyes were large and questioning.

"Please, don't question me; just trust me on this, okay? There's no need to worry," I lied, smiling through the fear. "It's just for tonight."

"Is it because of the bad man?" Alex's voice was barely above a whisper.

“What bad man?” Christine said. “What’s going on here, Mom? I have homework to do. I can’t just....”

“Please, don’t fight me on this,” I said to her, giving her a look I knew she would understand.

“I’m scared of the creepy man,” Alex said.

"Shh, no more of that," I hushed him, scooping up toiletries. "Let's just get in the car."

"Can I bring Mr. Fluffles?" Angel clutched her stuffed rabbit.

"Of course, baby." I ushered them downstairs, trying to keep my cool.

Matt was waiting by the door, balancing on his crutches, his face strained with effort and anger. "Come on."

"Everyone in the car. Now!" I didn't mean to bark the order, but urgency left no room for gentleness.

Matt struggled out the door, his movements hindered by the crutches but driven by adrenaline. I glanced around the shadowed yard, every rustle of leaves sounding like a footstep.

"Mom, are we safe?" Christine's hand found mine as we walked to the car.

"I won’t ever let anything happen to you," I promised. “This is just a safety precaution, nothing else.”

I helped Angel get into her car seat and strapped her down, then kissed her forehead and Mr. Fluffles, of course.

"Seat belts," Matt grunted, lowering himself into the passenger seat with a grimace.

"Head count. One... two... three." I clicked my belt into place, my eyes never ceasing their vigil. "All good."

"Let's go," Matt said, his tone harsher than intended. I was worried about scaring the children, but I believed Matt was right. You should never take a threat like that lightly.

I turned the ignition, the engine's roar slicing through the night's stillness. "We're going to be okay," I told them, more to convince myself than them.

"Damn right, we will," Matt echoed, his hand finding mine for a brief squeeze before I put the car into drive and pulled away from the only safety we knew.

As we reached A1A, the rearview mirror kept pulling my gaze, the silhouette of a car behind us morphing with each passing streetlight—too close for comfort, too constant to be a coincidence.

"Matt," I whispered, "that car... it's been with us since Minutemen Causeway."

"Change lanes," he said, voice low and steady. My hands tightened on the wheel as I obeyed, flicking the turn signal with a trembling finger. The other vehicle mimicked our path, its headlights an unwavering pair of eyes in the darkness.

"Speed up." Matt's command was terse.

I pressed the gas, the needle jumping as we sped along the deserted road. A glance in the mirror—still there, still following.

"Take the next right, then a quick left," he instructed, scanning the side mirrors with a frown.

"Is this going to work?" My voice betrayed the panic that was threatening to spill over.

"Has to."

Our tires squealed against the asphalt as I followed his directions, the sudden turns throwing us side to side. Angel let out a small whimper from her car seat.

"Mom?" Christine's whisper was shaky.

"Shh, there's nothing to worry about," I lied, hoping my voice sounded lighter than I felt. "We're like spies."

"Spies don't get caught," Alex piped up, trying to sound brave.

"Exactly," Matt said, casting me a grim look that belied his confident tone.

We zigzagged through streets, the suspense gnawing at my insides until, finally, a red light ahead gave us a chance. I made a sharp left into an alleyway, killing the headlights and holding my breath.

"Down," Matt ordered.

We all ducked, hearts pounding in the blind dark. Seconds stretched like hours until the sound of the other car roared past the alley's entrance.

"Go," he urged, and I fired up the engine again, pulling out in the opposite direction, leaving the specter of our pursuer behind.

"Are we... are they gone?" Christine's voice quivered.

"I think so." My relief was punctured by the fear of what could've happened.

THE HOTEL'S neon sign blinked a welcome as we pulled into the lot, a beacon in the consuming night. We shuffled inside, the lobby's sterile lights harsh against our strained eyes.

"Christine, Alex, Angel," I counted them once more, hugging each tightly, their small bodies solid and real in my arms. They were safe for now.

"Good job, Mom," Alex murmured, his face pale but trying to smile.

"Thank you," I whispered back, brushing a kiss on his forehead.

"Let's get to our room," Matt said, the strain evident on his face. He was trying to be the rock, but I could see his hands trembling.

"Okay, kids, race you to the elevator!" I forced a cheerfulness I didn't feel, anything to distract them from the ordeal.

"Last one there's a rotten egg!" Christine giggled, taking off with her siblings in tow.

"Hey, no fair! Wait up!" Alex yelled after her.

"Slow down!" I called, half-laughing, half-scolding.

Once inside our room, I surveyed our temporary haven: two queen beds, a TV, the mundane details offering a surreal comfort. The children clambered onto the nearest bed, their laughter a balm to my frayed nerves.

"Mom, can we watch cartoons?" Angel asked, her innocence a stark contrast to the night's events.

"Sure, sweetheart." I clicked the TV on, the animated chatter filling the silence.

Matt leaned against the wall, watching them, his jaw clenched. "They shouldn't have to go through this," he said.

"None of us should." I joined him, letting out a long breath as I took in their faces—my reasons for everything.

"Tomorrow, we figure this out," I murmured.

"Tonight, we rest," he replied, though the set of his mouth told me neither of us would find sleep easy.

"Tonight, we rest," I echoed, clinging to the semblance of peace as a shield against the fear that lingered just beyond the flicker of the TV screen.

The television's glow danced across the room, casting flickering shadows that played on the walls like specters of our fear. Matt's silhouette was rigid, a statue carved from worry and pain.

"Look at them," he whispered, his voice strangled with emotion. "They think it's an adventure, but it's a nightmare."

I turned away from the kids, their giggles belying the gravity of our situation. He threw himself on the bed. His crutches ended up discarded on the floor, a testament to his own battle that was still haunting us now. Was he ever going to be the same old Matt I fell in love with? The one who was afraid of nothing? The one who hunted criminals down fearlessly and never worried about his own safety?

I missed him.

"Matt, I—"

"Stop." He cut me off, his eyes searching mine in the semi-darkness. "You need to stop this. This isn't just about you anymore. It's all of us. You're putting us all in danger. This isn't even your case. Look what happened to me last time we went down this road."

I bit my lip, tasting the salt of anxiety and guilt. "I know."

"Then, why can't you see? This investigation is tearing us apart, putting our family in danger, and it's not worth it." His voice cracked at the last word, revealing the depth of his fear.

"Sarah didn't kill anyone," I said, my voice steady even as my heart raced. "If I back down now and let these threats scare me away, then everything I stand for means nothing. Justice, truth—it all becomes empty words. Sarah is innocent, and I can't turn my back on her."

"Even if it costs us everything?" His question hung in the air as heavy as the dread that clung to my skin. "Even if we have to go into hiding?"

"Someone is trying to silence me because they know I'm close to the truth. If we run scared now, they win. I can't live with that. I won't let our children live in a world where the bad guys get away because we're too afraid to stand up to them."

"Damn your principles!" The words exploded from him, a raw surge of desperation. "They keep getting us in trouble. They could have taken Alex today!"

"That's why I have to end this, Matt. I will find out who's

doing this and stop them. But I can't do it without your support."

He slumped against the wall, the fight seeping out of him. "Just promise me you'll be careful."

"Every step of the way," I promised, my resolve as unyielding as the darkness outside.

"Fine," he sighed, defeated. "But we do this together. No more lone-wolf antics. Agreed?"

"Agreed."

His hand found mine in the dim light, a lifeline amid the chaos. Together, in the quiet hotel room with the sound of cartoons playing softly in the background, we faced an uncertain future—one I was determined to meet head-on.

Chapter 47

The silence of the hotel room was a stark contrast to the turmoil raging within me. I sat on the edge of the bed, my fingers tracing the outline of my cell phone, willing it to ring with answers. The weight of Matt's gaze felt like an anchor, dragging me down into a sea of doubt.

"Are we doing the right thing?" My voice sounded small, almost foreign to my own ears.

Matt furrowed his brows in concern. "We're keeping our family safe. That's always the right thing."

"But at what cost?" I whispered, staring at my clenched hands. The image of Alex's frightened face flashed before my eyes, igniting a fresh wave of fear. But there was also something else.

Standing abruptly, I paced the cramped space, feeling caged. The flash drive—Pete Hancock's last secret—beckoned me, a siren call I couldn't resist. I couldn't stop thinking about it. I was sure it held the key.

"Where did I put it?" I muttered, rummaging through my

bag. Frustration mounted as each pocket revealed nothing—no flash drive.

"Looking for this?" Matt held up a pack of Peanut M&Ms, a teasing glint in his eye.

"Not funny." The realization dawned on me then, chilling and sharp. "I left it at the house."

I looked at Matt, knowing I could never tell him, forgetting that I had just promised him I would involve him. He would only tell me not to go.

"I just need to get some snacks," I lied smoothly, avoiding his knowing look. "I'm not in the mood for M&Ms. Keep the kids entertained."

"Be careful," he said.

"Always am." I forced a smile and slipped out the door.

The drive back to our street was a study in paranoia. Every shadow seemed to move, every car behind me a potential threat. I cursed myself for leaving the flash drive, for this reckless detour that could put us all in more danger. But I couldn't stop now.

The air was still as I stepped out of the car, my heart pounding a staccato rhythm against my ribs. Our house loomed in the darkness, its windows like hollow eyes. As I came closer, I realized the front door was ajar.

What on earth?

"Matt's going to kill me," I muttered under my breath, pushing the door open with a trembling hand. The other rested on my gun. The silence that greeted me was unnerving, the familiar transformed into something sinister by the events of the past few hours.

"Hello?" My voice was barely a whisper, betraying my fear. No answer came, only the echo of my heartbeat.

I reached for the light switch but stopped, my instincts

screaming at me to stay hidden in the shadows. I pulled out my phone, using its dim glow to navigate through the entryway. That's when I saw it—on the wall, a message scrawled in what looked like black crayon:

STOP NOW OR THE KIDS ARE NEXT!

A breath hitched in my throat, my fingers tightening around the phone. Fear slithered down my spine, but it was quickly chased by a flame of anger. They had come into my home and threatened my children.

"Is that supposed to scare me?" I hissed into the emptiness, defiance rising within me like a tide. I refused to be cowed by the faceless menace that lurked beyond the safety of our walls.

"Think again," I spat, the words bouncing off the walls and filling the space with my resolve. I snapped a photo of the threat, evidence of their intimidation. Coming here, thinking they could break me with threats and fear tactics, was a bold move.

"Mom always said, 'In the face of danger, you'll find your true strength,'" I whispered to the vacant rooms.

Determination stiffened my spine as I made my way toward my small office where I had left the flash drive. Each step felt like wading through quicksand, but I pressed on, propelled by the need to protect my family and clear Sarah's name.

"Come on; come on," I urged myself, rummaging through the mess they'd made, overturning papers and books until my hands finally closed around the small, plastic rectangle that held the answers we needed.

"Gotcha," I breathed, a small victory in the war that had been waged upon us. Clutching the flash drive, I backed out of the room, casting one last glance at the chilling message. It was meant to terrify, to paralyze me with fear. Instead, it served as fuel, igniting a fire that no threat could extinguish.

"Nice try," I muttered, pocketing the device and heading back to the sanctuary of the shadows outside. "But you're going to have to do better than that."

I washed the message away, then jammed the flash drive into my pocket and bolted out of there. My heart thrumming against my ribs, I darted to the car, casting paranoid glances over my shoulder. The world seemed too still, and every rustle seemed a potential threat.

"Come on," I muttered as the engine sputtered to life, coaxing it with more urgency than it deserved. Tires squealed against the pavement as I pulled away from the curb.

The neon glow of the Seven-Eleven sign was a beacon in the night, promising normalcy in its harsh fluorescent buzz. I grabbed a basket, tossing in bags of chips, candy bars—anything to sell the lie of a simple snack run. My hands shook as I placed each item on the counter, offering the cashier a practiced smile.

"Evening's getting warmer, huh?" he said, scanning the items.

"Feels like it," I replied, eyes darting to the door. "Summer is coming faster than we think."

"Be safe out there," he called after me as I hurried back into the night.

"Always am," I lied.

The hotel room door clicked shut behind me, and I leaned against it for a second, letting out a breath I didn't know I was holding. Matt looked up from his laptop, concern etching lines into his forehead.

"Got the snacks," I announced, forcing brightness into my voice as I held up the plastic bag.

"Great." He tried to smile, but it didn't quite reach his eyes. "Kids are asleep."

"Good." My gaze slid to their peaceful forms, guilt knotting in my gut. I couldn't tell him—not yet.

"Everything okay?" Matt asked, watching me too closely.

"Of course," I lied again, moving to the small desk in the corner. "Just need to check something for work."

He hesitated, then nodded, picking up where he'd left off. I waited for the hum of concentration before opening my laptop, the flash drive heavy in my hand. With a click, it was in, and I was holding my breath.

Folders appeared on the screen, cryptic labels giving nothing away. I clicked through them, files flying past in a blur until one caught my eye.

I double-clicked, and the screen filled with something that stole the air from my lungs.

"Sarah..." I whispered, heart sinking, gasping as the truth hit me like a freight train. "Oh, dear God, no."

Part IV

Chapter 48

The metallic clang of the cell door echoed through the corridor, pulling Sarah from her thoughts. She looked up to see a silhouette against the fluorescent glare.

"You're being released," the guard announced, his voice a detached monotone.

"What?" Disbelief laced her words as she rose to her feet, heart pounding against her ribs.

"The charges were dropped," he said, his gaze steady yet distant. "You can go. Now."

Her legs felt like they belonged to someone else as she stepped out of the cell. Relief flooded her, warm and dizzying, but it was chased by a tail of uncertainty that slithered up her spine. Why had they suddenly released her? What had happened? The walk toward the exit seemed surreal; each step toward freedom was weighed down by the invisible chains of apprehension.

In the property room, a dull gray bin awaited her. As she peered into its contents, her fingers trembled with an odd anticipation. One by one, she reclaimed the pieces of her former life: a crumpled jacket, a set of keys, and a wallet.

Then, her hand closed around the cell phone. It felt like grabbing onto a lifeline in a stormy sea. Every contact, every message, every photo—it was a digital key to a world she feared had forgotten her. Her grip tightened around the device, its significance far greater than its compact frame suggested. It wasn't just a phone; it was her chance to reconnect, to explain, to plead for the help she so desperately needed now.

Sarah's senses sharpened as she edged through the narrow corridor, the echo of her footsteps a rhythmic testament to her departure. The sterile scent of bleach clung to the air, mingling with the muted undertones of despair that seemed to seep from the concrete walls. Bars lined the path, their shadows casting striped patterns on the floor, a stark reminder of the captivity that had caged her.

"Watch your step," a disembodied voice murmured as she neared an uneven section of the flooring. Her eyes flicked up, meeting those of an inmate peering through the bars of another cell. There was no malice there, only the hollow recognition of shared misfortune.

"Thanks," she whispered, her voice a raspy ghost of its former self.

The clangs and shouts of the jailhouse faded into a dull hum as the exit loomed ahead, an illuminated rectangle slicing through the dimness. Anticipation quickened her pulse, each heartbeat a drum roll leading to the climax of her release.

And then, she was out. The heavy door shut behind her with a finality that sent a shiver down her spine. Sarah stood alone, the open sky stretching above her, a vast canvas of freedom marred by the uncertainty of what lay ahead.

"Okay, now what?" she muttered under her breath.

The outside world felt alien—a domain she'd been abruptly thrust back into without a map or compass. Cars zipped by in the distance, their drivers wrapped in their own realities, oblivious to the woman who had just reclaimed hers.

"Get it together, Sarah," she chided herself, scanning the perimeter for some semblance of direction.

“Victoria,” she whispered.

She took a deep breath. With tentative steps, Sarah moved away from the jail's oppressive shadow, clutching her cell phone like a talisman against the uncertainties that awaited her in the life she was about to re-enter.

Sarah pressed the phone to her ear. Her thumb circled the chipped corner of the device, the familiar gesture a lifeline in the sea of uncertainty that surrounded her.

"Sarah?" The line crackled with his response, a mixture of surprise and concern weaving through his tone.

"Can you come and get me? They... they released me," she rushed the words out, each syllable spiked with desperation. "I don't know where to go, I—"

"Where are you?" His question cut through the panic, tightening its grip on her chest.

"Outside the jail. I'm... I'm free, but I feel so lost." She clutched the phone tighter, her knuckles turning white against the black plastic.

"Stay right there, okay? I'm on my way. Don't move, Sarah." His steady voice was a solid anchor for her turbulent thoughts.

"Okay, I'll wait."

A sigh deflated her lungs, the relief manifesting in a shaky exhale. The knowledge that she wasn't alone—that he was coming for her—unfurled a fragile sense of security within her.

"Thank you," she whispered, the gratitude wrapping

around her like a warm blanket against the chill of the world outside her prison walls.

The car was nondescript, a shadow against the starkness of the jail's exterior—a charcoal gray sedan with tinted windows obscuring any glimpse of the driver. It glided to a stop just inches from where Sarah stood, the hum of its engine a soft purr in the stillness of her release.

For a moment, Sarah hesitated, her heart thumping audibly, a silent drumbeat to the anxiety that danced nervously through her veins.

The passenger door swung open with a quiet creak, breaking her paralysis. There, shrouded in the car's dim interior, sat a silhouette outlined by the faint glow of the dashboard. A hand emerged from the shadows, beckoning.

"Sarah," came from a calm and familiar voice—the voice that had promised to anchor her.

She approached, her steps tentative, pausing at the threshold of the open car door. Her gaze met his, and in the reassuring depths of his eyes, she found the flicker of trust she needed to step forward.

"Come on; let's get you out of here," he urged softly, his words a gentle nudge against her inertia.

With a shallow breath, Sarah slid into the seat, the leather cool beneath her. She pulled the door closed, sealing herself inside with her rescuer, and exhaled. The space between them was charged with unspoken questions, but for now, it was enough to simply be away from the cold bars and echoing footsteps of her cell.

"Adam," Sarah began, her voice barely above a whisper, as the car's purring engine filled the silence between them. "I can't.... Thank you isn't enough. You're here... after everything."

"Sarah," he replied, his tone insistent yet soft, "there's no debt between us. I'm where I need to be."

Her heart swelled with a mix of emotions too complex to untangle. There was gratitude and relief but also an entwining fear of the unknown road ahead. Yet, in his presence, she found a beacon of stability.

"Without you..." she started, but her words trailed off, lost in the labyrinth of her thoughts. “I feared I was all alone in the world.”

"Hey," Adam interjected gently, steering the conversation away from the dark roads of what-ifs. "We'll figure this out together. One step at a time."

The car glided forward, the world outside shifting from stark concrete walls to the blur of a life once familiar. She watched through the window as the imposing structure that had defined her recent existence shrank into the background. The jail became nothing more than a silhouette against the skyline—a piece of her past that no longer held her captive.

"Thank you, Adam," she said, turning to face him, her eyes reflecting the vulnerability and hope that danced within. "I knew I could count on you."

"Always," Adam affirmed, his hand finding its way to her thigh, a silent vow of solidarity. "I'm just happy you're out."

As the distance grew between Sarah and the jail, so did the realization of her newfound freedom. A tightness in her chest loosened, giving way to cautious optimism. The road ahead was uncertain, but it was theirs to travel—together.

Chapter 49

I was sitting in the hotel room the next morning when my phone suddenly rang. "Hello?

"Yes, this is Monica Chapman."

"Victoria's grandmother and the mother of Steven Chapman, yes, I remember you. How can I help you?"

"You left your card here when you were here to talk to Victoria, and now she's asking for you. She says she has something important to tell you, something she suddenly remembered, so I thought I'd...."

I sat up straight. "You did the right thing. I'll be right there."

"Thank you."

We hung up, and I grabbed my purse. I looked at Matt, who was napping on the bed with Angel. I had taken the two older kids to school earlier in the morning, but Angel had been allowed to stay home from preschool and Matt to skip his physical therapy—just for today.

Slipping into yesterday's jeans, lying crumpled on the floor, I fumbled with the buttons, my fingers clumsy with haste. My mind churned, trying to piece together the fragmented puzzle of Victoria's fractured memories.

Shoes. Keys. Wallet. Each item slapped into my palm as if gravity had intensified, pulling them toward me with the weight of the situation. I left Matt a note, then slid out. The door slammed shut behind me; the warm morning air slapped my face, jolting my senses awake.

The car tires squealed as I backed out of the parking lot, and the car's engine growled in response to my leaden foot on the gas pedal.

Turning onto Monica's street, the familiar sight of the house, now a sanctuary for Victoria, loomed ahead. It stood solemn and silent, holding its breath for the secrets it sheltered.

I killed the engine and leaped from the car, barely feeling the gravel crunch underfoot as I raced up the path. Every second counted; every heartbeat was a drumroll to revelation.

The door creaked open before my knuckles could rap against the mahogany. Monica's silhouette filled the frame, her face an ashen mask of worry.

"Thank God you're here." Her voice was a whisper lost in the cavernous hallway. She beckoned with a trembling hand, and I followed her lead.

The thick carpet muffled our footsteps as we navigated through the dimly lit corridor. Shadows clung to the corners, and the air hung heavy with the scent of antiseptic and something floral, trying to mask the truth of illness.

At the doorway to Victoria's room, Monica paused, her eyes locking onto mine. "She's been so fragile... and her eyes are sensitive to the lights lately; that's why I keep her in the darkness, but she's very determined to speak to you."

I nodded, swallowing the lump forming in my throat. Inside, the room was draped in darkness, curtains drawn tight.

The light from the hallway cast a soft glow over the bed where Victoria lay, a pale wraith amidst the tangle of white sheets.

"Victoria?" My voice felt intrusive in the hushed stillness.

Her head turned, and for a moment, her wide, clear eyes found mine. The ghost of a smile flickered across her lips as recognition sparked.

"Hey, Agent Thomas," she breathed out, the sound barely more than the rustle of leaves in the wind.

"Hey, yourself." I pulled a chair close, its legs scraping softly against the wooden floor.

Taking her hand—cool and fragile in my grip—I offered a reassuring squeeze. "Monica said you remembered something about the night your father was shot.... Can you tell me?"

Victoria's chest rose with a deep breath, and her fingers curled around mine, clinging to the lifeline I represented. Her lips parted, and she braced herself to once again confront the shadows of her past.

"Victoria?" My whisper cut through the heavy silence. Her eyes, brimming with unshed tears, met mine.

"Voices," she mouthed, her voice a thread of sound, frayed and delicate.

"Voices?" I leaned in closer, my ear almost touching her dry lips. "Can you say that again?"

"Before... Mama came." Each word was a struggle, clawing out from under the weight of memory.

"Before your mother arrived, you heard voices?" I repeated, ensuring clarity. There was no room for mistakes—not when so much was at stake.

Victoria's nod was almost imperceptible, a mere tremor through her frail form. "Yes."

"Whose voices, Victoria? Who did you hear?" My heart

hammered against my ribcage, each beat echoing her fear, her pain.

"A man...." The word fell like a stone into the room's stillness, sinking slowly into my consciousness. "My neighbor... Adam."

"Adam?" Surprise lanced through me, sharp and cold. "You're sure it was his voice?"

"Sure." Her affirmation was a sliver of certainty in a sea of doubts.

"Okay, okay, Victoria. That's huge." I squeezed her hand gently, a silent promise etched between our fingers.

My pulse quickened, a relentless drumbeat in the cavern of my chest.

"Are you all right?" Monica's voice sliced through the haze of my thoughts. She hovered at the edge of the bed, her eyes searching mine.

"Fine," I managed to say, though my tone betrayed the turmoil beneath the surface. "Just... processing."

"Of course, it's a lot to take in." She perched on the armrest of a nearby chair, the fabric whispering under her weight. "But remember, this is about Victoria. We need the truth—for her."

I nodded, feeling the gravity of responsibility settle on my shoulders. Her gaze held mine, steady and unwavering. There was strength in her stillness, assurance in her presence. I drew a breath, letting her certainty anchor me.

"Thank you, Monica." My words felt small in the expanse of what lay ahead. "For Victoria, we'll face whatever comes next."

Monica's hand found mine, her grip firm. "We're here to help," she said.

I offered a tight smile, the knot in my throat loosening enough to speak. "I can't thank you enough, Monica. Victoria," I glanced down at the fragile girl in bed, her eyes large and expectant, "you're incredibly brave. This... it's a big deal."

"Will it help?" Victoria's voice was a thread, nearly lost in the expanse of silence that followed.

"Every bit helps," I reassured her, tucking a stray lock of hair behind her ear. "You've given us something new, a direction. That's more than we had yesterday."

"Adam...."

"Let me worry about Adam," I said, firm yet gentle. "You just focus on getting better, okay?"

Victoria nodded, and I could see the trust she placed in me, a sacred charge I intended to honor. "I will find out what he was doing there that night. And if he had anything to do with your father's death, I'll bring him to justice. That's a promise."

"Justice," she whispered, her fingers tightening around mine before finally relaxing.

"Rest now," I urged, standing up but hesitant to let go. "We've got work to do, thanks to you."

"Be careful," Monica interjected, her voice carrying a mother's caution.

"I will," I replied with a smile that didn't quite reach my eyes. The room seemed to hold its breath as I stepped toward the door, acutely aware of the weight of truth and the relentless pursuit of justice that beckoned beyond the threshold.

I paused in the doorway. I turned to see Victoria's eyes flutter closed, her breath evening out. Monica stood by her side, a sentinel of maternal protection, yet her gaze followed me, sharp and knowing.

The dim light from Victoria's room spilled into the corridor, casting long shadows as I stepped out. I knew the dangers of what lay ahead; confronting Adam could unearth more than just the truth—it could provoke a predator cornered by his own deceit.

As I went outside, I thumbed my phone screen, pulling up Adam's contact information. My thumb hesitated over the call button. No, not yet. I needed to be smart about this and approach him with a plan, not just raw emotion. There was a lot to this story, and the pieces were falling into place slowly now. But I had to be clever about it.

The dangers were mounting, the stakes escalating with each passing second. And as I slipped out into the car, the chilling realization settled in my bones:

The hunter had just become the hunted.

Chapter 50

THEN:

THE LEATHER creaked as Sarah's fingers tightened around the steering wheel, knuckles whitening. The car hummed through streets lined with tall palm trees, their branches brushing a sky heavy with unshed rain. Every mile closer to the doctor's office was a silent battle against the siren call of a liquid crutch she had forsaken but not forgotten.

What she wouldn't give for just one small glass of wine. Or just a sip.

But no. She had been sober for five days now, and she couldn't give in to the desire. She had promised Steven that much.

"Almost there," Steven murmured, his gaze fixed on the passing scenery, a futile attempt to avoid staring at the tension etched in Sarah's profile.

"Uh-huh," she replied, a terse nod accompanying her words.

The car's interior was thick with unspoken fears, the air conditioning battling the heat from the two bodies enclosed in this moving capsule of anxiety.

The vehicle rolled to a stop in the parking lot of the pristine medical building, its facade a stark contrast to the turmoil brewing inside Sarah. She killed the engine, feeling the vibration ebb away beneath her, much like the resolve that threatened to slip through her fingers.

"Ready?" Steven asked, turning his attention back to her. He searched her face for the assurance he needed as much as she did.

"Let's go," she answered, pushing the door open and stepping out into the humidity that seemed eager to claim her.

They entered the doctor's office, a sanctuary of sterile smells and soft-spoken greetings. Behind the reception desk stood the doctor, an unexpected figure who could have stepped out of the pages of a glossy magazine. With his perfectly coiffed hair and a smile that seemed to pull at every heartstring, he extended a hand in welcome.

"Sarah, Steven, it's good to see you both," he said, his voice a melody of warmth that somehow eased the barbed wire wrapped around Sarah's chest.

"Doctor," Sarah greeted, her voice steadier than she felt. Her hand briefly clasped his. His touch was gentle, and his eyes reflected an empathy that didn't seem practiced or forced.

"Thank you for seeing us," Steven added, his handshake firm yet brief.

"Of course," the doctor replied with a nod, his smile unwavering. "Shall we?"

Sarah followed behind the two men, her heart pounding a frantic rhythm against her ribs, each beat a reminder of the reason they were here. She straightened her shoulders, casting a last longing glance at the exit before committing herself to whatever truths lay ahead.

Steven cleared his throat, his words slicing through the silence. "Doctor, Sarah's... well, she's been worried about Victoria's condition." His gaze flickered to Sarah, seeking silent permission before he continued.

"Sarah has her suspicions," Steven said. His voice was steady, but the concern in his eyes betrayed him. "She wants to know more about what's going on. Can you explain?"

The doctor's smile dimmed, the first sign of gravity settling into the room. He nodded, directing them toward the leather chairs that faced his polished mahogany desk.

"Please, sit down."

Sarah hesitated, feeling the weight of the room, the space between hope and despair narrowing with each breath. She perched on the edge of the chair as if ready to flee from whatever truth might unfold.

"As you know, Victoria is very sick," the doctor began, his eyes locking onto Sarah's. His tone had shifted, the melody now a somber hymn. "It started with leukemia, which slowly got better, but then we found cancer in her throat. The cancer that started in her throat...."

Sarah felt the air leave her lungs in a silent gasp, her knuckles whitening as they clung to the armrests.

"...has now spread," the doctor continued, his words deliberate, "to her lungs."

Sarah's heart raced, a thunderous echo in her chest that threatened to drown out everything else.

"Is there..." Sarah's voice cracked, and the struggle for composure was etched deeply into her face. "Is there anything we can do besides what we're already doing?"

"We're doing everything we can," he said. "The chemo and

the radiation. We're hoping it will eventually turn things around."

"Remission," Sarah whispered, the word a fragile hope that frayed with each shallow breath she drew. "I read... in her old medical journal. It said Victoria was in remission."

The doctor's expression softened, a crease of concern forming between his brows. He leaned forward, hands clasping together as if to gather his thoughts.

"Unfortunately," he began, his voice measured, "that was an error made by one of my colleagues. It set us back for a long time in her treatment." He reached for a stack of journals on his desk, the edges worn from frequent consultation. Flipping through the pages, he stopped at a chart dense with numbers and notes.

"Here," the doctor said, extending the open journal toward her. "You can see the progression...."

Sarah's gaze locked onto the pages, the stark reality displayed in clinical lines and cold data. The words "chemotherapy" and "metastasis" leaped out at her, branding themselves into her consciousness. She knew about all this, at least most of it, but Steven had kept their daughter's illness much to himself and told her to focus on her career while he took care of it. And whenever she asked about it, he told her not to worry, that he knew what he was doing. He was the one with the medical training, not her. Sarah had been subduing her pain by drinking, and that had made her numb. Now, she could feel it all for the first time in a long while. And it hurt.

"The chemo," the doctor continued, pointing to a series of entries, "it's keeping her alive, keeping the cancer at bay. But it's not making it smaller, I'm afraid."

"Alive," she echoed, the term both a lifeline and a sentence.

Sarah's eyes lingered on the graph, each point a heartbeat, each line a breath stolen from time.

Sarah's fingers trembled as she closed the journal, the weight of its contents pressing down on her like a physical burden. She looked up at the doctor, searching his face for any sign of reprieve, any sliver of hope that might contradict the grim prognosis laid bare on the pages before her. But his eyes only offered a solemn empathy, a reflection of her own despair. She had been wrong. Steven was right. She had been wrong to doubt him. It was like he always told her: What did she know about medical issues anyway?

"Thank you," she managed to stammer out, her voice a mere wisp in the sterile air of the office. "For... for being honest with us."

"Of course, Sarah," the doctor replied with a nod, his demeanor gentle. His hand reached out, open and waiting, and she placed her own within it—a brief connection, an attempt at comfort in the cold expanse of uncertainty.

The handshake was firm yet considerate, an anchor in the tumult of her emotions. She forced a tight-lipped smile, a social reflex masking the turmoil inside.

A flicker of recognition sparked in her memory as she withdrew her hand. "I've seen you before," she said, the thought surfacing unbidden. Her eyes narrowed slightly as she pieced together the image of him outside the professional confines of the clinic.

"I know where. You live on our street, don't you?"

The doctor's polite smile faltered for a fraction of a second, an imperceptible shift to anyone not scrutinizing as closely as Sarah was at that moment.

"Yes, as a matter of fact, I do," he confirmed with a nod,

regaining his composure. "Just a few doors down, close to the beach."

"Right," Sarah murmured, a sense of surreal familiarity washing over her. The handsome doctor, whom she had only known in the context of her daughter's illness, was suddenly cast in the mundane light of neighborhood normalcy. It was an odd thing, one that left her feeling momentarily adrift.

"Small world," she added, though the sentiment felt hollow against the backdrop of their current conversation. A small world, indeed, but one that seemed all too vast when filled with the echoing silence of unanswerable questions about her daughter's future.

"Big place, then?" Sarah's voice was light, but her mind churned with the implications of his proximity.

"Quite," the doctor said, the corners of his mouth ticking up in a muted smile that didn't quite reach his eyes. "The view of the water is rather calming."

"Sarah, we should go." Steven's hand closed gently on her elbow, a subtle yet firm reminder of their purpose. She glanced at him, reading the urgency in his posture, the slight crease between his brows.

"Of course," she complied, the word barely audible. Her gaze lingered on the doctor, tracing his jawline, searching for something undefinable in his expression.

"Thank you again," she managed, though her voice sounded distant to her own ears.

"Anytime, Mrs. Chapman," the doctor replied, his tone professional yet not without warmth.

Steven led her from the office, the click of the door shutting behind them echoing like a period at the end of a sentence. Their footsteps were muffled against the plush carpet of the hallway.

As they reached the exit, the warm air outside slapped against Sarah's cheeks, a bracing reminder of reality. She blinked rapidly as if waking from a trance. The world outside the doctor's office felt different, heavier somehow, laden with truths she couldn't unlearn.

"Home?" Steven's question hung between them, filled with everything left unsaid.

"Home," Sarah confirmed, her voice steady despite the tremor she felt within. They moved together toward the car, each lost in their own reflections.

Chapter 51

Tires screeched against the hot Florida pavement as I swerved around a slow-moving sedan, the Atlantic air whipping through my cracked open window. Cape Canaveral blurred past, a mosaic of sun-drenched storefronts and palm trees swaying with indifference to the urgency clenching at my chest. My fingers fumbled for my phone, the screen's glow a beacon of hope in the dimming light.

"Come on; come on," I muttered, tapping Detective Ryan's contact as if speed dialing could hasten his answer.

The line clicked, then buzzed—a voice called out. "Ryan."

"Detective, it's Agent Thomas." My voice was breathless, mirroring the pace of my heart. "Listen, I—"

"What do you want, Thomas?" His words cut through the static, sharp with annoyance.

"Something's come up," I pressed, steering with one hand, the other gripping the phone like a lifeline. "We need to talk about the Chapman case."

“Absolutely not. I'm done talking to you.”

"Ryan, I spoke to Victoria, Sarah's kid," I blurted out, the words tumbling over themselves. "She heard someone in the house that night."

There was a pause, long enough for me to hear the distant sound of seagulls mingling with my pounding pulse.

"And?" Ryan's voice was a mix of impatience and disinterest.

"Adam," I said, my grip tightening on the wheel. "Victoria heard Adam's voice before her mom got there."

"Thomas, you're grasping at straws." The detective's retort was swift, dismissive. "You can't just—"

"Grasping? She identified him by voice, Ryan!" My insistence bordered on desperation, the revelation too significant to ignore. “And there's something else”

"Look, Thomas," he sighed, the sound crackling over the line. "Adam's been through hell, lost his wife, and now you want to pin this on him?"

"You're not listening to me; there's more..." I shot back, feeling the sting of injustice as another piece slotted into the ugly puzzle of deceit and betrayal.

"Harassment is what it is," he countered coldly. "Back off, Agent Thomas."

But backing off wasn't in my nature—not when the truth was so close, or the stakes were this high.

"Ryan, listen to me," I started, the urgency clear in my voice. "Victoria's testimony could—"

"Thomas," he cut in, his tone sharper than broken glass. "Sarah Chapman's been released. Your mission is over. You won."

The words hit me like a freight train, and for a moment, the world outside blurred into streaks of color as my foot eased off the accelerator. "Released? On what grounds?"

"The chief thinks she's not our perp," Ryan said, and I could almost hear him shrugging through the phone. "Orders are orders."

"But that's the worst thing you could do!" I sputtered, my mind racing faster than my car. "You just put Sarah's life in great danger, Ryan."

"Look, I don't make the rules," he interrupted, his annoyance palpable. "Chapman's free to go until further notice."

"Damn it, Ryan!" I slammed my hand against the steering wheel. "If anything happens to her...."

"I can't win with you, can I? I thought you'd be happy. This was what you wanted," he said curtly. "But from now on, keep your nose clean, Thomas. No more wild theories."

"Wild theories?" I felt frustration knotting in my chest, tight and suffocating. "Are you just going to ignore this new information?"

"Enough, Thomas." There was finality in his voice, a closed door I couldn't open.

I took a deep breath, trying to steady the tremor of fear for Sarah's safety that threatened to overflow. My resolve hardened; I wouldn't let this go, no matter what Ryan said. Not when someone's life hung in the balance.

"Listen to me," I insisted, my words slicing through the tension. "Victoria heard him. Adam was there that night. Plus, I have something else I need to show you. We can't—"

"Stop." He cut me off with a force that nearly made me swerve. "I've had it with your rogue heroics. You're doing more harm than good, Thomas."

A hot coil of anger unfurled in my chest, but I clenched my jaw, forcing calm into my voice. "Then tell me, Detective, what would you have me do? Sit back and watch while the real culprit walks free?"

"Damn it, Agent Thomas!" The venom in his voice stung. "You think you're above the law?"

"I think I'm the only one trying to uphold it right now," I shot back, the car accelerating beneath me as though fueled by my own determination.

"Where are you going?" he demanded, suspicion lacing his words.

"Adam's," I said flatly. "He's got some explaining to do."

"Thomas, don't you dare—"

"Oh, but I will."

"Then, you're on your own."

"Goodbye, Ryan." I ended the call. My pulse thrummed in my ears, every beat fueling my resolve.

Adam would answer my questions—one way or another.

I threw the phone onto the dashboard; it skittered across the surface, coming to rest against the windshield—a small, insignificant rectangle of technology that had just delivered a heavy blow. My grip on the steering wheel tightened, knuckles turning white as I navigated the streets of Cape Canaveral, the Atlantic breeze doing nothing to cool my simmering fury.

Street signs blurred past, each one bringing me closer to Adam's doorstep. Houses in this part of town boasted well-manicured lawns and picket fences, starkly contrasting the chaos that churned within me.

Adam's place loomed ahead, its facade eerily serene beneath the Florida sun. I eased off the gas, the car slowing until it finally came to a halt in front of his driveway. The engine's hum fell silent as I turned the key; the sudden quiet pressing in on me felt like an accusation.

My hand lingered on the ignition, breaths shallow. Alone. Ryan's word echoed in my mind, but it didn't scare me. It emboldened me. This was the job—pursuing truth no matter how deep it buried itself.

I glanced at the house once more, noting the curtains drawn tight over windows that might as well have been eyes shut against prying gazes. Adam had answers, and I wouldn't leave without them.

I stepped out of the car, my service weapon a reassuring weight against my hip. The coastal air was heavy with salt and the promise of rain, but the storm inside me raged fiercer still.

The gravel crunched beneath my sneakers as I advanced. Each step was deliberate, practiced—the gait of an agent who had walked down this path of confrontation more times than she cared to count. Yet, a singular unease knotted my stomach, coiling tighter with every breath.

"Answers," I muttered, a mantra to focus my resolve. This wasn't just about Sarah's freedom any longer; it was about justice, about the lurking shadows of doubt that refused to dissipate. I texted Matt to let him know where I was going. He texted me back to be careful and to call for backup if needed, even though it wasn't our jurisdiction. Call first, then explain later. Then he added that he was happy I shared where I was with him.

My fist raised to the door, and before I could second-guess the force of my resolve, I knocked. Three sharp raps—enough to command attention, sufficient to signal I meant business.

Chapter 52

Monica stood in the kitchen, a bastion of warmth and savory aromas. The pot of soup before her, a cauldron of comfort, bubbled gently as she stirred. Her hand was steady, the ladle an extension of her will, swirling through the thickening broth. A contented smile played upon her lips, one that reached the crinkles at the corners of her eyes.

The spoon clinked softly against the sides of the pot, a rhythmic sound that grounded Monica in the moment. Every motion was deliberate, each stir a careful choreography of love translated into culinary form. She assessed the soup's readiness by sight and scent, the rich melding of herbs and vegetables telling her all she needed to know.

With a final swirl that gathered every flavor, Monica placed the ladle on the ceramic rest beside the stove, the delicate chime of wood meeting stone punctuating the end of its journey. Then, with hands that had known both the tenderness of cradling a child and the resolve of weathering life's storms, she grasped the pot's handles, her grip secure yet gentle.

She shifted the weight of the pot from the stove, the

liquid inside offering a silent, rolling protest, and turned the knob with a decisive click. The flame tucked itself away, retreating beneath the iron grate, obedient to her command. Satisfied, she saw the surface of the soup settle, a mirror now calm, reflecting back at her the years of care woven into every meal, every bowl filled, every promise kept.

Monica's gaze wandered from the soup's quiet stillness, drifting across the gleaming countertop. There, amid the daily clutter, a tray caught her eye, its contents meticulously organized. Medication bottles, their labels facing outward, stood like sentinels beside a kaleidoscope of pills.

Her fingers, still warm from the kitchen's heat, reached out. They danced over the plastic caps with practiced ease, pausing at the first vial. With a gentle squeeze and twist, the childproof seal gave way under her insistence. One by one, the capsules and tablets found their way into her palm—oval, round, some oblong—each shape a testament to the care prescribed by doctors.

She lined them up, a tiny regiment awaiting their call to duty. Each pill was a promise, a vow to maintain the strength needed for the days ahead, for the love yet to be given.

"Can't forget you," she said, a hint of affection in her voice as she plucked the last tablet, white and innocuous yet vital as a heartbeat. It joined its companions, completing the array, a colorful mosaic of survival and determination.

The kitchen lights cast a soft glow on Monica's face as her eyes glazed over, not seeing the tray of pills but instead a sunlit past. A young boy with hair the color of autumn leaves laughed as he chased bubbles across the lawn, his small hands reaching up to the sky.

"Look, Mommy! I'm gonna catch the rainbow!"

"Be careful, Stevie!" Her voice was light, threaded with laughter as her heart swelled like the summer clouds above.

"Got one!" he squealed, triumphantly holding up a glistening sphere, his reflection mirrored in the iridescent surface.

"Always my brave boy," she murmured, the memory as vivid as if it were unfolding before her now.

The clack of the pill bottle closing snapped Monica back to the present. The kitchen was silent, save for the tick of the clock, marking both the passage of time and the weight of her promise. Steven, her brave boy, had left more than memories; he'd entrusted her with his most precious treasure.

"Victoria needs me," she said to no one, her resolve hardening like the set of her jaw. She would be the fortress against the world's chaos, just as she had been for him. For her granddaughter, she would be a sanctuary, a place of love and safety, where no harm could breach the walls she built with care.

Monica's lips parted gently, a soft melody weaving through the silence of the kitchen. The tune was familiar and warm, a lullaby once sung under starry skies to a wide-eyed child who clung to her every note. Now, the hum flowed from her with the same tenderness, a musical thread binding the past to the present.

"Everything's going to be just right," she whispered into the steam rising from the soup, her voice mixing with the tune. The melody curled around her, infusing the room with the echo of her joy, the contentment that came with the sacred duty of care.

With each hum, the weight of the tray in her hands felt lighter. Her fingers wrapped around the edges, securing the ceramic plate beside a steaming bowl, its contents promising warmth and comfort. She navigated the path toward Victoria's bedroom, each footstep measured and deliberate, a dance of precision born from years of practice.

"Steady now," she murmured to herself, eyes fixed on the hallway ahead, the humming a constant companion. The rhythm in her chest matched the cadence of her feet as Monica crossed the threshold. The promise she carried was reflected in the careful balance of nourishment and love upon the tray.

"Victoria, love, dinner's ready," Monica's voice caressed the air, a soft call weaving through the hall's stillness. The warmth in her words was a gentle embrace, an affectionate nudge against the silence that blanketed the house.

"Vicky?" she tried again, a note of playfulness threading into her tone as she neared the door, her heart sending out waves of care with each syllable. She pictured Victoria's bright eyes, the way they'd light up, the shared smiles that seasoned their meals with more than just herbs and spices.

Monica's hand, a delicate shadow against the wood, paused on the doorknob. The hum of anticipation buzzed in her ears, a silent drumroll for the moment of reveal. Her fingers tightened, feeling the cool metal beneath them, and with a breath held tight in her chest, she pushed.

The door swung open, easing into the quiet room beyond. A sliver of space widened and grew, inviting her in with the promise of what lay inside.

"Victoria?" The name floated into the room, a feather drifting on a breeze of hope and worry, painting the air with anticipation.

Monica's breath hitched. The room—Victoria's sanctuary—was silent. Too silent. The gentle creak of the opening door seemed to thunder in the stillness.

"Victoria?" she called again, her voice now a sharp note slicing through the quiet. No response. The warmth drained from her tone, replaced by an edge of urgency that had no place in this nightly ritual.

She stepped inside, the tray balanced with practiced poise. Something was off. Her eyes darted, catching fragments of the room.

"Victoria?" The word shattered, splintering into silence.

Monica's fingers loosened their hold involuntarily, the tray tilting, a slow-motion dance of china and silver. It slipped from her numb grasp, the clatter of dishes exploding against the hush like a clap of thunder, soup splashing onto the carpet in a wild arc of amber.

The shock rooted her to the spot, the echo of broken porcelain filling the room, rebounding off walls that should've bounced back laughter, not this hollow sound of distress.

"But it's... that's impossible...."

Her granddaughter's bed was empty, the sheets still crumpled, the pillow devoid of the little head that should've been denting it. Her wheelchair was by the side of the bed. The girl hadn't been able to walk for years.

A chill crept up Monica's spine, whispering dread into her ear.

Where in the world was Victoria?

Chapter 53

Rapping sharply on the door, I waited for Adam's response. Silence hugged the air, thick and unyielding. A second attempt, louder this time. Nothing. Hand steady, I reached out, grasping the doorknob. It turned with ease, a silent invitation into the unknown.

"Federal Bureau of Investigation!" My voice boomed through the open doorway, slicing the quiet. "I'm coming in!"

Stepping over the threshold, my senses sharpened. Eyes darting, gun held in a practiced grip by my side, I advanced, every nerve tingling with the possibility of what lay ahead.

The air felt cold in the house, the kind that seeps into your bones and settles there. I walked, my steps measured and heavy, toward the foot of the stairs where Nicki's life had spilled out onto the polished wood. The stain was still there, a darker patch that whispered of the violence it had witnessed. My chest tightened, my heart sinking as I stopped at the edge of the scene.

I thought about the suitcase they had found by the stairs,

packed with her belongings. It didn't make sense. The pieces didn't fit.

"You were leaving... not ending," I muttered to the silence, trying to piece together the shattered logic of it all. She'd been planning something, going somewhere.

"Why were you running, Nicki?" I asked the empty room, knowing no answer would come but asking nonetheless.

I started with the living room, eyes scanning for anything out of place. Dust settled on picture frames—memories frozen in time, smiles that hadn't faded even as the people in them had.

"Focus," I whispered to myself.

The kitchen next. Dishes piled up in the sink. Upstairs, the hallway was silent, save for the soft creaking of floorboards beneath my feet. Bedroom doors ajar, begging me to delve into their secrets.

"Adam?" No answer came. I didn't expect one.

Their bedroom felt hollow. I flicked on the light, squinting against the sudden brightness. My gaze swept from corner to corner, hungering for a clue, a sign, anything.

"Nothing? Really?" My frustration simmered. Then I saw it —the slightly open closet door beckoning. I approached with my heart drumming a steady beat of anticipation.

"All right, let's see what you're hiding."

Hangers clinked together, too many empty spaces where Adam's clothes should have been. Shirts, jackets, pants—all gone. A neat freak like Adam leaving his wardrobe gutted? It churned my stomach. Unease crept in, and suspicion bloomed.

"Where'd you go, Adam? Running or chasing?"

I ran my fingers along the vacant rods, each empty hanger an accusation, a question left hanging in the air.

The vibration in my pocket jolted me from the emptiness of Adam's closet. I fished out my phone, eyes still roving over the barren wardrobe.

"Agent Thomas speaking."

"Agent, it's Monica—Victoria's grandmother." Her voice trembled like a leaf in a storm, each word heavy with dread. "She's... she's gone."

My pulse skipped. Gone? I crossed to the window, peering out as if Victoria might magically appear on the lawn below.

"Monica, slow down for me. What do you mean 'gone'?"

"Her bed—it's empty," Monica gasped between shallow breaths. "I went to check on her, and she's not there. Her wheelchair... it's just sitting there like she vanished into thin air!"

"Okay, Monica. I'm here; I'm listening." My hand tightened around the phone. "Did you see or hear anything unusual tonight?"

"Nothing! We both took a nap. I just woke up and... and...." She trailed off, the sound of her panic replaced by the quiet sobbing of a woman unmoored by fear.

"Stay where you are," I instructed firmly. I was already moving toward the stairs, my mind shifting gears.

"Please," she whispered. "Her medication," Monica's voice crackled through the phone, "she can't miss a dose."

"Understood." The words were sharp, clipped with urgency. I paced, feeling the weight of every second slipping by.

"Find her," Monica pleaded.

"Doing everything I can," I assured her, though my gaze was locked outside, searching for a sign, any clue to latch onto.

That's when I saw them through the windowpane, Adam and Sarah, their silhouettes huddled together in the house next door. Their proximity was too close, and their body language was too tense. Suspicion coiled within me like a spring.

"Monica," I said, keeping my voice level while my eyes tracked Sarah and Adam's every move, "I need you to stay calm. Can you do that for me?"

"I'll try," she breathed out, the quiver in her voice betraying her terror.

"Good." My hand hovered above my gun as I took in Sarah's furtive glance and Adam's hurried whisper. Something wasn't right. I could feel it in my bones.

"Agent Thomas?" Monica's anxious tone broke through my focus.

"Stay put, Monica. I'm on it." With those words, I ended the call, my resolve hardening like ice. It was time for a little visit next door.

I slipped the phone back into my pocket. My gaze flickered once more to the window, to the shadows moving within the neighboring house.

It was time to act. Quick, measured steps took me from the room, instincts honed from years in the field guiding my movements. Every sense was alert, every muscle primed for what was to come.

Adam and Sarah, I had questions, and they were going to give me answers, whether they liked it or not.

I pushed through Adam's front door, a careful silence wrapping around me as it closed. Sarah's house loomed next door, its windows dark, secrets tucked behind the curtains. I moved swiftly, feet barely whispering against the concrete.

My eyes swept left to right, once and twice. There were no signs of life or of Victoria.

"Watch yourself," I muttered under my breath.

Closer now, I spotted the wheelchair ramp winding up to

Sarah's front porch, an empty testament to accessibility and care. It was too still, too vacant. The hairs on my neck rose. Suspicion pulsed in my veins.

I was steps away from the door when a shape shifted inside. My hand found the gun at my hip, fingers brushing cold metal. Not yet—not until I have to.

"Sarah!" My voice was firm and controlled. "Adam! Open up."

Silence greeted me first, then the sound of a lock disengaging. The door cracked open, a sliver of light cutting through the growing darkness.

"Evening, Agent." Sarah's voice was smooth, too smooth. "What brings you here?"

"Victoria's missing," I said, watching her face for any flicker, any tell. "Have you seen her?"

"Missing?" She looked surprised. "What do you mean missing?"

"Mind if I come in?" I didn't wait for an answer, stepping past her into the dimly lit hallway. My senses were on high alert, every shadow a potential hiding place, every creak a whispered secret.

"Of course," Sarah replied, but her tone was tight. She knew I wasn't just there for pleasantries.

"Look, if you're suggesting—" Sarah started, but I cut her off with a raised hand.

"Where's Victoria, Sarah?" This time, my question was a blade, sharp and direct. "And Adam? He was here a minute ago. I saw you two. Kissing. You're having an affair, the two of you?"

Her eyes flinched, guilt flickering like a shadow across her face.

"Agent, I swear, I don't—"

"Save it." I started moving again, each step purposeful, closing the distance between suspicion and truth. "We can do this the easy way or the hard way."

"Easy," she whispered, her resolve crumbling. "Please."

"Then, start talking." I leaned in, my presence filling the space, leaving no room for lies.

Chapter 54

THEN:

THE BOTTLE of wine felt like a grenade in Sarah's grasp, her knuckles whitening as she seized it from the counter. It was a silent kitchen accomplice to her seething rage. With a swift twist, the cork surrendered, releasing a soft pop that echoed mockingly throughout the room. She slammed it down, her breaths shallow and ragged, the anger churning inside her like a storm.

"Come on; come on," she muttered, sloshing the dark liquid into the glass with more force than necessary. The crimson swirl promised a reprieve, a momentary ally against the onslaught of emotions warring within her.

Sarah wrapped her lips around the glass, tipping it back, the wine cascading down her throat in a fiery trail. She welcomed the burn and let it spread through her chest, imagining it as liquid courage pooling in her heart, steeling it for what was to come.

"Steven," she hissed under her breath, the name a curse, a battle cry. Her mind's eye painted the upcoming confrontation with vivid strokes, each thought another layer of determination lacquered onto her resolve. He had pushed her to this edge, and she teetered there now, fueled by wrath and the heavy blanket of betrayal that had settled over her shoulders.

She took another gulp, larger this time, the glass barely leaving her lips before she refilled it. Sarah could picture him, could almost feel the weight of his deceit filling the space around her, suffocating her. Her hand shook, not from the alcohol but from the sheer intensity of her fury.

"Tonight, Steven," she whispered into the empty room, "tonight, you'll hear me."

The screech of rubber on the aluminum ramp tore through the silence, a harbinger of the storm to come. Sarah's spine stiffened, a primal alertness seizing her senses. The wine glass, now a fragile grenade in her grasp, threatened to shatter with the tension that gripped her.

"Steven," she whispered venomously, the name searing her tongue.

She hurled herself toward the door, her pulse hammering a frenetic cadence against her temples. With a swift motion born of rage rather than grace, she flung the door open and was met with the sight of him.

"Sarah," Steven began, but his voice was drowned out by the cacophony of her own heartbeats.

The wine, an unintended traitor, betrayed her resolve with its scent clinging to her breath. His eyes narrowed, the familiar accusation already forming on his lips before it sliced through the thick air between them.

"You've been drinking again, Sarah," he spat, the words cloaked in a bitter frost that could chill the warmth from any room.

Her voice, when it came, was a quivering blade—a tremble that betrayed both fury and anguish.

"How dare you accuse me?" she retorted, the irony of his judgment a slap to her face. Her hand, still clutching the glass, shook, not from the alcohol coursing through her veins but from the sheer force of betrayal that had compelled her here to this precipice where civility crumbled away like a cliffside under siege.

"Look at you, Steven," she continued, her voice climbing as though it could scale the walls of his indifference, "always so quick to judge."

The air hung heavy with unspoken histories, the silence a taut wire strung with years of grievances unvoiced and wounds unhealed. The standoff, a tragic dance of two silhouettes cast against the dying light, held the promise of a storm on the brink of eruption.

"Enough!" Sarah's shout echoed, her body a coiled spring released as she lunged for Steven. The glass slipped from her grasp, shattering on the floor, a crystal echo to their discord.

"Get off me!" Steven's arms flailed, seeking to ward her off, but determination had given Sarah reckless strength.

"Admit it!" Her hands found his shirt, twisting the fabric in a vise grip. "You think you're better than me?"

"Sarah, stop this madness!" Steven's voice was strained, his attempts to remain calm crumbling beneath her onslaught.

Their bodies crashed together with a force that shook the pictures on the wall, a testament to the ferocity of pain and anger. Grunts punctuated each movement as they struggled, an intimate ballet of rage.

"Let go!" he demanded, his words muffled against her shoulder as they fell to the floor, a tangle of limbs and resentment.

"Never," she hissed, her fingers digging into his flesh, searching for the truth in a way words never could.

A picture frame hit the floor beside them, glass splintering like ice underfoot. They were heedless of the chaos, of the shards that mirrored their shattered relationship, of the world beyond their private war.

"Sarah...." Steven's protest was cut short as they rolled, the ground unsteady beneath them.

"Say it!" Each word was a hammer strike, her resolve as unyielding as the hardwood floor beneath them.

"Enough," he gasped, but it wasn't surrender that edged his voice—it was something else, something darker.

"Get off!" Steven's breath was hot and ragged against her cheek, his voice desperate.

"Never," Sarah spat back, her hands clawing at him as they grappled on the floor. The taste of iron and sweat mingled in her mouth, a bitter cocktail of their struggle.

"Sarah! Please!" Steven's voice now had a pleading note that she would have found satisfying if not for the consuming fury that drove her every action.

"Shut up!" she snarled, her fingers finding his throat.

From outside, the distant wail of sirens sliced through the cacophony of their conflict. They were noise without meaning, a background score to the crescendo of their fight.

"Police," Steven choked out, his eyes widening with the realization.

"Police!" echoed a shrill cry from beyond the walls—the neighbor, no doubt, having borne witness to their strife.

"Damn it, Sarah!" Panic edged Steven's words as he struggled beneath her grip. "We need to stop!"

"Too late for that," she hissed, but the growing volume of the sirens penetrated her haze of anger. Blue and red flashes danced across the air, a disco of impending doom.

Her heart hammered against her ribcage like a bird desperate for escape. Her mind screamed at her: stop, think. But her body was a creature of its own, fueled by betrayal and hurt.

"Sarah, listen!" Steven's voice broke through, insistent and scared. "Please."

The urgency in his tone finally reached her, a cold splash of reality against the heat of her rage. She released him abruptly, both of them panting, staring at each other as the sirens grew deafeningly close.

"God, what have I done?" She scrambled back, her hands shaking as she wiped her mouth. Her chest heaved with the weight of her actions, her thoughts racing to assemble some semblance of defense.

"Sarah, it's over," Steven said quietly, struggling to sit up. His face was etched with pain and resignation. "It has to be."

She knew he was right. The sirens were a herald of consequences, a reminder that the world outside would hold them accountable for what happened within these four walls.

"Steven, I—" Her plea was cut short by the sound of car doors slamming, heavy footsteps approaching, the inevitable closing in.

"Save it," Steven muttered, his gaze fixed on the door as if, by sheer will, he could delay the intrusion.

The blue and red lights painted the room in stark, alternating strokes, highlighting the disarray, the scattered remnants of their life together. There was no time left—only the reckoning that awaited them both.

The door shattered the silence, an explosion of wood and authority as it flew open. Black uniforms surged into the chaos of Sarah's house, a storm of order clamping down on the tempest she had become.

"Police! Hands where I can see them!" The command was all-encompassing, brooking no argument.

Two officers, their badges glinting with purpose, closed in. One gripped Steven's arm, easing him away from Sarah's reach. The other, a stern-faced woman with an unyielding grip, took hold of Sarah's wrists, pulling her hands behind her back.

"Ma'am, you need to calm down!" She was firm and professional but not unkind.

Sarah struggled against the cuffs snapping shut, the cold metal a stark contrast to the heat of her boiling blood. "I didn't do anything wrong!"

"Easy," the officer said, guiding her with a practiced hand.

And then they saw them—the scratches on Steven's face and throat.

“We're taking this one in,” the officer said, looking at Sarah.

"Steven!" Sarah called out, her voice breaking. Her eyes searched for his, seeking some semblance of understanding, begging him to explain this wasn't how it was supposed to end.

"Sarah, stop resisting," the officer warned as they led her through the remnants of her life, now strewn across the floor like so many forgotten dreams.

"No, you don't understand!" Her protests were met with the resolute faces of law enforcement, faces that had seen this scene play out a hundred times over. Faces that didn't know her story, her pain, or her love.

"Please, just listen to me!" Her plea echoed off the walls, a desperate cry swallowed by the finality of the moment.

"Keep moving," the officer instructed, her voice devoid of emotion.

"Steven!"

"Never show your face here again, Sarah," Steven's voice cut through the chaos like a knife, sharp and cold. His eyes were two flints, sparking with anger as they bore into her. "You're nothing but a drunk."

His words stung, venomous, branding her with an accusation that made her insides churn. Sarah felt a sob claw its way up her throat, but she swallowed it down, refusing to give him the satisfaction.

"Steven, please—" Her voice was a whisper, a futile attempt to reach whatever shred of compassion he might have had left.

The officer's hands were firm on her shoulders, propelling her toward the door, but it was his dismissal that shoved her out into the night. The porch light cast long shadows, stretching out like fingers trying to pull her back inside, back to a life now crumbling around her.

"I'm not a drunk!" She hurled the words over her shoulder, hoping they would pierce through his armor of disdain. But they seemed to dissolve in the air, powerless against the fortress he had built around himself.

Sarah's feet stumbled over the threshold as the officers escorted her down the steps, her resistance ebbing away with each step. The sirens had quieted, leaving only the sound of her ragged breaths and the distant hum of the city.

"Listen to me; I didn't do anything!" Her protests were faint now, the fight draining from her voice as the reality of her situation settled in like a heavy shroud.

"Move along, ma'am," one of the officers said, devoid of emotion, just another voice in the cacophony of her downfall.

As the police car swallowed her up, Sarah's pleas became muffled, the steel door muffling her cries of innocence. And then, with a finality that echoed in her very bones, Steven slammed the front door shut, severing the last thread connecting her to the home she once knew.

"Steven...." Her voice was nothing more than a whisper lost to the night as the car pulled away, leaving behind the shattered remains of what was meant to be a sanctuary.

Inside, Steven stood alone, the silence enveloping him like a cloak. The aftermath of their confrontation lay scattered around him—a broken vase, a spilled glass, a love that had turned into something unrecognizable. He had won the battle, but at what cost?

Chapter 55

The air felt electric, charged with a heaviness that clung to my skin. The room was still, too still, as if the house itself held its breath. My gaze locked on Sarah, her eyes wide and darting between Adam and me. Adam had come out from his hiding place. His presence was like a shadow, silent but weighing down every inch of the space behind her.

"Sarah," I said, my voice low and steady despite the drumbeat of my heart, "I know. I know why you did what you did to him—the day they cuffed you and took you away. I read about it in your file. You were charged with domestic violence. But you had reason to attack him. It wasn't the affair since you were both guilty of that. It was something else, but no one would listen to you, especially not because you were drunk."

Her lips parted slightly, a tremor passing through them that betrayed her façade of calm. She blinked rapidly, once, twice, a flicker of confusion before she masked it with a forced stillness.

"Wh-what are you talking about?" Her words came out in a whisper, barely pushing past the tension that seemed to thicken with each passing second.

"Steven," I pressed on, my resolve hardening. I know the truth about that day. It has to be why you attacked him—because you found out what he had done."

I held her gaze steady and unflinching. There was a moment—the briefest flicker of fear in her eyes before she masked it again with confusion.

"How do you know?" Her voice cracked around the edges, a picture of vulnerability wrapped in a veneer of strength.

"Journals." I leaned in closer, my words deliberate, piercing the veil of uncertainty that hung between us. "Medical journals—originals and altered ones."

"Altered?" Sarah's brows furrowed, a crease forming as if her mind was racing to catch up with the pieces I laid out before her.

I nodded, the grim reality settling like dust in the silence that followed. "I found them at Dr. Hancock's house," I continued, letting each word sink in. "Dr. Pete Hancock. He had them on a flash drive."

Recognition sparked in her eyes, and a connection was made. She knew what had happened to him; we all did.

"Someone killed him too," she whispered, the word hanging heavy in the air.

"Those journals," I said, my voice slicing through the stillness, "they were tampered with... pages replaced, dates altered. Replaced with false diagnoses." I paced a tight circle on the worn carpet, each step punctuating my words. "They fed us Steven's narrative, Sarah. But Victoria—she was in remission. Years ago."

Sarah's hands knotted together, white-knuckled as if holding onto the last shred of a reality she thought she knew.

I stopped pacing and turned to face her squarely. "Victoria should've been thriving, not... not like this."

"I know," she murmured, her voice barely audible. She looked up, her eyes searching mine for a flicker of deceit. Finding none, something within her seemed to break. "I found something, too." Her voice was stronger now, tinged with anger and hurt. "On the day he threw me out. A bag of medication. Steven brought it home from the hospital."

"Medication?" I prompted, though I felt the truth clawing its way to the surface.

"Drugs he used on Victoria." Sarah's breath hitched, her control fraying at the edges. "To make her sick. To keep her looking ill."

"Christ," I exhaled sharply, the pieces clicking into place. There it was—the ugly truth laid bare between us.

"Steven played us all," I added softly, my gaze fixed on her. "He was a sick man. I had to look into it, but it's a reality. It's not just women who suffer from Munchausen by proxy," I said firmly, taking a step toward her. "Men can harbor that same twisted need to be needed, to orchestrate sickness."

Her eyes, wide with the horror of understanding, remained locked on mine.

"It's a disease? I didn't know what was wrong with Steven," she whispered, the name a poison on her lips.

"It is."

I reached out, placing my hand gently on her shoulder. The tremor beneath my fingers spoke volumes. "He took control by making Victoria ill—playing the doting husband. She was sick as a young child; she had leukemia, but he enjoyed the attention so much that he hid from you that she was actually in remission a few years later. He kept making her sick to get the attention he craved from doctors and nurses when taking her to the hospital. The seizures and the unusual reactions and symptoms that they couldn't quite diagnose were all from the medication he was poisoning her with. And he kept you away from her to remain in control."

"Control…." The word seemed to shatter in her mouth, fragments of the life she thought she had known scattering like glass. "That's why he was always there, always…."

"Playing the caretaker," I finished for her. "While all along, he was the cause."

Her frame shook as if the ground beneath her feet had given way. A sob clawed its way up from the depths of her being, a raw sound that resonated with the pain of betrayal. She looked away, her chest rising and falling in jagged rhythms.

"I was so certain when I found those meds that he was making her sick on purpose, but I thought I had to be crazy for thinking like that," Sarah gasped, the reality of it hitting her like a physical blow. "The appointments, the treatments… It was all him."

"All him," I confirmed, the bitterness of the truth tasting like ash. "You weren't crazy."

"I tried to tell everyone, but no one would listen. I tried everything for Victoria…." Her voice broke, the name of her daughter wrapped in layers of guilt and sorrow.

"Victoria was a pawn in his sickness." My voice felt distant and clinical, even as anger seethed within me.

Sarah's face crumpled, and she collapsed into herself, a small, broken figure consumed by the enormity of what she knew. With each ragged breath, she grappled with a reality that had been manipulated beyond recognition—a life torn apart by the man she had vowed to love and trust.

"Steven…." Tears streaked down her cheeks, her body convulsing with sobs that had been held back for far too long.

"Sarah," I crouched before her, my hand finding hers and squeezing tight. "We'll make this right—for you and Victoria."

Adam's shadow loomed over us, a silent sentinel to our charged exchange. His eyes never left Sarah, sharp and calculating, as if trying to piece together a puzzle only he could see.

"Sarah," I began, my voice steady despite the vortex of emotions swirling in the cramped living room. "I've seen what he's done—the lies he's woven into the very fabric of your lives."

Her eyes, red-rimmed and wide, lifted to meet mine. "No one has believed me before."

"The evidence doesn't lie, Sarah. The journals, the medications—he manipulated them all to paint a picture that served his narrative."

A shiver ran down her spine, and Adam shifted his weight behind her, a wordless gesture that seemed to tether her to the here and now.

"Everything points to Steven, not you." My words cut through the thick air, each syllable a promise. "I will not stop until everyone sees that. Until Victoria gets the life she deserves, free from this... this charade."

"Can we really expose him? After everything?" Doubt shadowed her face, but beneath it, a spark of something fierce flickered to life—a mother's protective rage, perhaps, or the dawning realization of empowerment.

"Trust me," I said, and it was more than reassurance; it was a vow. "We have the truth on our side. And I'm not just going to sit back and watch an innocent person suffer for crimes they didn't commit. I know you didn't kill him, even though you had the motive."

Adam's presence was a quiet force, his breathing a steady counterpoint to Sarah's uneven gasps. He didn't speak, didn't need to. His vigil spoke volumes.

"Thank you for believing me," Sarah's voice broke into a whisper, barely audible over the storm brewing outside. Her eyes, misted with unshed tears, locked onto mine, a silent testament to her fragile state. "I thought I was alone in this."

"You're not alone," I replied firmly, squeezing her hand. "I'm here now, and we're going to fix this mess."

Her nod was almost imperceptible, but it carried the weight of her world—a world turned upside down and shaken until all she thought she knew spilled out like loose change from a pocket.

"Sarah, whatever it takes, we will—"

"That night," she said. "The night Steven died, I had... I just couldn't stand it anymore. I knew he had her in the house with him and that he was poisoning her. I kept thinking of all the seizures, all the times he had taken her to the hospital because she was unresponsive. And all the attention he always got from it, from our families and friends, who always felt so sorry for him because he was the caretaker. And it was all a lie? And he was still doing it to her? I couldn't take it, so I fell off the wagon and had a drink. I had to try and stop him. And maybe, if someone else hadn't killed him, well...."

"Don't think like that," I said. "You're not a murderer."

"But I was happy that he was dead," she said. "And that made me feel bad."

"You can't blame yourself for"

The click of the door handle cut me off mid-sentence, snapping our focus to the room's entrance. Time seemed to stutter as the door inched open, the ominous creak mingling with the howl of the wind.

"Who's there!" Adam's voice, finally breaking its silence, was sharp and commanding.

Instinctively, we turned to look just as a figure stepped through the threshold, a gun clasped in their unsteady grip, the barrel glinting ominously in the dim light. My heart slammed against my ribs, each beat a drumroll in the tense silence that followed.

Chapter 56

With my pulse throbbing a frantic rhythm against my ribs, I stared at the figure looming in the doorway. Each heartbeat was a thunderous echo in my ears, drowning out all other sounds. The gun—a stark, terrifying contrast to the dust motes floating in the stagnant air—seemed to draw all the light into its dark, lethal form.

Adam's face blanched, his voice a strangled cry that shattered the stillness. "Oh, dear God," he breathed out, stumbling back a half step.

The intruder stepped forward, the gun unwavering in her grip. She was diminutive, her features soft and unlined, belying a fragility that contrasted sharply with the deadly weapon she brandished. A shock of dark hair framed her face, too young-looking to be called a woman, even though she was one, a young one. Her eyes, though, held a worldliness that no child could possess; they flickered with an intensity that spoke of years beyond her apparent age.

"Put the gun down," Adam's plea sounded weak even to my ears, the desperation clawing at the edges of his composure.

"Victoria?" The name tumbled from Sarah's lips, barely a whisper but slicing through the tension like a blade. Her daughter, the girl she'd lost to shadows and silence, stood there, a ghost made flesh.

"Mom," she cooed, the mocking lilt of her voice wrapping around them all like a chill. "Surprised?"

Sarah crumpled, knees hitting the floorboards with an unforgiving thud, tears betraying her as they streamed down her face. The gun in Victoria's hand, that monstrous extension of her will, seemed to waver for a heartbeat—just long enough for a sliver of hope to pierce my despair.

"Sweet tears, Mom. Genuine, are they?" Victoria's smirk twisted her once angelic features. The mockery stung more than any slap.

"Victoria, all these years... could you walk?" Sarah's voice cracked, a mix of hope and anguish threading through the syllables.

She circled us slowly, gun unwavering, like a shark with its prey. Her eyes met mine, gleaming with an unsettling resolve. I still had my gun and wondered if I could pull it fast enough. I didn't want anyone to be hurt today.

"Oh, Mom," she said, voice dripping with venomous sweetness, "you have no idea."

"Tell me." Sarah's plea was raw.

My heart kept pounding against my ribcage while Sarah was begging for the truth that seemed as elusive as her presence had been all these years.

"Father liked his little secret," she confessed, the word "father" tainted with scorn. "He said I was frail and needed protection. I was sick. But he lied. To everyone."

"Protection?" Adam echoed with disbelief painting his features in broad strokes.

"Control, more like it." Victoria's lips curled into a bitter smile, the gun still pointed with an eerie steadiness. "He made sure I never took a step outside that room. Not until I realized the chains were all just smoke and mirrors."

"Chains?" Sarah repeated. She looked like her world was tilting on its axis as the puzzle pieces of their shattered life refused to fit back together.

"Metaphorical ones, Mom. The kind that bind you deeper than any lock or key ever could." Her gaze held Sarah's, unflinching and resolute, revealing the depth of deception they had been entangled in.

"Victoria, I...." Words failed Sarah; the enormity of the reality—a reality twisted by secrets and lies—threatened to swallow her whole.

"Medicine. Every day, little vials of lies," Victoria spat out the words like they were poison. Her arm didn't waver, the gun a steady reminder of the stakes at play.

"Poison?" Sarah sounded like she was choking.

"Medication I didn't need. Enough to keep me weak in bed... make me too sick to complain or speak my mind." Her eyes flicked away for a fraction of a second, haunted by memories. "Daddy's little invalid."

"Jesus, Sarah." Adam's voice was a tortured whisper. "How come no one found this out?"

"Because he was a master of illusion," Victoria sneered, her finger tightening around the trigger. The mockery of a childhood spent under lock and key was etched in the pallor of her skin, as were the dark circles under her eyes that Sarah had always attributed to her "illness."

"Your doctor visits..." Sarah started, but her voice broke, tears choking the words. "It was all fake."

"He paid them all," she said with chilling calmness. "He

handpicked them to tell you what he wanted you to hear. Dr. Hancock was his closest ally. He'd do anything for money."

"Victoria, I'm so sorry," Sarah sobbed.

"Sorry won't change the past," she shot back, her voice cold as ice.

"Nor will that gun," Adam interjected, his hands raised placatingly.

"Maybe not. But it makes you listen, doesn't it?" There was power in her stance, in the way she held onto her anger like a shield.

The silence that followed was loaded, a ticking bomb with no countdown. We were trapped in the shockwaves of revelation, each truth detonating closer to the core of their family facade. Victoria's betrayal by her father, Sarah's blindness until it was too late, and the neighbor's misplaced trust—the pieces lay scattered, shards too sharp to piece back together without drawing blood.

"Victoria, please," Sarah whispered through tears, the finality of the moment pressing down on us all, "we can help you now."

"Help?" The word came out twisted and unrecognizable. "I don't need help anymore, Mom. I needed it then."

Chapter 57

The room was a charged circuit, each of us a conductor for the surging tension. Sarah's sobs punctured the silence like heartbeats, her shoulders quaking as she knelt on the floor. Adam, a looming figure wrought with anguish, placed a tentative hand upon her heaving back. His eyes, two dark pools reflecting a storm of emotions, never left Victoria.

"Please, Victoria," he implored, voice thick with desperation. "Why did Nicki have to die?"

Victoria stood statuesque, the gun in her hand an extension of her unwavering resolve. Her arm didn't tremble, but her eyes betrayed a storm that threatened to shatter her cool exterior. The weapon felt impossibly heavy in the space between us.

"Adam...." Her voice broke, then steadied like a ship righting itself after a rogue wave. "You don't understand."

"Help me understand!" Adam's plea sliced through the stale air. "Help me see why she deserved this!"

I held my breath, afraid to move or to speak—afraid of breaking the delicate balance that kept us all alive in this moment. My heart drummed a frantic rhythm against my ribs, a silent prayer that no one would crack under the strain.

"Nicki was everything to me," Adam continued, the words tumbling out, a torrent of pain and confusion. "And now she's gone because of what? Some twisted sense of justice?"

"Justice?" Victoria's laugh was hollow, void of any true humor. "You think this is about justice?"

"Then tell me what it's about!" Adam's voice rose, a crescendo of grief and fury.

Sarah's cries softened, a low moan of fear as the standoff stretched taut. I could almost see the threads of our fates, interwoven and fraying, ready to snap. Every muscle in my body tensed, prepared to leap into action or brace for impact.

"Because I can't make sense of any of this without her," Adam finished, his voice barely above a whisper, raw and exposed. “I loved her even though she betrayed me. I betrayed her, too.”

Victoria's finger hovered over the trigger, her resolve flickering like a candle in the wind.

"Victoria, stop!" The words burst from me, shrill and desperate, as I pushed myself off the wall. "You're not thinking this through!"

She whirled to me, the gun wavering between Adam and my direction. Sarah's sobs hitched in her throat, a silent witness to the madness unfurling before her.

"It wasn’t because of the affair," I looked at Adam, my voice steadier than my trembling hands. "She knew."

Confusion marred Adam's face. "What are you talking about?"

"Steven," I said, spitting out the name like it was poison. "Nicki knew about him... about the abuse. She saw him and what he did. She knew, and she did nothing. Out of love, perhaps, to protect him, or maybe even fear. We'll never know."

"She did nothing?" Adam's mouth hung open, disbelief etching his features.

"Nothing," I repeated with a nod, the weight of the truth anchoring me to the spot.

"But... I loved her. Nicki loved me despite everything," Adam whispered, more to himself than to us. But his eyes searched mine for a lie that wasn't there. "I thought I knew her?"

"Love has blind spots," I murmured, knowing how hollow it would sound to his ears.

"Shut up!" Victoria's shout echoed off the walls, her grip on the gun tightening. "I did it. I killed her. I killed my dad and the doctor."

Sarah let out a loud shriek.

"No," I countered, shaking my head, feeling the certainty of my own conviction. "You didn't."

"Yes, I did."

I shook my head. "No, you didn't. You were too weak to be able to do it. You'd been poisoned for years. You were bedridden and feeble. You could barely walk after years of not using your muscles. The real killer helped you get back on your feet after killing your dad, her only son. She nursed you back, and now you stand here in front of us, finally strong enough. She was scared we were figuring out the truth, and she confided in you. That's why you told me you heard Adam's voice that night—to remove focus. And then your mother was released and tried to contact you. You knew we had figured out it wasn't Sarah. So you decided to grab the gun and sneak out. Your plan was to find me and confess. To protect her. Because she had done so much for you, she was the only person who cared enough actually to do something to help you. And you feel like you owe her. But you don't deserve to be in another prison, Victoria. What was done to you wasn't your fault."

"Victoria," Sarah said, crying. "What she is saying is true. You deserve your freedom. Please, Victoria, don't do anything stupid now."

A tear escaped Victoria's eyes, and she didn't wipe it away. She looked at her mother, who stood and reached out both arms. "Victoria. I'm sorry. You don't know how sorry I am."

A sniffle emerged from Victoria, and then violent sobs broke out, causing her torso to tremble. "Mo-om... I...."

Victoria's grip slackened, and the gun fell with a clatter to the floor. The absence of the weapon's threat filled the room with a sudden, heavy silence.

"Victoria!" Sarah's urgent cry cut through the stillness as she leaped forward and grabbed her daughter, who deflated in her arms. She wrapped her arms around Victoria, pulling her close. Their bodies shook with sobs that spoke of betrayal and pain intermingled with relief.

I stood there, watching them, the bond between the two women unspoken but undeniable. Healing had begun through tears and broken breaths, but so had our real hunt—for truth and justice.

Chapter 58

The wheel spun under my grip, a sharp pivot that cut through the hum of routine. My foot pressed harder on the gas, urgency bleeding into the motion as the car veered off course. The therapy center sign became a blur in the rearview mirror, shrinking behind us.

"Hey!" Matt's voice, laced with confusion and concern, broke the silence. "Where are you taking us?"

"Shortcut," I lied, not meeting his gaze.

We passed the familiar storefronts and street corners, all drowned in the golden wash of a morning sun desperate to pierce through gathering clouds. Then, without warning, I swung the car onto a gravel-lined path, the tires crunching a staccato against the loose stones.

"Since when is a cemetery a shortcut to physical therapy?" Matt said, his voice rising an octave. He gripped the dashboard, knuckles white.

"Trust me." The words came out terse, my focus narrowing.

I pulled up beside a wrought-iron fence, overgrown with ivy, the shadows of the headstones stretching like fingers across the ground. Killing the engine, I grabbed the keys and flung open the door. Matt reached for my arm, a silent plea etched into the lines of his face.

"Eva Rae, what are you doing?" His eyes searched mine, looking for the plan, the method in the madness.

"Stay here," I commanded, more forcefully than I intended. "I'll be right back."

"Right back? You can't just—" But I was already outside, slamming the door shut on his protests.

"Matt, please." I leaned down, meeting his bewildered gaze through the window. "Just wait for me."

"Fine," he grumbled, though his fingers drummed an anxious rhythm on the dashboard.

"Thank you." A hollow thanks, but it was all I could offer before turning away.

I didn't look back as I strode toward the sea of stone and marble, leaving him alone with the idling hum of the vehicle and the unspoken tensions that hung between us like ghosts.

Gravel crunched under my sneakers, the solemn rows of gravestones passing in a blur. My breath came in short gasps, misting in the chilly air as I wound my way through the cemetery's silent occupants. Ahead, a solitary figure hunched over a grave, shoulders shaking with quiet sobs.

"Monica," I called softly, not wanting to startle her more than necessary.

She jerked upright, turning toward me with red-rimmed eyes. "Eva Rae? How did you know?"

"Your house... it's swarming with cops and empty." I knelt beside her on the damp grass, ignoring the cold seeping through the fabric of my pants. "This place," I gestured around us, "your son's grave seemed like somewhere you might go."

Monica's gaze dropped, her fingers tracing the engraved name on the stone before her. "I had nowhere else."

"Understood." My voice was low and steady despite the adrenaline that still coursed through me. I kept my eyes locked on hers, searching for something beneath the grief and desperation.

"Monica."

My voice was barely above a whisper, the cemetery's silence amplifying the weight of my question. "Why did you kill Steven?"

She looked up, her eyes hollow. "My grandchild," she murmured, almost to herself. "He would've destroyed that little girl's life. He already had."

She paused and shook her head.

"Someone had to stop him." Monica's voice grew firmer, her conviction piercing the humid air between us. "And apparently, I was the only one capable enough."

I exhaled slowly, the moral quandary settling like frost over the grass. "I understand why you did it, Monica. But you know I can't just let this go."

Her head bowed, a nod acknowledged the inevitable. "I know, Eva Rae."

"Come on." I offered my hand, palm open and steady. "Let's get you out of here."

Monica's hand trembled as she placed it in mine. With a gentle tug, I helped her to her feet, feeling the weight of her surrender.

The chill of the gravestone's shadow clung to my skin as we moved away, Monica's hand still resting in mine. Her steps were hesitant and unsteady, like she was walking through a nightmare she couldn't wake from.

"Left foot, right foot," I muttered under my breath, a mantra to keep us both grounded. The wind whispered through the leaves above, an audience of ancient oaks and weathered stones to our grim procession.

"Thank you, Eva Rae," she breathed out, her voice quivering with fear and gratitude.

"There really isn't much to thank me for," I replied, eyes scanning the horizon for any onlookers. The cemetery lay deserted, its silence a heavy blanket over us.

A sharp click broke the quiet. My gaze snapped toward the sound, and my heart stuttered.

"Monica, what—?"

"Sorry." Her apology was a ghost of a whisper, her eyes pained. "I can't let myself go to prison."

The gun trembled in her grasp, but her intent was crystal clear. Silver muzzle—a slash of dread—pointed straight at me.

"Monica, don't do this," I pleaded, voice steady despite the thudding of my pulse in my ears.

"I can't be stopped now." There was a finality in her tone, a resignation that chilled me more than the weapon she wielded.

"Think about Victoria," I tried, reaching for the woman who had sacrificed everything already.

"A little late for that."

And then, it happened.

She swung the gun's handle at my head. All I saw was a flash of movement, a blur of regret etched into her features, and then pain exploded across my temple. The world tilted, a kaleidoscope of color as I crumpled, the damp earth rushing to meet me.

Distantly, I heard the rustle of footsteps retreating. Blood warmed the side of my face, a stark contrast to the chill seeping into my bones. Through the haze of agony, I realized Monica was gone, leaving me alone with the betrayal and the throbbing wound she'd inflicted.

Grit and gravel embedded in my palms, I pushed against the ground. Every pulse sent a fresh wave of agony from the wound on my head. My vision blurred, painting the world in smears of gray and red. But Monica was out there, somewhere beyond the rows of silent stones.

"Monica!" The name wrenched itself from my throat, raw and desperate. There was no answer but the whispering wind.

Legs unsteady as a newborn fawn's, I forced myself upright. Blood snaked down my neck, warm and insistent. I stumbled forward, one step, then another, driven by the need to find her, to end this.

"Come on." It was a mantra, a plea to my own body not to fail me now.

The cemetery gates loomed ahead, iron bars that seemed to mock my sluggish pace. I broke through, gasping for air that did nothing to ease the fire in my lungs or the pounding in my skull.

I got out into the street, and there he was. Matt was standing sentinel on the sidewalk, leaning on one of his crutches, holding the other in the air like a soldier's rifle. Monica lay crumpled on the pavement, one arm twisted beneath her, her chest rising and falling with shallow breaths. The gun she'd brandished lay just out of reach, an ironic twist of fate that left her defenseless.

"Eva Rae?" Concern was etched deep in his voice, his eyes scanning me from head to toe.

"What happened?" The words were thick with urgency.

"I—I tripped her," he said, the corner of his mouth lifting in an attempt at levity despite the situation. "Guess these things are good for more than just walking."

"Tripped her?" A bubble of incredulous laughter escaped me, but it popped as pain ricocheted through my head. “With your crutch?”

"Yeah," Matt nodded, steadying himself. "She was running, and I just... I couldn't let her get away."

"Good man." I reached him, leaning heavily against his sturdy frame. My legs threatened to buckle, but Matt held firm.

"Let’s just hope she stays down long enough for the police to arrive," I murmured, pressing a hand to the back of my head. The world swam, but with Matt's help, I remained on my feet, ready to face whatever came next.

Fumbling for my phone with unsteady hands, I dialed 911. The operator picked up instantly, her calm voice a stark contrast to our ragged breaths.

"Police and an ambulance," I managed to say between gasps. "Suspect apprehended. Officer hurt."

"Location, ma'am?" the voice prompted efficiently.

"Greenwood Cemetery entrance," I replied. The words felt like they were being dragged from my lips. "Send them fast."

"Help is on the way. Can you confirm the suspect is secured?"

"Unconscious," I confirmed, glancing at Monica's still form. "And disarmed."

"Stay on the line, ma'am. Are you able to administer first aid to yourself or the suspect?"

"First aid...." My vision blurred at the edges, dark spots dancing before my eyes. "Not sure—"

"Matt?" I leaned into him, my knees giving out.

"I got you, Eva Rae," he assured, his grip tightening. Just hang on."

"Officers are en route," the operator's voice sounded distant. "Hang tight; help will be there shortly."

"Thanks," I whispered, the darkness creeping closer. "Matt... you really saved the day."

"I always have your back," he murmured, his voice solemn as we waited for the sirens to cut through the graveyard's silence.

Epilogue

ONE WEEK LATER

Chopping. The rhythmic sound of the knife against the cutting board set a beat to my thoughts, each slice a reminder of the normalcy I craved.

"Dinner's almost ready!" My voice carried over the sizzle of vegetables in the pan.

"I'm hungry now, Mom!" Alex shouted back without tearing his eyes from the screen where pixels danced in rapid-fire succession. His fingers moved over the controller, every tap and swipe as precise as the moves I made when disarming a situation—or a suspect. At least, I'd like to think so.

"I'm doing it as fast as I can," I called out, glancing at the clock.

"Look, Mommy!" Angel's voice, bubbly with enthusiasm, pulled me away from the stove. She was on the floor, surrounded by a fortress of multicolored blocks, her small hands deftly placing the final piece on her makeshift castle. "It's our house!"

"Beautiful, honey." I smiled, wiping my hands on the apron before kneeling beside her to admire the creation.

"Careful, don't knock it over," I warned playfully as she beamed up at me, her pride as clear as the sky outside our window.

Alex let out a victorious cheer, snapping us back to his digital world. "Yes! Take that, bad guys!" He pumped a fist in the air.

"Your real-life hero is right here, you know," I said with a chuckle, standing up to stir the pot once more.

"Uh-huh," he mumbled, already lost again in his game, chasing pixelated justice while I stood guard in reality, ensuring the villains we faced could never reach them here. I had faced Detective Ryan and gotten him to admit that he approached my son after school and wrote a threat on my living room wall. He also admitted to following us in his car that night when we went to the hotel. I had reported him, and he was immediately fired.

The simmering pot on the stove filled the kitchen with a hearty aroma, but it was the weight lifting from my shoulders that truly warmed the space. I leaned against the counter, a long-held breath escaping me. Monica had confessed to all three murders, and it still echoed in my mind, her words not just closing a case but locking away the nightmares that had haunted me. Her description of how she had tried to make them all look like suicides by placing the bodies afterward and putting a gun in their hand made a lot of sense. Only, at Steven's house, the gun had slid out of his hand, and the magazine had fallen out after she left. Sarah had arrived and picked it up, shocked at her discovery. The guns, Monica had bought illegally. It was easy for her to slide in and out of houses unseen, as no one found an old woman suspicious. Adam and

Sarah were now together. They had decided to sell both their houses and try to move on together. Adam explained he had been scared when seeing another murder scene on his street. He worried that the police would arrest him because we had been so suspicious of him early in the investigation. That's why he packed and decided to leave. But then Sarah called him while he was staying at a motel where he spent the night, and he decided to go back. He wanted to help her, realizing that running away wasn't the solution.

"Mom, is food ready?" Angel's voice pulled me back to the present, her eyes wide and curious.

"Almost, baby girl," I replied, stirring the stew with more vigor than necessary. The relief felt tangible like the steam rising from the bubbling broth. Each stir was a churn of emotions; every bubble breaking the surface was a tiny celebration. Monica behind bars meant safety and justice served, but most of all, it meant peace for those restless souls she'd wronged in her quest to punish those who had helped her son poison Victoria.

"Good. I'm starving!" she giggled, returning to her blocks, oblivious to the gravity of what had transpired. Her innocence was the purest form of happiness I knew, untainted by the darkness I faced daily.

"Mom, when's dinner? I'm dying here!" Alex called out, his voice cracking in mock desperation from his virtual quest.

"Patience is a virtue, Agent Alex," I teased, glancing at the clock. "Ten more minutes."

"Okay... but I'm holding you to that," he bargained, eyes never leaving the screen.

A glint of sunset reflected off a car window outside. My hands stilled. The sound of an engine cutting out pricked my ears, and curiosity pulled me toward the window.

Matt emerged from the sedan, his tall frame unfolding from the car, a pair of crutches wedged under his arms. He paused, surveying the short trek to our front door with the calculating gaze of a detective scoping a crime scene. Then he took a steady step, leaning on his crutches, followed by another, the metal tips of his crutches clicking against the concrete with rhythmic certainty.

"Daddy!" Angel squealed, abandoning her fortress of colorful blocks to join us at the window.

"Let him concentrate, kids." I held up a hand, but pride swelled within me as I watched Matt navigate his way to us, each step a testament to his determination. His dark hair was tousled, likely from the frustration of rehabilitation exercises. Yet, there was an unmistakable lightness to his movements—a dance between man and crutches that spoke volumes of his progress.

"Look at him go, Mom," Alex breathed out, his usual jest replaced with awe.

"Like a superhero," Angel chimed in, her tiny hands pressed against the glass.

"Exactly," I agreed, my heart thrumming a rapid beat. "Our very own superhero."

"Should we help him with the stairs?" Alex asked, torn between the urge to rush out and the respect for Matt's hard-won independence.

"No, let him do this," I said, my voice barely above a whisper.

We were a silent cheer squad, watching Matt close the distance with unwavering resolve. Each click-clack of the crutches on the path and stairs was a drumbeat pushing away the ghosts of the pain we'd all endured. When his eyes finally met mine through the window, they sparkled with triumph. Then we all ran to the door.

I waved through the open doorway, catching Dan's eye as he backed out of the driveway.

"Thank you!" My words hitched a ride on a gust of wind, hopeful they'd reach him. He nodded, his silhouette framed by the fading sunlight before the car disappeared around the corner.

"Hey there, beautiful."

"Hey, handsome. Good day?"

"Got some good news," he beamed, a boyish grin stretching across his face.

"Share with the class?" I teased, closing the distance between us.

"Prosthetic leg." His words were nearly tripping over each other. "Dan says I'm ready, that I'll be walking on my own two feet sooner than we thought."

"Really?" I couldn't help but feel the excitement bubbling in my chest.

"Really," he affirmed, his confidence infectious. Dan's been talking to the specialist. They're optimistic. They said I've got the grit for it."

"Of course you do." I reached out, running a hand through his tousled hair. "You're unstoppable."

"Seems so." He chuckled, the sound wrapping around me like a warm blanket.

"Unstoppable," I echoed, allowing the word to fill the room and seep into the corners where doubt liked to linger. "That's you."

"Guess I am a superhero, huh?" Matt jested, throwing a glance toward the kids.

"Superhero, indeed." My heart sang.

“I’m actually thinking of going back to work once I’ve gotten used to it.”

"Work? You mean back to the force?" My voice hitched, a note of alarm threading through the question. The sight of him, so full of life and chatter about his new prosthetic, had been a beacon of hope. But this? This was an unforeseen gust, threatening to snuff it out.

"Of course, I mean work." He reached for my hand, giving it a gentle squeeze. "I'm not going to let this," he gestured to his crutches, "keep me from what I love."

"Matt...." The word was a soft exhale, a mother's instinct clashing with the admiration for the man before me. His dedication was one of the things that drew me to him, but at what cost?

"Hey, I'll be careful. Desk duty, promise." His thumb caressed the back of my hand, a soothing rhythm against my racing thoughts.

"Desk duty," I echoed, the words rolling off my tongue with skepticism as my mind conjured images of shootouts and narrow escapes—the very memories that haunted our dreams.

"Cross my heart." Matt's smile was meant as reassurance, but it did little to silence the parade of what-ifs marching through my head.

"Okay." I managed a nod, though it felt like agreeing to let him waltz into a fire. My heart thrummed against my chest, a silent drumbeat of worry.

"Okay?" He searched my face, looking for the truth behind the acquiescence.

"Okay," I repeated, stronger this time. If I knew anything about Matt, it was that holding him back wasn't an option. Not when it came to his calling. Not when it came to serving others. And I was happy to see him smile again.

"Thank you," he whispered, pulling me close. His scent, a mix of determination and aftershave, filled my senses.

"Stay safe," I murmured into his shoulder, allowing myself this one plea.

"Always." His lips pressed against my forehead in a kiss that spoke of promises and battles yet to come.

"Mom, I'm hungry!" Alex's voice cut through my lingering concerns, his small frame dashing past us. Angel's giggles followed, her tiny feet pattering on the hardwood floor as she went in pursuit of her brother.

"Table, guys," I called out, my voice steadier than my nerves felt. The clink of silverware and the shuffle of chairs filled the space, grounding me back to the present.

"Smells good, babe," Matt said, easing himself into his seat with practiced grace despite the crutches propped against the chair.

"Thanks." I placed the last dish on the table, a spread that spoke of normalcy and family routines that we fought so hard to maintain. Christine joined us without looking up from her phone as usual.

"Can I help?" Matt reached out, but I shook my head.

"Sit. You've done enough."

"Peas, please!" Angel's request was more of a song than a sentence. Her hands clapped together in delight as I obliged, spooning bright green orbs onto her plate.

"Did you win your game, champ?" Matt asked, turning toward Alex, who was already shoveling food into his mouth.

"Uh-huh! Beat the boss level!" he mumbled, bits of carrot escaping his lips.

"Awesome!" Matt's enthusiasm matched Alex's, his eyes crinkling at the corners. It was these moments, this effortless bond between them, that sometimes took my breath away. His son Elijah was still with his grandmother, and he was enjoying living there for now and had made a lot of friends in the area where Matt's mother lived, so we had decided to let him stay there for now on the condition that he came here and ate with us at least once a week. He, too, was growing up so fast.

"More peas, Mommy!" Angel chimed in again, oblivious to the weighty conversations that had come before her simple request.

"Of course, sweetheart." I smiled, serving her more, watching as she balanced one pea at a time on her fork with intense concentration.

"Looks like you've got competition, Matt. Our little lady here might just be the next sharpshooter in the family," I teased, glancing at him with an affection that mingled with my lingering worries.

"Hey, I'll take a partner with such focus any day," he chuckled, winking at Angel, who beamed with pride.

"Let's eat up," I encouraged, settling into my chair, the five of us enclosed in the warm light of the dining room, the scent of stew mingling with the lemony tang of freshly steamed vegetables.

I reached across the table, my fingers brushing against Matt's. The roughness of his skin, marked by the ordeals he'd been through, was familiar and comforting in its resilience. I laced my fingers through his, feeling the strength that had once wielded a weapon with precision, now holding onto me with tenderness.

"Hey," I whispered, tugging gently at his hand.

He turned to me, a half-smile playing on his lips, his eyes reflecting the soft light that enveloped us.

"Hey, yourself," he replied, the timbre of his voice grounding me further into the moment.

Our kids' chatter became a distant hum as I leaned in closer, closing the space between us. His breath mingled with mine, a prelude to our lips meeting in a kiss that held the promise of new beginnings and unspoken oaths of love. It was soft yet certain, a silent language only we spoke.

Pulling back slightly, I stared into his eyes, finding an echo of my own happiness.

"We've come so far," I murmured, more to myself than to him.

"Thanks to you," he said, his voice hushed, filled with gratitude and awe.

"Us," I corrected, squeezing his hand, "we're a team, remember?"

"Always," he agreed, the corner of his mouth lifting higher.

Around us, the clinking of cutlery on plates and the murmur of contented conversation all wove together into the tapestry of family life. It was a melody I'd feared losing but now played stronger than ever.

"Mommy, look, I'm using chopsticks!" Alex exclaimed, brandishing his utensils with an exaggerated flourish, rice grains tumbling back onto his plate. He had a thing for anything Japanese lately: cartoons, food, and utensils, so I let him use chopsticks and practice whenever he wanted to.

"Wow, buddy, you're becoming quite the pro," I said with a laugh, turning to share the moment with Matt.

"I wanna do that," Angel piped up, her face alight with the simple joy of being included in her brother's adventures.

"Sure thing, Angie." Alex handed her the sticks and showed her how to hold them. He had come to enjoy his role as big brother, one he wore with pride, while Christine rolled her eyes at them. I had spoken earlier with Olivia, and she was still doing well at college. She said she was coming home the following weekend, and I couldn't wait to see her.

I sat back, my heart brimming over as I absorbed the scene before me: my children growing and thriving, my partner recovering and smiling, and the sense of peace that had seemed so elusive now cradling us gently. This was happiness, not just a fleeting emotion but a state of being woven through the fabric of our everyday lives.

"Family," I whispered, barely audible over the sound of our shared existence.

"Forever," Matt echoed, understanding without needing me to speak louder.

We finished our meal amid laughter and stories, each bite savored, and each glance exchanged a reminder of what we had overcome and what lay ahead. As the last plates were cleared and the children's yawns grew longer, the contentment within me swelled. I was home, truly home, surrounded by love, lulled by security, and ready for whatever tomorrow would bring.

THE END

Afterword

Dear Reader,

Thank you for purchasing Rest In Peace (Eva Rae Thomas #15). The idea for this story came to me when I heard about Gypsy Rose Blanchard, as you can probably already guess if you know about it. It's the story of a little girl growing up with a mother suffering from Munchausen by proxy, where she claimed her daughter was sick, and everyone believed her, but she was, in fact, the one hurting her. One day, the daughter met someone online and had this person kill her mom so she could finally be free. The story was a big inspiration to me. I researched whether men could also have Munchausen by proxy, and as I found out that they could, I knew I had to write about it. For those of you who haven't heard about the case or the illness, here are links to some inspiration:

https://www.biography.com/crime/gypsy-rose-blanchard-mother-dee-dee-murder

https://www.webmd.com/mental-health/munchausen-by-proxy

https://medium.com/california-dreaming/jack-barron-munchausen-by-proxy-dad-bd44531fb3b8

As always, I want to thank you for all your support and remind you to leave a review of this book if you can. It means so much to me.

Take care,

Willow

What's coming next from Willow Rose?

Get on the list to find out about coming titles, bargains, give-aways and more.

Join Willow Rose's VIP Newsletter to get exclusive updates about New Releases, Giveaways, and FREE ebooks.

Just scan this QR code with your phone and click on the link:

SCAN ME

INTRODUCTION TO EXCERPT

Find out how Eva Rae Thomas startet as FBI agent.
SO WE LIE is a prequel to the Eva Rae Thomas Series.

"What do we do when the truth hurts too much?

Fresh out of the national academy - mother of two - **FBI profiler Eva Rae Thomas** is in over her head on her first assignment in multi-million-copy bestselling author Willow Rose's breath-taking mystery."

Excerpt of SO WE LIE

A GRIPPING, HEART-STOPPING MYSTERY NOVEL

Prologue

WASHINGTON, D.C.

They only ever fought when they were drunk. Mindy Lynn and Tuck Bowman had been together for a little more than seven years now and were known among their friends as the stable couple, the ones who never fought, who agreed on almost everything. And that was the truth, at least for the most part—until they both had a little more than they should to drink. Then it took nothing to set both of them off, and as they were driving home from the Grillfish, where they had been drinking at the bar for hours after finishing dinner, they were at each other's throats.

"Don't give me that," Tuck said, accelerating to rush through a yellow light. "I saw how you looked at him when he came over to you."

Mindy threw out her arms. "I don't even know who you're talking about, for crying out loud."

Tuck turned his head and stared at her, his blue eyes growing narrow and angry. Mindy worried that he wasn't looking at the road ahead.

"Do you love me?"

"Please, keep your eyes on the road," she said, placing her hands nervously on the glove compartment.

"I'll darn well keep my eyes where I want them," he hissed, then glared briefly ahead of them before looking at her again. He clasped her thigh hard. Pain shot through her body. Tuck had never laid a hand on her like that before. His eyes were glossy, staring blankly at her, his lips growing into a tight line. Mindy felt dizzy. She really shouldn't have taken those last two shots. She could still taste the tequila and would be so sick tomorrow. It was her problem. When they reached a certain level of drunkenness, it was like she couldn't stop. She wanted more and more. It wasn't often she allowed herself to go this far, and typically, she would have stopped a lot earlier before she reached that point of no return. But since Tuck got laid off from his construction job, things hadn't been good. They had struggled financially, and Tuck had found it hard not to be able to provide as he ought to. Not that they had any children yet, but they wanted to. They had been trying for years and struggling to face the fact that the pregnancy hadn't happened yet. Mindy often talked about seeing someone—a professional—about it but hadn't dared to mention it to Tuck yet. If something was wrong with him, it would break his heart. It would simply crush him.

"It'll come. You just need to give it time," her mom had said. "Who knows? Maybe you're worrying too much about it. It'll come when you least expect it. Heaven knows you were a huge surprise to your father and me. It's easier when you don't have any expectations."

So that's what Mindy tried not to have. Expectations. It was harder said than done, for sure. After three years of trying, it was getting difficult to ignore the facts. And tonight, she had brought it up, stupid as she was, over the fried fish platter, the same dish she always ordered in that place.

"It's been three years, Tuck. Do you think maybe something is off?"

Those were her words. That was all she had said. But it was enough. Tuck's eyes grew distant, and he barely blinked.

Before she could say anything else, he had downed his beer and asked for another one, which he drank without speaking a word to her. Mindy had cursed herself for bringing it up. It was supposed to have been a night of celebration for them because Tuck had finally landed a new job—one that paid well for once. They had been so happy up until that moment when she asked that dimwitted silly question when there was no reason to. Why did she have to ruin everything?

He had taken the drinking to the bar, and she had followed him, trying to put him in a better mood. After a couple of shots, he had finally eased up on her, and they had talked normally again. It wasn't until they made it to the car that the fighting began. Now, Tuck was accusing her of flirting with some guy she didn't even remember talking to. As always, they were avoiding what was really bothering them. They kept fighting as he turned onto Wisconsin Avenue, the car swerving on the road.

"I can't believe you," he said. "But I guess you don't love me anymore. If you loved me, you wouldn't cheat on me."

Mindy scoffed. "Cheat on you? Where is this coming from?"

"Oh, come on. How stupid do you think I am?" Tuck yelled, tapping a finger on his temple. "I know you. You've been acting so strange lately, and the other day you wouldn't let me look at your phone. You don't think I notice the signs, huh? But this is so typically you. You..."

"Please, keep your eyes on the road, Tuck!" Mindy yelled as a truck came rushing toward them, blaring its horn, blinking its headlights. Tuck pulled the wheel and turned away from it just in time. Mindy clasped her chest and breathed heavily as the truck blasted by them.

"There it is again," he said, looking at her angrily. "You thought I'd hit that truck, didn't you? You don't trust me."

That was the worst thing in Tuck's eyes—when Mindy didn't trust him to protect her. He always pulled that card when he was drunk. He would gather episodes in his mind and then rattle them off when he'd had too much. Starting with the time she asked him about the letters from the IRS that kept coming in the mail. Mindy closed her eyes with a sigh. Her head was spinning, and she felt a headache approaching behind her eyes.

"Of course, I trust you, Tuck," she lied, trying to calm him down, to make him feel better. She had done that a lot these past few years when he got like this. It usually worked, but she wasn't sure it would this time. "I was just scared. You know how nervous I get when driving after...."

Mindy trailed off when thinking about her best friend, Amy. She had been in a car crash when they were still in high school, and a car slammed head-on into hers. She had been killed on the spot.

Mindy looked out the front as a set of headlights hit them and almost blinded her.

"That car is coming toward us really fast," she said, her voice trembling.

Tuck turned to look and saw the car rushing toward them, swerving from side to side. "Oh sh...." Tuck said, turning the wheel abruptly as the car whooshed by them.

"Whoa!" Mindy exclaimed, and they both looked in the rearview mirror, following its path as it continued, then crashed into a tree on the side of the road.

Part 1

SIX YEARS LATER

Chapter 1

I paused for a second as I showed the uniformed woman behind the glass my badge. It was still so shiny that it was hard to hide how new it was.

"Eva Rae Wilson? Agent Wilson?"

Her eyes lifted and met mine through the glass. The sound of my name made me wince slightly. After being married five years and changing my maiden name—Thomas—out with Wilson, I still hadn't gotten used to being called that. I had discussed it intensely with my husband, Chad. I had wanted to keep Thomas because I loved that name, but he got very offended that I didn't want to carry his name, so in the end, I caved. I just liked the sound of Agent Thomas better than Agent Wilson. Don't ask me why. I guess I wasn't prepared for losing my identity like that. In my mind, I was still Eva Rae Thomas as I had been my entire life.

"I don't think I've met you before. You new?"

I nodded, blushing slightly. "Yes. Got with the bureau just recently."

She gave me an annoyed look, then lifted her eyebrows. "And you're here to see Frank Woods?"

"Yes. I've filled out all the paperwork."

"Okay, looking fine..." she said, looking at the papers I had handed her when arriving. "You got the signature there, and on the back as well... and your initials on page three, yes. I guess you're good to go."

She leaned over and pressed the button to open the locks on the double doors leading inside the prison. This bunker-like building only housed the worst of the criminals in the D.C. area. It was my first time there, and I wasn't without jitters. I walked through and showed my badge once again, just lifting it so the guard could see it. I enjoyed showing it still, as it was something I had worked really hard to achieve. Becoming an FBI profiler with the BAU, Behavioral Analysis Unit, was a lifelong dream of mine, and it had finally come true. I had taken four years of psychology in college, then gone through training at the FBI Academy before being stationed at a field office in D.C. for three years before applying for the BAU. I couldn't believe that I had been selected for training, and after two and a half years, I was a fully functioning FBI profiler. Now, it was time for me to show them my skills. And I knew exactly how to impress them all. The solution was standing right in front of me a few seconds later when I sat down in the interview room, and the door was opened.

"Frank Woods," I said to the guy in the orange jumpsuit. His hands and feet were chained together as he was guided inside, flanked by two guards with stern looks on their faces. He wasn't as handsome as in the pictures I had in my file in front of me, but he was still a good-looking guy. The salt and pepper on the sides of his hair suited him, and it was clear he had spent the last six years on the inside working out. He was a lot more muscular now than he had been when convicted for murdering his wife.

I pointed at the chair in front of me, smiling politely, trying my best to hide just how nervous I was.

"Have a seat. You and I have a lot to talk about."

Chapter 2

THEN:

Online dating was more challenging than she had expected it to be. Mary Ellen Garton scrolled through yet another profile on MillionairesMatch.com. She could hear her sister Frances' voice in the back of her head, telling her it was a scam, that there were not actually millionaires on this dating site.

"I mean, if you were really a millionaire, why would you need to look for a date on a website? All you'd get would be gold diggers."

Mary Ellen disagreed. It was true that most of the guys who had written to her had turned out not to be worth her time, but at some point, she was certain she would find Mr. Right. It wasn't that he needed to be a millionaire; it would just be a nice addition—like a bonus. Even though Mary Ellen was a single mom with four children, she wasn't exactly struggling. She was doing okay for herself and had taken care of them by herself for three years now while climbing the career ladder at her company. She was actually quite the businesswoman herself, and money was tight some months, but not severely. And she had finally been able to buy the house she had rented for the past five years, and with the house skyrocketing in value this past year, she had learned she now had a positive net worth.

Yes, Mary Ellen could take care of herself and her children just fine, even though her sister never believed she could. There was a lot more to Mary Ellen than her sister gave her credit for.

"I'll find the perfect match, and you'll be so jealous, Frances, while eating your own words," she mumbled to herself, scrolling through the profiles, looking at the pictures. Mary Ellen paused at one, then clicked the profile. This guy's photo showed him playing golf in those awful pants they always wore. He had a cute face, but she couldn't really deal with the fact that he was a golfer. That usually took up a lot of a man's time, and she would never see him when he was off work. That could be both good and bad. It was good to have time apart—to miss one another and not rub elbows all the time, but then again, she'd end up sitting alone with the kids all weekend and have to drive them alone to all their activities while grumbling about him being on the golf course, again. Mary Ellen's friend Jennifer had that problem with her husband, and it drove her nuts. Nope, there was no way she was going down that road. Mary Ellen shook her head, then deleted this guy's request to connect. She wasn't taking any chances. This time, the guy had to be absolutely perfect for her. And she just knew he would be. He was there somewhere, waiting for her to find him. She knew it in her soul.

"Where are you, my future husband?" she said with an expectant smile as she scrolled further down, looking at pictures, discarding the men one after another. "I know you're in here somewhere."

She sighed as she looked at a guy she liked but then realized that he lived in France. She wasn't up for a long-distance relationship. Not that he needed to live in her backyard or even in the same county. She didn't mind driving a few hours, but she couldn't do a whole other country. She simply didn't want to.

"Nope," she said and left his profile, slightly sad that he wasn't the one since she really liked his deep blue eyes.

"It's gotta be just right. And I know it will be once I...."

Mary Ellen paused when seeing the picture of a man who had already requested to connect with her. She stared at the picture, then took a deep breath and clicked his profile, expecting to find something wrong at first glance, as she had done with the rest of them. But to her surprise, it didn't happen this time. This guy lived only three hours away, and he was about the same age as Mary Ellen, older by two years, which was perfect. He had no children and hadn't been married before, only been in a long-term relationship with a woman who didn't want to get married. They split because of *different interests.*

And he was actually a millionaire. He wrote that he had his own house with a pool and had made money on investments that made it possible for him to retire last year at the age of only forty-eight.

This means I will have plenty of time for a new partner in my life. And I will do my utmost to keep you happy.

Mary Ellen stared at the picture of him standing by a willow tree, leaning against it in his black jeans and blue shirt, smiling handsomely.

She leaned back in the chair, sighing comfortably, feeling a few butterflies appear in her stomach.

"There you are, Mr. Perfect. I was wondering when you'd show up."

Chapter 3

"Let me get this straight. You want to reopen my case?"

Frank Woods looked at me from behind his bangs that had grown long and fell into his eyes. Being in his mid-fifties, he was almost twenty-five years older than me, yet I couldn't help but find him attractive. His smile and his eyes bore a secret in them that drew me in. He had been described as a womanizer and a player in the media, but that wasn't what I saw. He was charming, yes, but not in a bad way. He wasn't flirting with me, and sitting across from him didn't make me feel as uncomfortable as I had expected. The media had painted an ugly picture of him back then, and I was beginning to think it was quite unfair.

He leaned forward, and his chains rattled.

"Do you mind elaborating?"

I smiled. "I understand why you're confused."

He scoffed. "Confused is quite the understatement. Do you have anything to base this request on? I've admitted to killing her. What can you possibly have that will prove I didn't?"

I looked down at my file, then shook my head before lifting

my gaze again. "I don't have anything solid, and that's why I came to you first. I need you to give me access to your wife's things. I think they might have missed something important when going through it all six years ago, but I can't prove it. I assume you still have all your old stuff from the house? Maybe in boxes somewhere?"

He cleared his throat. "Well, my sister-in-law lives in the house with the kids now. She takes care of them. You'll have to ask her. I guess."

"I thought that maybe if I got you to give me permission, then it might be easier. I'm assuming she's not interested in helping you?"

That made him laugh. "Oh, no. She hates my guts. I can't blame her. I would hate me too."

"That's what I'm hoping to be able to change," I said. "I hope to clear your name and give you your life back. I think you're innocent."

That made him laugh again. "You think I'm innocent?"

I nodded nervously. "Yes."

"You're crazy, do you know that?"

"I'll have to get used to being called that. I have a feeling I'll hear that a lot if I pursue this further."

He leaned back and gave me a suspicious look. "Are you even a real agent? You're pretty young."

I showed him my badge and photo ID. "But I am. A profiler."

"That looks brand new; how long have you had it?"

I blushed. "That's beside the point."

"Ah, I see. Young and eager to prove our worth, are we?"

"Maybe, but that shouldn't...."

"Tell me, why should I trust you?"

"Do you have a choice?" I asked, fighting to sound as confident as possible. "I don't see anyone else here trying to help you."

He shrugged. "I can say no."

"That's your choice, yes, of course. But then you'll have to rot in here for the rest of your life while sticking to your little lie that you killed your own wife."

Frank Woods paused. His smile went stiff, and he leaned back in his chair again. He stared at me for a few seconds, biting the inside of his cheek.

"I think our little chat is over."

"No, please," I said, placing a hand on the table. "I'm sorry if I offended you. I really need to do this. It's been driving me crazy. We went over your case during training, and it kept bothering me; it kept me awake at night."

Frank scoffed again. "Really?"

"Yes, really."

He narrowed his eyes. "You genuinely believe that I'm innocent?"

"Yes. That's what I've been trying to tell you all along."

"Even when I tell you that I'm not?"

"Yes."

He whistled. "Wow, either you're the smartest agent alive or the dumbest. I can't seem to figure out which one."

"Maybe let me be the judge of that," I said, grinning. I had been thinking the same thing repeatedly these past months when going over Frank's case in my mind, unable to let it go.

"So, what do you say? Will you give me access to your house and your things?" I asked hopefully.

He glared down at me. I couldn't blame him for being cynical. He had claimed his innocence for a long time, but no one believed him. In the end, he had finally told them he did it. I thought he had just caved because the pressure was too much, and he knew he couldn't win. That was one of my theories. Another was that he had admitted his guilt to protect someone else—someone dear to him. But I knew he would never tell me, so I didn't ask, at least not yet.

Then, he nodded. "Okay, little miss profiler. You have my permission. I'll have my lawyer write a letter to my sister-in-law and make sure she doesn't get in your way. Let's see what you can do."

That made me smile widely. "You won't regret it, Mr. Woods."

"I sure hope not," he said with a wink as the guards came back in and pulled him to his feet. He shuffled forward toward the door when he suddenly stopped and looked back at me.

"Let me ask you this, miss profiler... why my case? Of all the cases? Lots of people in here claim to be innocent. I don't. Why me? Why now?"

I sighed. I had asked myself that same question over and over again, trying to convince myself to leave it alone.

"Let's just say your profile didn't exactly fit this killer. As I said, we reviewed your case in class, and I didn't believe you did it at any point. I promised myself I'd take a closer look once I was hired. I don't think I can sleep until I do."

"You seem very sure, even though I say I killed her."

"I don't believe you. I know a liar when I see one."

That made him laugh, and as he was escorted out, he mumbled, "I like her."

Chapter 4

He was watching the kids playing in the yard across the street. The little boy, who wasn't so little anymore as he neared the age of eight, was on the swings, while his older sister, by two years, was playing in the high grass with her small dolls.

Stefan Mark sighed deeply while seeing this. It wasn't often he got to see them anymore as they were playing more inside—probably watching TV or playing computer games like more and more children did these days. Or just tapping away on some mindless game on the phone. It saddened Stefan because he believed that children ought to spend time outside every day, as much as possible. Not that he had been a particularly outdoorsy kid himself, but still. He would like to see them more.

"Stop growing," he said and placed a hand on the window. "I can't keep up."

Stefan walked out on the porch with his coffee cup in his hand and sat down on the old porch swing. From here, he could hear the kids laughing, which was the most soothing sound in the world. How he wished he could go over there and hug them again like he used to. How he wished their little faces would light up and they'd run to him with open arms, yelling Uncle Stefan, and the little one would simply plop into his lap like the most natural thing in the world.

Like he belonged there.

But that was long ago now. Now, the kids only looked at him with big eyes like he was a stranger, and their aunt would pull them inside the house if he came near it. He was no longer welcome in their lives.

And that made him so sad.

Because he loved those little munchkins.

Stefan sipped his coffee while watching them play, enjoying the sound of their voices being carried across the cul-de-sac by the eastern wind. He couldn't hear exactly what they were saying, but they sounded happy, and that was enough for him. He stayed in this house for their sake, to be able to keep an eye on them and follow them as they grew. They were the only reason he hadn't left when the incident happened. This place brought him nothing but sorrow and deep sadness otherwise.

The girl, little Izzy, was playing quietly until her brother, Ben, jumped off the swing, ran to her, and took one of her dolls out of her hand. He took off laughing while Izzy screamed angrily. Then she got up and ran after him. Stefan watched them as she tried to catch him, and Ben squealed with joy, holding the doll up high in the air over his head so his sister couldn't reach it, even when jumping. In turn, Izzy pushed him hard, and he fell back, hitting his head on the asphalt driveway. Now, Ben was crying while Izzy triumphantly wriggled the doll out of his grip and was about to walk away when their aunt came running out to them. She helped Ben get up, then grabbed Izzy by the hand and pulled her forcefully toward the door while scolding her for pushing her brother. Stefan rose to his feet, feeling awful for poor Izzy, and as he did, their aunt turned her head and spotted him. Her eyes glared directly at him, and he felt it like icicles on his skin. Shivering, he turned around and went inside the house while Izzy cried on the other side of the cul-de-sac, being dragged toward the door.

End of excerpt... Get ***SO WE LIE*** today on Amazon.

About the Author

Willow Rose is a multi-million-copy best-selling Author and an Amazon ALL-star Author of more than 90 novels.

Several of her books have reached the top 10 of ALL books in the Amazon store in the US, UK, and Canada.

She has sold more than six million books that are translated into many languages.

Willow's books are fast-paced, nail-biting pageturners with twists you won't see coming.

That's why her fans call her The Queen of Plot Twists.

Willow lives on Florida's Space Coast. When she is not writing or reading, you will find her surfing and watching the dolphins play in the waves of the Atlantic Ocean.

Join Willow Rose's VIP Newsletter to get exclusive updates about New Releases, Giveaways, and FREE ebooks.

Just scan this QR code with your phone and click on the link:

Win a waterproof Kindle e-reader or a $125 Amazon giftcard!

Just become a member of my Facebook group **WILLOW ROSE - MYSTERY SERIES**.

Every time we pass 1000 new members, we'll randomly select a winner from all the entries.

To enter go here: https://www.facebook.com/groups/1921072668197253

Follow Willow Rose on BookBub here: https://www.bookbub.com/authors/willow-rose

Follow Willow on BookBub

Connect with Willow online:
https://www.facebook.com/willowredrose
https://twitter.com/madamwillowrose
http://www.goodreads.com/author/show/4804769.
Willow_Rose
https://www.willow-rose.net
Mail to: contact@willow-rose.net

facebook.com/willowredrose
x.com/madamwillowrose
instagram.com/madamewillowrose

Books by the Author

MYSTERY NOVELS

EVA RAE THOMAS MYSTERY SERIES

- So We Lie (Eva Rae Thomas Mystery, prequel) - Click here
- Don't Lie To Me (Eva Rae Thomas Mystery #1) - Click here
- What You Did (Eva Rae Thomas Mystery #2) - Click here
- Never ever (Eva Rae Thomas Mystery #3) - Click here
- Say you love me (Eva Rae Thomas Mystery #4) - Click here
- Let Me Go (Eva Rae Thomas Mystery #5) - Click here
- It's Not Over (Eva Rae Thomas Mystery #6) - Click here
- Not Dead Yet (Eva Rae Thomas Mystery #7) - Click here
- To Die For (Eva Rae Thomas Mystery #8) - Click here
- Such A Good Girl (Eva Rae Thomas Mystery #9) - Click here
- Little Did She Know (Eva Rae Thomas Mystery #10) - Click here
- You Better Run (Eva Rae Thomas Mystery #11) - Click here
- Say It Isn't So (Eva Rae Thomas Mystery #12) - Click here
- Too Pretty To Die (Eva Rae Thomas Mystery #13) - Click here

- Till Death do us part (Eva Rae Thomas Mystery #14) - Click here
- Rest In Peace (Eva Rae Thomas Mystery #15) - Click here

HARRY HUNTER MYSTERY SERIES

- All The Good Girls (Harry Hunter Mystery #1) - Click here
- Run Girl Run (Harry Hunter Mystery #2) - Click here
- No Other Way (Harry Hunter Mystery #3) - Click here
- Never Walk Alone (Harry Hunter Mystery #4) - Click here

MARY MILLS MYSTERY SERIES

- What Hurts the Host (Mary Mills Mystery #1) - Click here
- You Can Run (Mary Mills Mystery #2) - Click here
- You Can't Hide (Mary Mills Mystery #3) - Click here
- Careful Little Eyes (Mary Mills Mystery #4) - Click here

JACK RYDER MYSTERY SERIES

- Hit the Road Jack (Jack Ryder #1) - Click here
- Slip Out the Back Jack (Jack Ryder #2) - Click here

- The House that Jack Built (Jack Ryder #3) - Click here
- Black Jack (Jack Ryder #4) - Click here
- Girl next door (Jack Ryder #5) - Click here
- Her final word (Jack Ryder #6) - Click here
- Don't Tell (Jack Ryder #7) - Click here

EMMA FROST MYSTERY SERIES

- Itsy Bitsy Spider (Emma Frost #1) - Click here
- Miss Polly had a Dolly (Emma Frost #2)- Click here
- Run, Run, as Fast as you Can (Emma Frost #3) - Click here
- Cross your Heart and Hope to Die (Emma Frost #4) - Click here
- Peek A Boo I See You (Emma Frost #5) - Click here
- Tweedledum and Tweedledee (Emma Frost #6) - Click here
- Easy as One Two Three (Emma Frost #7) - Click here
- There's No Place like Home (Emma Frost #8) - Click here
- Slenderman (Emma Frost #9) - Click here
- Where the Wild Roses Grow (Emma Frost #10) - Click here
- Waltzing Mathilda (Emma Frost #11) - Click here
- Drip Drop Dead (Emma Frost #12) - Click here
- Black Frost (Emma Frost #13) - Click here

REBEKKA FRANCK MYSTERY SERIES

- One, Two... He is Coming for You (Rebekka Franck #1) - Click here
- Three, Four ... Better Lock your Door (Rebekka Franck #2) - Click here
- Five, Six ... Grab your Crucifix (Rebekka Franck #3) - Click here
- Seven, Eight... Gonna Stay up Late (Rebekka Franck #4) - Click here
- Nine, Ten... Never Sleep Again (Rebekka Franck #5) - Click here
- Eleven, Twelve... Dig and Delve (Rebekka Franck #6) - Click here
- Thirteen, Fourteen... Little Boy Unseen (Rebekka Franck #7) - Click here
- Better not cry (Rebekka Franck #8) - Click here
- Ten little Girls (Rebekka Franck #9) - Click here
- It Ends Here (Rebekka Franck #10) - Click here

MYSTERY/HORROR NOVELS

- Edwina - Click here
- To Hell in A Handbasket - Click here
- Umbrella Man - Click here
- Black Bird Fly - Click here
- In Cold Blood - Click here

HORROR SHORT STORIES

- Eenie, Meenie - Click here
- Rock-A-Bye Baby - Click here

- Nibble, Nibble, Crunch - Click here
- Humpty, Dumpty - Click here
- Chain Letter - Click here
- Better Watch Out - Click here
- Mommy Dearest - Click here
- The Bird- Click here

FANTASY, SCI-FI AND PARANORMAL ROMANCE/SUSPENSE

THE VAMPIRES OF SHADOW HILLS

- Flesh and Blood - Click here
- Blood and Fire - Click here
- Fire and Beauty - Click here
- Beauty and Beasts - Click here
- Beasts and Magic - Click here
- Magic and Witchcraft - Click here
- Witchcraft and War - Click here
- War and Order - Click here
- Order and Chaos- Click here
- Chaos and Courage - Click here

THE AFTERLIFE SERIES

- Beyond (Afterlife #1) - Click here
- Serenity (Afterlife #2) - Click here
- Endurance (Afterlife #3) - Click here
- Courageous (Afterlife #4) - Click here

- The Surge - Click here
- Girl Divided - Click here
- In One Fell Swoop - Click here

THE DAUGHTERS OF THE JAGUAR SERIES

- Savage (Daughters of the Jaguar #1) - Click here
- Broken (Daughters of the Jaguar #2) - Click here

THE WOLFBOY CHRONICLES

- Song for a Gypsy (The Wolfboy Chronicles) - Click here
- I am WOLF (The Wolfboy Chronicles) - Click here

BOX SETS

- Eva Rae Thomas Mystery Series: Book 1-3 - Click here
- Jack Ryder Mystery Series Box Set: Vol 1-3 - Click here
- Jack Ryder Mystery Series Box Set: Vol 4–6 - Click here
- Mary Mills Mystery Series Box Set: Vol 1-2 - Click here

- Mary Mills Mystery Series Box Set: Vol 1-3 - Click here
- Rebekka Franck Series Vol 1-3 - Click here
- Rebekka Franck Series Vol 4-6 - Click here
- Rebekka Franck Series Vol 1-5 - Click here
- Emma Frost Mystery Series Vol 1-3 - Click here
- Emma Frost Mystery Series Vol 4-6 - Click here
- Emma Frost Mystery Series Vol 7-9 - Click here
- Emma Frost Mystery Series Vol 1-5 - Click here
- Daughters of the Jaguar Box Set - Click here
- The Vampires of Shadow Hills: Books 1-3 - Click here
- The Vampires of Shadow Hills: Books 4–6 - Click here
- The Vampires of Shadow Hills: Books 6–9 - Click here
- The Afterlife Series (Books 1-3)- Click here
- Horror Stories from Denmark - Click here
- The Wolfboy Chronicles - Click here

Published by BUOY MEDIA LLC

Cover design by Juan Villar Padron, https://www.juanjpadron.com

Special thanks to my editor Janell Parque http://janellparque.blogspot.com/

To be the first to hear about new releases and bargains from Willow Rose, sign up below to be on the VIP List. (I promise not to share your email with anyone else, and I won't clutter your inbox.)

- Tap here to sign up to be on the VIP LIST -

Follow Willow Rose on BookBub:

BB Follow me on BookBub

Connect with Willow online:

Facebook

Twitter

GoodReads

willow-rose.net

madamewillowrose@gmail.com

Contents

Part 1

www.ingramcontent.com/pod-product-compliance
Lightning Source LLC
Chambersburg PA
CBHW030340310726
48979CB00001B/119
9781954938557